BREAKDOWN

BREAKDOWN

A "Nameless Detective" Mystery

by **BILL PRONZINI**

Delacorte Press

M
Pronzini

Published by
Delacorte Press
Bantam Doubleday Dell Publishing Group, Inc.
666 Fifth Avenue
New York, New York 10103

The trademark Delacorte Press® is registered in the U.S. Patent
and Trademark Office.

Library of Congress Cataloging in Publication Data
Pronzini, Bill.
    Breakdown : a "nameless detective" mystery / by Bill
Pronzini.
        p.   cm.
    ISBN 0-385-29896-X (hc)
    I. Title.
PS3566.R67B7   1991   90-38196
813'.54—dc20   CIP

Manufactured in the United States of America
Published simultaneously in Canada
February 1991

10 9 8 7 6 5 4 3 2 1

BVG

For Ed Gorman—
—a kindred spirit

BREAKDOWN

Chapter 1

I WAS LATE getting to the tavern that Monday night because I let myself put in too much overtime on a routine skip-trace. Not that being late mattered much. After three barren weeks, this angle on the Lujack case had turned into a protracted waste of time. If it weren't for the fact that all the other angles seemed to be just as dead-ended, I would have dropped it by now.

Besides, working nights kept me from brooding too much about all the bad things that had darkened Kerry's life—and mine—during the past few months.

I parked my car near the foot of Taraval, where it ends at 48th Avenue. It was a raw late-January night, with a chill wind herding a low scudding mist in from the ocean a few hundred yards away. From where I parked, you could see no more than fifty feet beyond the Great Highway, which parallels 48th here; all of Ocean Beach was obscured behind shifting traceries of gray. The pedestrian-crossing signal at the Great Highway glowed an eerie red, like a disembodied hand caught and held in motionless warning by the mist.

At the moment there was no traffic of any kind in the

vicinity, even though it was only eight thirty. There were
lights in some of the squat row houses and two-unit apartment buildings along this block of Taraval, and in the scattered few business establishments in the block back across
47th, but the people were all shut away behind closed doors
and drawn curtains. Life at this western edge of the city—Out
There at the Beach, San Franciscans call it—is nothing like
life at its teeming inner core. It has a closed-off, clannish
ambiance, a different taste and texture than any other neighborhood. Part of the reason is a heterogenous mix of conservative and funky architectural styles and life-styles; of residents old and new, blue-collar and white-collar, Asian and
Anglo, neo-hippies and newlyweds, and a large percentage of
retirees. The other part is intangible. Maybe the salty air and
the heavy fogs and cold winds have something to do with it;
maybe living on the edge—of the city, of a great land mass, of
earthquake country—has something to do with it too. The
reshaping and landscaping of much of Ocean Beach and the
Great Highway, part of an ongoing beachfront sewer project
and the need to control the hazard of windblown sand, has
done little to alter the strangeness. And if anything, the devas-
tating 7.1 quake in October has increased it. You can feel it as
soon as you go Out There.

I donned the cloth cap I always wore to the tavern. Or
rather, that Art Canino, shop steward for a South San Francisco plumbing contractor, always wore. Then I buttoned the
collar on my overcoat and got out into that freezing wind.

Quiet here, too, on a night like this. If it weren't for the
foghorns, bleating distantly like lost strays, you could imagine
yourself in one of the small seacoast towns upstate. The pulse-
beat of the city was faint here on clear days, and when it was
muffled by the fog you couldn't hear it at all. I went at an
angle across the empty street, back toward 47th. Several
blocks away, the headlight on one of the big L Taraval street-
cars probed dimly through the fog; but even though those
LRVs make a lot of noise, and even though I could feel the
vibration from this one as I crossed the tracks, I couldn't hear

it yet—as if it were approaching through a different dimension.

The tavern's entrance was just a narrow storefront between a dry-cleaning establishment and one of the two-unit apartment buildings. Above the door, a blue-neon cocktail glass cast a faint glow that had no particular warmth or welcome to it. The lower two-thirds of the adjacent window was covered by heavy blue cloth suspended from a horizontal pole; you couldn't see inside through the upper third unless you happened to have a stepladder handy. The name of the place was painted on the window glass in flaky blue lettering that I couldn't read until I was just a few feet away:

HIDEAWAY

I went in. Most of the regulars were there, maybe a dozen altogether tonight, all but one comfortably arranged at the cluster of tables along the right-hand wall and in the rear booths. The man seated alone at the bar was not Nick Pendarves. The regulars all looked my way as I entered, but none of them smiled or nodded or offered words of greeting. Three weeks was not enough time to make me one of them; three months might not be enough. But they knew me now, and no longer seemed to resent my presence, and they were friendly enough on an individual basis.

At the far end of the bar, where I usually sat, I hoisted myself onto a cracked leather stool. Pendarves wasn't anywhere in the long, narrow room. The door to the men's john was open, which meant that he wasn't in there either.

The bartender took his time coming my way. But that didn't mean anything; he took his time serving everybody. His name was Max. If he had another name, nobody had spoken it within my hearing. He was a pudgy little guy in his early fifties, muscular through the chest and shoulders, with an egg-shaped head covered with spiky tufts of gray-black hair that made you think of pig bristles. He wouldn't gossip or let you buy him a drink; he held himself aloof even from the regulars.

And he used words sparingly and grudgingly, as if he had been given a small allotment and was afraid of using it up.

"What'll it be?"

"Usual," I said.

"Bud Light?" He had a good memory for what people drank.

"Bud Light."

He set me up with the beer and a frosty glass, then moved a plastic bowl my way. Well, well, I thought. I had finally reached the intermediate beer-nut level of acceptance.

"Nick been in yet tonight?" I asked him.

"No."

"Wonder how come. He's usually here by eight."

Max shrugged.

"Working late, maybe," I said.

Max shrugged again and went down to the other end of the plank.

I sat nursing my beer, waiting. I would give Pendarves the better part of an hour—long enough to maintain my cover as the newest of the neighborhood barflies. Ten minutes walked away dragging their heels. I was in no mood for passive sitting tonight, and there was little enough here, other than the regulars, to absorb my attention. The Hideaway had no jukebox, and the small TV over the backbar was seldom turned on except by special request; an old-fashioned dartboard was about the only standard tavern diversion. The talk was muted, an irregular background drone that I didn't feel like contributing to. I tried to keep my thoughts neutral but Kerry was there, Kerry and her mother, worrying at the edges of my mind. Finally I got up and went to the dartboard and began tossing darts at it, just to have something to do.

There are all sorts of neighborhood taverns in a city of neighborhoods such as San Francisco is. Straight and gay, white-collar and blue, ethnic and cosmopolitan, rough-trade and genteel, pickup joints and "family" watering holes; hangouts for the literati and holding pens for the illiterati; places dripping with authentic local atmosphere, adorned with phony atmosphere for the benefit of suckers and slumming tourists, completely lacking in atmosphere of any kind. But there aren't many taverns like the Hideaway anymore, in San Francisco or anywhere else in the country. They're a dying breed, soon to enter the same extinct category as black-tie supper clubs and dime-a-dance emporiums. They'll survive only as long as circumstances permit and enough of their patrons remain above ground to make them marginally profitable.

The Hideaway was just what its name suggested: a sanctuary, a literal hideaway for the men and women who frequented it. It was as much a social club and senior-citizens center as a place for the consumption of alcohol, the drowning of sorrows, and the celebrating of small victories. Most of the clientele were over fifty and had been coming here for years, or at least had lived in the neighborhood for a long time —retirees and near-retirees, widows and widowers, loners and misfits; the disabled and the forgotten, the has-beens and the never-wases. They came for the companionship of others like themselves, and because it was a place close by where they could escape the loneliness and frustrations of their private lives. That was why outsiders, casual drop-ins, were tolerated but never encouraged: They were threats to the sanctuary's delicate balance, reminders of the uncaring world-at-large that the regulars sought to avoid.

An old tavern, the Hideaway, in business continually since just after Repeal and operating under its present name for more than forty years. It was owned now by the widow of Sam Delaney, the man who had christened it Hideaway. She was in poor health, and there was some concern among the regulars that when she died her relatives would sell the property and the new owners would shut it down. If that happened, it would be a serious tragedy in their lives. There were other bars in the neighborhood, but not in the immediate vicinity and none like the Hideaway. Without it, some of these people would be lost. More than one of them, I thought, would not survive its closing for very long.

There was not much to the place, as far as the decor went. Just an oblong, high-ceilinged room, ill-lighted and musty with the smells of alcohol and tobacco, of salt-damp and age and the flavors of all the people who had made it their second home for over half a century. Long bar on the left as you came in; half a dozen well-used tables and chairs and one long cushioned bench along the wall on the right; four low-backed booths built into the far right-hand corner, two on the back wall and two on the side wall. Ancient linoleum on the floor, worn through in several places so that you could see the dark oiled boards underneath. Walls adorned with faded black-and-white photographs of a vanished San Francisco: the original Cliff House, Ocean Beach in the thirties, this neighborhood when it was all salt grass and sand dunes, before Dolger and the other developers bought up the land and covered it with "affordable" housing.

The first time I'd come here, just after the new year began, the Hideaway had struck me as a drab, cheerless bar ruled by ghosts and despair. But after three weeks, I had a different impression. This may have been a haven for the elderly and the disaffected, but they didn't come here to mourn or exchange bitternesses or sit around morosely waiting to shake hands with the Grim Reaper. Most of them were vital people; they brought their hobbies, opinions, insights, and verbal pleasures in with them, and shared them freely. There was sadness here, and a sense of tragedy, but there was laughter and joy too—and a kind of warmth and camaraderie that I found enviable.

Each of the two booths along the back wall had a green-shaded droplight over it. In one of them now, a retired civil servant named Harry Briggs was playing chess with fat, fortyish, painfully shy Douglas Mikan, the youngest of the regulars, who had inherited just enough money from an overprotective mother so that he didn't have to work. They played often and well and were very serious about their chess; they almost never spoke to each other while a match was in progress. In the other back booth, Peter Vandermeer sat reading a

pamphlet with great concentration. He was nearly eighty, thin
and sinewy, once a cable-car motorman and now an amateur
historian who probably knew more obscure facts about California history in general and San Francisco history in particular than most college professors. A couple of nights ago he
had spent twenty minutes telling me more than I ever wanted
to know about the Panama-Pacific Exposition of 1915.

The only person at the bar, down at the far end, was Ed
McBee, a longshoreman whose wife had died not long ago.
Over at the tables, there was Charlie Neale, who had a crippled right leg as the result of some sort of industrial accident.
And Kate and Bob Johnson, who belonged to different political parties and had evidently spent most of their married life
arguing politics. And Annie Stanhope, constantly knitting
from a huge bag of yarn while she drank vast amounts of dry
sherry that never seemed to have any effect on her. And
Frank Parigli, who had some kind of night watchman's job
and who spent his mornings combing Ocean Beach for driftwood and shells; his hobby was making collages, which he
sold to gift shops for the tourist trade. And Lyda Isherwood,
big and brassy, with a loud voice and a louder laugh; she
claimed to have once run a whorehouse in Nevada (nobody
seemed to believe her), and told bawdy stories in a surprising
variety of accents and dialects. There were others too, some
whose names I had learned and some I knew nothing about.
But their faces were all familiar now, and even though I was
here under a false name and false pretenses, and in another
week or so my life would no longer intersect with theirs, I felt
an odd sort of kinship with them. If I lived Out There at the
the Beach instead of in Pacific Heights, if I didn't have Kerry
—and, to a lesser degree, Eberhardt—this was the kind of
place and these were the kind of people I might find myself
gravitating to.

Kerry. I threw another dart, too hard and a little wildly.
Thinking: I *don't* have her now, do I? And what if this thing
with her mother gets worse, drags on and on?

Outside, somewhere close by, there was the sudden squeal

of tires on pavement, the crescendo-and-fade of a car passing at high speed. Nice driving on a foggy night, I thought. And promptly forgot about it.

But not for long.

Just about a minute had passed when the tavern's door whacked open. I felt the night's gusty breath all the way over where I was standing by the dartboard—and I watched Nick Pendarves blow in.

Pendarves was a tallish, gangly man in his mid-fifties, a couple of years younger than me. He wore his usual gray work shirt and gray work pants and gray-and-black plaid jacket, but you didn't think of him in terms of gray; you thought of him in terms of rusty. He had rust-colored hair, the kind of voice that sounded as if it were corroded, and a slow, jerky way of moving, as if all his joints needed oiling—the Tin Man of Oz left out too long in bad weather. But there was something different about him tonight; I saw it even at a distance and it put me on instant alert. His movements were quicker and more agitated than usual, and he paid no attention to the other regulars as he came down the bar. He leaned up against it between two of the stools, clutching at the beveled edge as if for support.

I moved over to where he was. When I got close enough I could see that his craggy face was pale, that the fire of bitter anger blazed in his eyes. He paid no attention to me, either, as I claimed one of the stools near him.

"Bourbon," he said to Max. "Double shot."

Max cocked his head, as much of an expression of surprise as he was ever likely to betray. Like me, Pendarves was a beer-drinker; in three weeks I had never seen him order anything else.

"Well? What the hell you waiting for?"

I watched Max get busy, Pendarves light an unfiltered Pall Mall with unsteady hands. Then I asked, "What's up, Nick? You look kind of shook."

"Son of a bitch tried to run me down," he said without looking my way.

"Who did?"

"Tried to kill *me,* by God."

"When? Just now?"

"Come out of nowhere while I was crossing the street. Couldn't of missed me by more than a couple feet. I hadn't jumped when I did . . . Christ!"

Max put the double shot down in front of him. Pendarves threw it off as if it were water, rubbed the back of his hand across his mouth. His eyes looked as hot as the tip of his cigarette.

"Kids?" Max said.

"Kids my ass. One guy, no goddamn headlights. He done it on purpose. Swerved right at me."

I said, "Who'd do a thing like that?"

"Thomas Lujack, that's who."

". . . Guy you're testifying against?"

"Him. Yeah."

"You sure it was him?"

"Sure enough."

"So you got a good look at him this time too?"

"Too dark. But it was Lujack—who the hell else? Tried to run me down like he done his partner. Well, he won't get away with it."

Max said, "Call the cops, Nick."

"Hell with the cops."

"What if he tries it again?"

"I'll make sure he don't."

"How?"

"Never mind how. That's my business."

"Better just leave it to the cops," I said.

"Hell with the cops," Pendarves said again.

"Fix him in court then, on the witness stand. If you didn't see the driver you can't be positive who it was . . ."

Pendarves wasn't listening. His head was down, his face set so tightly it was full of spasming nerves and ridges of muscle. He smoked his Pall Mall in fast, deep drags, as if he were trying to burn it up as quickly as he could.

Pretty soon he said, talking to himself, "Rivas . . . yeah, that's it. Make damn sure the bastard leaves me alone. Him and that brother of his both."

"Who's Rivas?"

No answer. What was left of his cigarette seared his fingers; he said, "Shit!" and jabbed it out viciously.

"Nick, who's Rivas?"

The sudden pain had brought him out of himself. His head snapped around my way and his eyes focused on me for the first time. "Canino," he said, "what the hell you sucking around for?"

"Hey, I was just trying to help—"

"Keep your questions to yourself." He shook himself, the way you'd shake off a sudden chill. "Max, give me another double."

"Sure."

Another voice, shy and halting, said, "Nick . . ."

Pendarves swung around. When I looked back I saw Douglas Mikan standing a couple of feet away, fingering the knot in his tie.

"What *you* want?"

"I just . . . make sure you're all right . . ."

"Leave me alone, you fat wimp."

Mikan backed off, staring at Pendarves like a hurt puppy. All the other regulars were staring at him, too, now. Conversation had died.

"What's everybody gawking at?" he demanded.

Down the bar Ed McBee said, "Don't take it out on us, Nick. We're on your side."

"Yeah."

"Notify the cops, that's good advice—"

"Butt out, Ed, huh? All of you just mind your business and let me take care of mine."

He swung around again as Max set him up with his second double. He put that one away as quickly as the first, then shoved away from the bar and stalked to the door in his rusty-jointed stride and was gone into the night.

I stayed where I was for about ten seconds. Then I shook my head and said, "Ah, the hell with it," as if I had lost my taste for beer and bar-lounging. I got up and went after Pendarves.

He was down the block a ways, just crossing Taraval—doing it cautiously, head twitching left, right, left, right. I went in the same direction but on this side of the street. I saw him get into his car, a beat-up Plymouth Fury with a loose rear bumper; heard the starter grind as I hurried across 47th Avenue. Thirty yards separated me from my car when he maneuvered out of the parking space; twenty yards when he made a too fast turn out of sight on 47th, heading north.

I was on the run by then, with my keys in my hand. It took me less than fifteen seconds to get the door unlocked, the car started and into a fast U-turn across the streetcar tracks. When I made the swing onto 47th, the Plymouth was two blocks away, approaching the Rivera Street intersection. Almost immediately its taillights flashed bloodily in the blowing fog and Pendarves turned right onto Rivera. I accelerated to close the gap—but I needn't have bothered. Two blocks east, the Plymouth had slowed again and was just turning into the weedy driveway next to a weathered yellow-brown corner house.

The house belonged to Pendarves. The way it looked, he was not going anywhere but home.

He quit his car, leaving it in the drive rather than putting it away in the sagging garage that crouched at the rear edge of his property. I drove past as he disappeared through a gate between the garage and the house. In the next block I made another U-turn and pulled in to the curb and cut my lights. From there I could see the mist-wreathed front of his house, the Plymouth sitting dark in the driveway.

Pretty soon lights went on inside the house. And stayed on. I sat there for twenty minutes: Pendarves did not come back out. Whatever he intended to do about Thomas Lujack, he apparently wasn't going to do it tonight.

Well, all right. That part of it was on hold. As for the rest of it . . .

For three weeks I had been working on Pendarves at the Hideaway, the only public place he frequented with any regularity, trying to pry some sort of useful information out of him; and now for the first time all that effort had paid some dividends. In fact, this was the first real break Eberhardt and I had had since we'd undertaken our investigation. The only trouble was, it was potentially disastrous in more ways than one. If Thomas really had tried to run Pendarves down tonight, it blew us right out of the water.

Thomas Lujack was our client.

And we were trying to prove him innocent of one hit-and-run murder charge already.

Chapter **2**

BEFORE I ENDED MY VIGIL on Pendarves's house, I used the car phone to call Thomas Lujack's home in the San Carlos hills. I wanted to hear what he had to say about tonight's incident, and I wanted to alert him to the threats Pendarves had made. I also wanted to find out if he was there, because if he was, he couldn't have tried to run Pendarves down. It would take a professional race-car driver to get from this part of San Francisco to his place in not much more than half an hour.

There was no answer.

I didn't like that much, either.

IT WAS AFTER TEN when I got to my building in Pacific Heights. A crack in the front stoop was the only damage it had suffered in the earthquake; the landlord still hadn't repaired it. Except for most of my collection of pulp magazines being dislodged from their shelves, and some broken crockery, my flat and personal possessions had come through all right too. The only real damage I'd had to deal with was at the office, where I'd been when the quake hit, and even that was pretty minor.

Tonight the flat had a barren, comfortless feel—the way the homes of some of the Hideaway's disaffected must feel to them, I thought. Reaction to the mood I was in. And to the fact that the place needed cleaning, tidying . . . no, hell, what it needed was Kerry. What *I* needed was Kerry.

She hadn't been here in ten days; I hadn't been to her apartment in Diamond Heights since before Christmas. For the second straight year we hadn't been able to spend the holidays together. Nor had we been able to spend a night together since Cybil's arrival. We'd been to bed only twice in all that time—my saggy old bed on a pair of stolen afternoons. Momentary releases of tension, that was all they were, quick and passionless and almost painful. What made it worse was that they were the only things I'd been able to do for her since the twenty-first of November—the only things. I was on standby: waiting until I was needed.

I hung up my overcoat and cap, turned up the thermostat. It was cold in here; that damned January wind was sharp enough to penetrate steel. Into the bedroom then, where I keep the telephone and answering machine, to check for messages. There weren't any. The bed looked as though it had been ransacked: I had not slept well the past few nights. I sat on the edge of it and punched out Eberhardt's number.

I'd tried to call him on the car phone, but the line had been busy both times. It was free now and he answered on the third ring, with an un-Eberhardt-like lilt in his voice.

"Hello to you too," I said. "Who'd you think it was? An obscene caller?"

"Ha ha," he said. Eberhardt is my best friend as well as my partner, and the salt of the earth, but he has absolutely no sense of humor. He thinks the funniest man who ever lived is Bob Hope. "I just got through talking to Bobbie Jean; I thought she forgot something. What do you want this late?"

"Development on the Lujack case, finally. But I don't like most of it and neither will you." I told him about the alleged hit-and-run attempt, the fact that there had been no answer at Thomas's house when I called.

"Hell," he said, "none of that has to mean anything. Could've been a case of careless driving and Pendarves over-reacted."

"Sure. Or it could be Thomas is guilty as hell on both counts."

"You call Glickman yet?"

Glickman was Paul Glickman, Thomas's attorney—one of the better criminal lawyers in the Bay Area, and the man who had hired us to work as defense investigators. I said, "No. That can wait until morning. I'll call him first thing and have him set up a meet with Thomas."

"You don't think Pendarves'll do anything crazy to-night?"

"I doubt it. He was pretty sore, making threats, but he's no hotheaded kid. Besides, everybody in the tavern heard him. He'd have to be a fool to try anything after that."

"What kind of threats?"

"Nothing specific. Said he'd fix Thomas, that kind of thing."

"Doesn't sound too serious."

"No. The name Rivas mean anything to you?"

"Rivas, Rivas . . . why?"

"Pendarves mentioned it. Some vague connection to the Lujack brothers."

". . . Familiar, but I can't quite place it."

"Somebody Pendarves works with at Roofco, maybe?"

"That's it," Eberhardt said. "Rivas, Antonio Rivas. I talked to him the first day I was out there."

"Friend of Pendarves?"

"Just coworkers, according to Rivas."

"So maybe he lied."

"Why would he . . . oh, I get it. You think Rivas might be the third witness."

"Possible, isn't it?"

"Possible, sure. If there really was a third witness. But why would Pendarves cover up for a guy like Rivas?"

"You talked to him. What kind of guy is he?"

Silence on the line; Eberhardt was thinking about it, working his memory. "Friendly, outgoing," he said at length. "Little dude in his twenties, been in this country three or four years, speaks broken English. Nothing in common with Pendarves that I can see."

"They get along all right?"

"No gripes from Rivas. No love and kisses, either. Just two guys who work together, different as night and day."

"Rivas wouldn't be the hardcase type, would he?"

"No way. Why?"

"I was thinking Pendarves might try hiring somebody to do some strong-arm work on Thomas."

"Forget it. Rivas'd be the last person for that."

"Suppose he's got a mean friend or relative?"

"I don't see him as a go-between either."

"Okay. I'm just shooting blind here. Have another talk with him tomorrow, see if you can find a connection. You *can* get to him when Pendarves isn't around?"

"I can try. I doubt they eat lunch together."

"I'm eating mine with Kerry tomorrow, but I should be back by one," I said. "I'll have Glickman set up the meet with Thomas for sometime after two."

"Right."

I drank a glass of low-fat milk and then tried to watch something on TV. My powers of concentration were nil tonight. Finally I took some calcium lactate, which Kerry had once told me was as effective as Nembutal in helping you sleep, and undressed and put the bedclothes more or less in order and got in among them.

And lay there in the dark, with my mind going clickety-clickety-clickety. The calcium lactate was no good tonight; about the only thing that would have worked was a blow on the head with a hammer.

I was aware of the ticking of the bedside clock, like a

counterpoint to the wind. Time, passing time. More than ten
months now since the end of my private taste of hell, when I
had been kidnapped by a madman and chained to the wall of
an isolated mountain cabin and left there to die slowly of
starvation. I was mostly healed now; the last crippling anxiety
attack had been almost three months ago, just after the earthquake, and I no longer seemed to constantly need people
around me to ward off the fear of being trapped and alone.
But there were scars, deep and disfiguring scars. I had been
changed by my ordeal, profoundly and irrevocably. I had lost
the virtue of patience, for one, and gained a capacity for sudden rage, sudden violence; I was capable of things that once I
would have considered unethical, unthinkable. Such as the
resolution I had brought to a case last May, up at Lake
Tahoe. If the truth about that had come out, I would have
lost my license and maybe my life. I'd been aware of this at
the time but I had done it anyway. And would again, if I had
it to do over.

Once I had known myself pretty well, known what I
would do in just about any situation. Not anymore. There was
a new, dark side to my personality that I did not know at all,
and that for the rest of my life I would have to be on guard
against. . . .

Outside the wind was gathering strength. Making banshee
noises as it rattled window glass, shook unseen objects. Pacific
Heights is one of the city's hillside neighborhoods, close to the
ocean and the bay, and when the wind blows it blows stron-
gest up here. Most nights I don't mind it. Tonight, it added to
my restlessness.

To keep from listening to it, I swathed my head in blan-
kets and pillows. And to keep from thinking broody thoughts
about myself, or about Kerry and her mother, I tried the
subject of Eberhardt and Bobbie Jean Addison, his soon-to-be
bride.

They had been seeing each other for more than a year
now, seriously for eleven months. He'd first popped the question last May, and kept popping it until she finally relented. I

was happy for both of them, because for both of them it was a
good match. Not only did they love each other, they were
perfectly suited in temperament and emotional needs. Eb had
lived alone for years, since his divorce from his first wife,
Dana, and hated every minute of his enforced bachelorhood;
he was the kind of man who needed a wife and the illusion
that he was "being taken care of." Bobbie Jean had suffered
through two bad marriages, had raised two daughters on her
own, professed to be soured on matrimony, and seemed to
enjoy her independence. In spite of that, she was the kind of
woman who needed to prove to herself that she could make a
relationship with a good man work; that she had not become
selfish, closed off in her feelings, incapable of giving as well as
receiving love.

They were planning an April wedding. Why April? I'd
asked them. Neither had a satisfactory answer. They'd just
decided on April, that was all—one of those mutual decisions
two people make for no reason other than that it seems right
to them. As if it had been divinely ordained. I didn't believe in
that theory of life and the universe, and yet there were things
in my life, too, that seemed predetermined or inevitable—
some right, others wrong, as if I were being manipulated by
outside forces. . . .

The hell with that. I threw another mental switch, re-
routed my thoughts onto the Lujack case.

It was a strange one, all right. Full of complications and
enigmas that seemed to defy rational explanation even after
three weeks of both routine and creative investigation. The
facts were these:

Thomas Lujack and his brother, Coleman, owned and operated a small factory off Bayshore Boulevard, just across the
Daly City line. The factory—Containers, Inc.—manufactured
a variety of cardboard and fiberboard cartons for industrial
and commercial use. The two men had founded it in the early
seventies, weathered a couple of rough years, and with the
financial aid and marketing expertise of a man named Frank
Hanauer, had gradually built it up into a successful operation

that currently employed some thirty people full-time and grossed close to three million a year. The Lujacks each owned forty percent of Containers, Inc.; Hanauer, in return for his early investment, owned the other twenty percent.

According to everyone we'd talked to, the Lujacks and Hanauer got along fine: no personal or business rifts of any kind. Yet on the evening of Tuesday, December 5, Frank Hanauer had been deliberately run down and killed by a Cadillac Seville belonging to and allegedly driven by Thomas Lujack.

The two men had worked late that night, long past the company's five o'clock closing, on the feasibility of opening a branch factory in Fresno. Coleman Lujack had stayed late, too, but only until six fifteen. When he left, his brother and Hanauer were the only ones on the premises. Both Lujacks swore that the work had gone smoothly, with not even a minor disagreement.

A little after seven o'clock, Hanauer had left the premises alone and set out on foot along Industrial Way, the dead-end street on which Containers, Inc., was located. That morning he'd left his car at an auto body shop a block away, to have a dent in the fender repaired; the shop was closed by that time, but because Hanauer had expected to work late, he'd made arrangements with the shop's owner to leave the car locked outside. He had walked about a hundred yards when Thomas Lujack's Caddy swung off the factory grounds, accelerated, veered into Hanauer when he tried to dodge out of the way, continued to the open end of the street at a high rate of speed, and disappeared east on Bayshore Boulevard.

There were two known witnesses to the hit-and-run—and maybe an unknown third. Industrial Way is just what its name implies, a street lined with a variety of small manufacturing companies and warehouses; none of the businesses operates at night, so at 7:00 P.M. the street is virtually deserted. On this particular Tuesday, however, the Lujacks and Frank Hanauer weren't the only ones working late. An accountant named Allen Dinsmore, employed by Soltech, a solar-heating equipment company, was finishing up an overdue profit-and-loss statement. And Nick Pendarves, shop supervisor at a roofing supply outfit called Roofco, who had put in some overtime checking a late-arriving shipment of shingles, had just locked up and was about to get into his car.

The hit-and-run happened right in front of Roofco, less than fifty feet from where Pendarves was standing. It was dark, but there was a moon that night, and a streetlamp not far away; Pendarves claimed he'd had a clear look at the man driving the Caddy. It was Thomas Lujack, he said, and no mistake. He knew Thomas by sight, recognized him instantly. Allen Dinsmore could neither corroborate nor refute Pendarves's ID. He had been more than seventy-five yards away, too far to tell much of anything about the driver.

Dinsmore did contribute one potentially important observation: After the car struck Hanauer and roared away, he saw Pendarves come running out to where Hanauer lay in the street; and he said he had an impression that there was another person standing near Pendarves's car, someone who had also witnessed the hit-and-run. But he couldn't be sure because of the distance, the unsure lighting, and the fact that it had all happened so fast; it might have been nothing more than a shadow. There was no sign of a third witness when he ran outside and joined Pendarves. And Pendarves had flatly denied that anyone had been with him on the Roofco lot.

It was Dinsmore who called the police. Two patrol cars and an Emergency Services ambulance arrived within fifteen minutes. Hanauer was beyond help; the Daly City coroner said later that he must have died instantly. The ambulance had been there about a minute when Thomas Lujack came hurrying on foot out of the Containers, Inc., yard—lured to the scene, he claimed, by the ambulance siren. He expressed amazement, dismay, bewilderment at the death of Hanauer and Pendarves's accusation that he had been driving the car. He said he'd been in his office working since Hanauer's departure; stated that as far as he knew, his Cadillac was still parked on the factory lot; admitted that yes, he'd heard the screeching tires and gunned engine a few minutes earlier but assumed it was just wild-riding kids. Why would *he* run down Frank Hanauer, for God's sake? They'd been friends and business partners for close to twenty years.

The police had checked the Containers, Inc., lot and found Thomas's Cadillac missing. It hadn't taken them long to locate it, abandoned on Bayshore Boulevard less than a quarter mile from the entrance to Industrial Way. The right front fender was caved in, fresh blood and skin tissue and bone fragments adhering to the grille. The key was still in the ignition—a spare key, Thomas said, one he'd kept in a magnetized container behind the rear bumper. His other key was on his ring, and the container was no longer behind the bumper. Who knew he'd kept it there? Why, nobody except his wife and brother. But it was a common hiding place for a spare key; or maybe someone had seen him getting it at the factory one day a couple of weeks ago, when he'd misplaced his key ring. Somebody must be trying to frame him, he said . . . but he had no idea of who or why.

They didn't believe him. Pendarves stood fast to his ID of Lujack as the Caddy's driver; Thomas admitted to being the only person at the factory after Hanauer left; and there was the fact that the Caddy had been abandoned close by. The police theorized that Thomas had returned to Containers, Inc., on foot through the old railroad yards that paralleled Industrial Way to the east. He'd had plenty of time to do that, and to concoct his story on the way; and it being night and the area deserted, he could have managed it without being seen. The evidence was enough so that they'd arrested him on a charge of vehicular homicide.

He'd hired Paul Glickman, who convinced a judge to set a reasonable bail. Meanwhile, the police turned up no apparent motive for Thomas to have murdered Hanauer—but this was canceled out, as far as they were concerned, by the fact that Thomas had a violent temper and an arrest record: He had once been charged with aggravated assault in a restaurant dispute. The week after Christmas, the San Mateo County

DA's office decided to prosecute on a charge of second-degree homicide. The DA refused to plea-bargain, but Thomas said he wouldn't have pled guilty to a reduced charge anyway because he was an innocent man. If and when the case came to trial, Glickman would defend him on that basis.

And that was where Eberhardt and I came in.

Our job was to a) prove Thomas Lujack's innocence by finding out who had stolen his car and run down Hanauer, and why; or b) discredit Pendarves's damning testimony by proving that he was an unreliable witness. In three weeks we hadn't been able to do either. Dozens of interviews and background checks, and my nightly fishing trips at the Hideaway, had produced zero answers and zero leads.

No one seemed to have any motive for doing away with Frank Hanauer. He had been well liked by everybody; had never spoken of problems with Thomas or Coleman Lujack or anyone else at Containers, Inc. For all intents and purposes, he was as unlikely a candidate for murder as you could find.

Similarly, no one seemed to have the kind of grudge against Thomas that would lead to a murder frame. *He* was mostly well liked, despite his roughhouse temper; happily married and afflicted with no major vices. The only possible enemy we were able to turn up was the man he'd had the fight with in the restaurant. But that had happened five years ago; and the other party—a salesman—said he barely remembered the incident, and besides, he'd been in New York on a business trip on December 5.

There were no black marks against Nick Pendarves, either, unless you counted the fact that his wife had divorced him in 1984 for unspecified reasons, and refused to talk to us when we contacted her at her present address in Chico. He had worked for Roofco for twenty-three years and was considered a valued employee; he lived alone in his house on Rivera Street and had never had any problems with his neighbors; he spent part of almost every evening at the Hideaway, the only socializing of any kind that he indulged in. He had no close friends—no friends at all, apparently, except for other patrons of the tavern. He was a taciturn man, one who kept to himself for the most part and was not easy to know. But if nobody particularly liked him, nobody particularly disliked him either. We couldn't find any reason why he would have lied in his positive ID of Thomas Lujack as the hit-and-run driver, or why he would lie about the presence of a third witness. Nor could we find even a mote of evidence to verify that there had been a third witness. None of the other Roofco employees had been given permission to work overtime that night, and Pendarves had been alone in the building when the last of his coworkers left. That seemed to rule out a Roofco employee as the ethereal witness; and the deserted nature of Industrial Way at 7:00 P.M. on a Tuesday night seemed to rule out a passerby or someone who had come for a personal rendezvous with Pendarves.

So there we were as of today, flat up against failure. And now a new and confusing wrinkle had been added—the alleged attempt on Pendarves's life tonight.

If it *had* been a deliberate attempt, then who else but Thomas Lujack? He'd been increasingly nervous of late, fretting about the lack of results. Given his anxiety, and his temper, it was possible that he'd lost control tonight—as he'd allegedly lost control for some reason on the night of December 5—and set out to eliminate the one man who could assure his conviction.

And yet, was he screwy enough to have tried doing it with a car—a method that would point straight at him? I didn't want to think so. But the fact was, I did not know enough about what went on inside the man, or about the motives behind Hanauer's murder, to make a proper judgment.

There were two other alternatives: Somebody else had tried to run down Pendarves tonight; or it had been an accident, one of those crazy coincidences that happen sometimes, and Pendarves's imagination had blown it up into something sinister. The first of the two made sense only if the somebody were acting on Thomas's orders, somebody he paid to eliminate Pendarves; but where was the sense, looking at it from

Lujack's point of view, in premeditating a murder that would surely backfire on him, prejudice his defense, and probably convict him on *two* counts of vehicular homicide? The second alternative was much more likely. It was also the one I wanted it to be, because it negated an ugly twist in a case that was already too complicated and frustrating.

We'd have a better handle on that part of it tomorrow, after we found out what Thomas had to say and after I saw Pendarves again later on. If it was just a false alarm . . . well, that was fine. But in any event we were still smack up against a stone wall on the Hanauer killing.

If Lujack hadn't run him down, then who had? And why?

Chapter 3

TUESDAY WAS ANOTHER gray, blustery day, with a steady drizzle thrown in for added discomfort. I awoke to it late, feeling dull and logy from less than half the sleep I needed, and I was still out of sorts when I got down to the office at nine thirty—as gray inside as the day itself. Not even the prospect of seeing Kerry for lunch cheered me much.

The office Eberhardt and I share is a big converted loft in a building on O'Farrell Street, not far off Van Ness. Before we took it over a few years ago, when we became partners, it had housed an art school whose owner had had a skylight installed. The skylight had shattered during the big quake. The world's ugliest light fixture had also come crashing down, things had fallen off walls and desks, and cracks had spiderwebbed the ceiling. I had been there to see it all happen —alone in the office at four minutes past five that October evening, rinsing out the coffeepot in the alcove sink. If I'd been at my desk instead, the damn light fixture might have done *me* some damage, because it caromed off the desk and knocked my chair over.

As a San Francisco native I've been through a lot of

quakes; but as soon as that one hit, with such jolting violence, I knew it was a bad one—maybe the Big One. My first thought had been for Kerry's safety; I'd believed then that she was still at work on an upper floor in one of the untested new Financial District high rises. In fact she'd left early that day, had just entered her apartment, and hadn't been hurt or even shaken up too badly. But it was a couple of chaotic hours before I found that out, and several more tense hours until I learned that Eberhardt and Bobbie Jean, who had been together in Marin County, had also survived unhurt.

There had been no structural damage to this building, so we were spared having to vacate and find new office space. Over the next couple of weeks, we had prodded our somewhat sleazy landlord into repairing the ceiling, putting in a new skylight and a new (and much less offensive) light fixture, and had otherwise gotten on with our business and our lives. But you don't forget an experience or a tragedy of that magnitude. It hadn't been the Big One after all, but it had given us all a bitter taste of what the Big One would be like.

Seismologists are now predicting a one-in-three likelihood of a 7.5 temblor on the Hayward Fault within the next thirty years, with a projected five thousand dead and forty billion dollars in damages. Those are frightening odds, grim figures. But what do you do in the face of them? Pack up and move away? There's no place that is perfectly safe; natural disasters can happen anywhere. Besides, your chances of dying from a fall in your own bathtub are greater than dying in the worst earthquake; knowing that, how many people get rid of their bathtubs? What you do is to learn the lessons taught by this last quake, the Little Big One, and learn them well, and then put your trust in providence and the law of averages and go on without fear. A life lived in fear is no life at all. . . .

On this January morning the office was cold and bleak, with the weight of the day pressing down against the rain-streaked skylight. I put on the steam heat, put water on to boil for coffee, and checked the answering machine. No messages. Then I called the law offices of Glickman and Crandall, on Pacific Avenue downtown. Paul Glickman wasn't in yet but was expected within the hour. I left a message to have him return my call as soon as he arrived.

It took me thirty minutes to type a report and billing invoice on yesterday's skip-trace. Eberhardt had treated himself to a New Year's present of a small computer, but I'd held firm about not getting one for myself. In an age when detective work is dominated by electronic devices and young three-piecers specializing in high-tech industrial espionage and hostile corporate takeovers, I take a certain amount of pride in being a technophobic throwback. *I* specialize in old-fashioned, low-tech investigative work. I've never been able to fathom the inner workings of Big Business; and anything more mechanically complicated than an electric typewriter makes me nervous. I feel about computers the way aborigines once did about cameras: I'm afraid the damn things will try to steal my soul.

Even so, I might have succumbed to their timesaving lure by now if it weren't for their users' constant proselytizing. There is something about owning a computer that turns normal, even meek individuals—and Eberhardt was no different since he'd gotten his—into slavering zealots who will never rest until they've convinced you to become one of them. Not long ago, a guy I know called me a dinosaur because I don't own a computer; and he got angry, actually angry, when I told him I had no intention of ever owning one . . . as if I'd said I had never been to church and was a budding Satanist besides. Computer technology: the New Religion. I would rather listen to a pack of Jehovah's Witnesses trying to convert me to their brand of the Old Religion than I would to one computer disciple telling me in reverent terms how much his life had changed for the better since he'd gotten his Apple or Kay-Pro, and how *happy* I'd be if only I would renounce my heathen ways and come to worship at the electronic shrine.

It was ten fifteen, and I was making a telephone background check for another client, when Glickman called on the other line. I cut my conversation with the TRW credit people short, then spent five minutes giving Glickman a detailed account of what had happened last night.

He listened without interruption. Unlike some criminal attorneys, he was neither egocentric nor publicity-seeking; and he operated on the principle that other professionals knew their business as well as he knew his and would go about doing their jobs in the most effective ways possible. That made him easy to work with—a rarity among high-powered lawyers these days.

When I was done he asked, "Do you think Pendarves was telling the truth?"

"About the car almost running him down? Yes. There's not much doubt he had a close shave."

"But it could have been an accident."

"Sure. It could also have been deliberate and somebody other than Thomas Lujack was driving the car. Pendarves admitted it was too dark to see clearly. Naming Lujack might have been an emotional response."

"Pendarves isn't normally an emotional man, is he?"

"No."

"Is it likely, then, that he'll follow through on his threats?"

"I'd say no but I can't be sure. He's a hard man to get a fix on."

"I don't want to go to the police if it can be avoided," Glickman said, "especially if he didn't report the near-miss. Our position is shaky enough without this kind of inflammatory thing getting into the record."

"You'll talk to Thomas right away?"

"As soon as I can reach him."

"I'd like to have a few words with him myself. Would you mind arranging a meeting later today at your office?"

"Not at all. I expect to be free after three, if that's convenient for you."

"Fine."

"I'll get back to you as soon as I've spoken to our client."

I was still waiting at twenty past eleven, when I finished

my background check, and still waiting at eleven thirty. That was long enough. I switched on the answering machine, locked up the office, and went to keep my lunch date with Kerry.

LUCY'S CAFÉ, one of those trendy nouvelle cuisine places that caters to the Financial District business crowd, was near the foot of California Street, within hailing distance of the Ferry Building and my former office on Drumm. The ad agency where Kerry worked as a senior copywriter, Bates and Carpenter, maintained a permanent reservation on three tables there; and when one or more of them were not being used for business purposes, B. & C.'s employees were allowed to use them for personal luncheons.

I had been there ten minutes when she arrived. Usually she was prompt for appointments. Usually, too, she came into a place, public or private, with an air of self-possession and good cheer. Not today, though. Not for the past two months. She came in slowly, shoulders rounded a little, and even from a distance you could tell that she was under a strain. Up close, the signs were obvious. She had lost weight again, so that she had the same gaunt-cheeked, hollow-eyed look I had confronted when I came back from my three-month kidnap ordeal. Hurt lay in her gray-green eyes, and it hurt me to see it there and not be able to do something, anything, to wipe it away.

We smiled at each other as she sat down and shrugged out of her coat, untied a scarf that protected her auburn hair. She tried to make her smile bright, but it did not come off. It had a pale, brittle quality at the edges.

"Sorry I'm late," she said. "Damn meeting."

"No problem."

After a few seconds she said, "I look like the wrath of God, don't I?"

"No. You look fine."

"Liar. There seem to be mirrors everywhere I turn these

days. I never realized there were so many mirrors in this city."

"Cold outside," I said, to change the subject. "You want something hot to drink?"

"No, I'd rather have some wine."

I signaled one of the waiters and when he came she ordered a half carafe of chablis. She didn't look at me as she spoke, as if she were afraid I would say something censorious; she had a tendency to drink too much when things were difficult, and we both knew it, and in the past there has been some friction between us because of it. But I hadn't said anything yet in this case and I wouldn't. Only a self-righteous jerk would chastise a woman for drinking too much when she had recently lost her father and her mother was a borderline basket case.

When we were alone again I reached over and took her hand. It was cold, the skin dry, papery. She said, "What I wouldn't give for a good night's sleep. I doubt if I slept four hours last night."

"Cybil?"

"She was up until dawn. Pacing."

"Is that something new?"

"More or less. Around her bedroom, up and down the hall—nonstop. She tries to be quiet but I still hear her."

"You talk to her about it?"

"This morning. She promised she wouldn't do it anymore. God, she's so vague, so abject. She keeps saying what a burden she is and how sorry she is for being one; she's constantly begging me to forgive her. She's so afraid."

"Of you putting her in some kind of home."

"That, and of being dependent on strangers, and of dying alone. I keep trying to reassure her but it doesn't sink in. Nothing sinks in."

I said gently, "You're sure she's not suffering from Alzheimer's or something similar?"

"Sure enough. Her memory is fine . . . too fine. She talks on and on about the past, about Ivan. It's grief and depression and something else too, I'm not sure what." Kerry shook her head; her eyes were moist. "I used to think she was strong, stronger than my father, better able to handle a crisis. But now . . . she's not the same person I grew up with, that I've known all my life. She's changed, and I don't just mean because of Ivan's death."

She got old, I thought. In spirit as well as years. One day not so long ago, even before Ivan's fatal heart attack, she woke up and she was old.

I didn't say that to Kerry; it would have been cruel. I said, "She still won't talk to a grief counselor?"

"No. She breaks down and cries every time I suggest it. She won't see or talk to anyone but me. Won't leave the apartment for any reason now. When I'm there she follows me around like a puppy. When I'm not there she just sits and stares at the TV. Or cleans; she's scrubbed the kitchen floor three times in the past week."

"Maybe *you* ought to talk to somebody, then—a doctor who specializes in geriatric cases."

"I've thought of that. Psychotherapeutic medication might help Cybil's depression, except that she wouldn't take it voluntarily. She's never believed in drugs. And a reputable doctor wouldn't prescribe medication anyway without examining her first."

"I meant for counseling," I said. "Advice on how to cope with the situation, what to do about it."

"Maybe you're right. I've got to do something, I know that. I still want to believe she'll snap out of it on her own, but I know in my heart she won't."

The waiter arrived with her wine, and a silence developed between us while we looked at the menus. I found myself remembering Cybil the first time I'd met her, at a convention of pulp writers and collectors like myself, several years ago—the same convention at which Kerry had come into my life. Cybil had been in her sixties then, yet still vibrant, attractive, young at heart; a mature version of the beautiful woman she must have been in the 1940s, when she and Ivan both made their living writing stories for the mystery and fantasy pulp magazines. Russell Dancer, another pulpster who had long carried the torch for her, called her "Sweeteyes"—a name that fit her perfectly. Cybil Wade had been a sweeteyed presence that the years had failed to damage.

I thought then of the last time I'd seen her, the week before Christmas when Kerry and I picked her up at the airport. I had barely recognized the frail, stooped, white-haired woman whose eyes were dim and haunted, no longer sweet. Even now I could hear the thin, unfamiliar voice saying to Kerry on the ride back to the city, reliving what she had already relived a hundred times, "He was out in the garden all afternoon, tending his flowers. . . . It was a warm day and I told him to wear his sun hat but you know your father, he never listened, he was such a stubborn man. . . . I was in the kitchen making an early supper when I heard him come inside. . . . I poured a beer for him and took it in and he was sitting in his chair, so still, I knew immediately he was dead. . . . He never spoke a word, isn't that just like him, he simply sat down in his chair and died. . . ." Cybil Wade: seventy-five, recently widowed, and unable to cope with either death or life, unable to remain in the Los Angeles home she and Ivan had shared for over fifty years because "I see him everywhere in that house. . . . I'll go out of my mind if I stay there. . . ."

She hadn't said much to me that day, had seemed hostile. The hostility had burgeoned over the holidays, gotten to the point where I couldn't even call Kerry at home without triggering an emotional outburst in her mother. The reason was simple: I had never cared for Ivan Wade and he had never cared for me and we'd made no secret of our mutual dislike. More than once he'd tried to break up Kerry's relationship with me; he felt I was too old for her, worked at a dangerous profession, was unworthy for other reasons that had to do with paternal expectations and jealousy. More than once we'd had angry words. Cybil and I had always gotten along well, but since Ivan's death she had translated my troubles with him into a mistaken belief that I was glad he was dead, and so she had grown to hate me for my imagined callousness.

Kerry knew what kind of man her father had been, and what kind of man I was; she didn't resent me as Cybil did. Yet she also knew, without it having been mentioned by either of us, that while I wasn't happy Ivan was gone, I felt no real sorrow at his passing. That knowledge was like a small wedge between us, one that only time would work loose. It had made the last few weeks that much more difficult for both of us.

We each ordered a seafood salad for lunch. Kerry picked at hers, then abandoned it completely in favor of what was left of her chablis. The wine put a darker flush on her cheeks than the cold had done. It seemed to relax her, too, so that we were able to maintain a pretense of ease in each other's company. But a pretense is all it was. Even though we didn't talk any more about either Cybil or Ivan, they were there at the table with us like a pair of ghosts.

We didn't linger over coffee. Outside, I walked with her to the building in which Bates and Carpenter had its offices. When we entered the lobby she drew me away from the nearest people, leaned close with her fingers tight on my arm, and murmured against my ear, "I think I can get off a little early tomorrow, around three thirty. How about you?"

"Sure. I don't have anything pressing."

"I could meet you at your place around four."

"I'd like that."

"I need you," she said. "You know?"

"I know, babe. I need you too."

"Call me after lunch tomorrow, just to make sure."

I said I would. She kissed me quickly, and touched my cheek, and hurried away across the lobby. I watched her until she got into one of the elevators; then I went back out into the wet afternoon.

Thinking: Assignation made in a public place. Like two new and furtive lovers living for the present because the future is uncertain.

It made me sad, and a little excited, and a little afraid.

Chapter **4**

WHEN I GOT BACK to the office I found Eberhardt waiting. He was lounging at his desk, fouling the air with smoke from one of his stubby old briars. I'd given him a good Danish tobacco for his birthday, but predictably enough he'd gone back to smoking his favorite blend—an evil black mixture of latakia and dried horse turds, judging from the smell of it.

"I got to Rivas right at noon," he said, "and we didn't talk long. So I figured I might as well come back here."

I nodded. "Glickman call?"

"No messages on the machine, no calls since I came in."

"Damn. Means he hasn't been able to locate Thomas."

"Doesn't have to be anything in that."

"I know, but I don't like it."

"You won't like this either," he said. "Pendarves didn't show up for work today."

"Oh, fine. He at least call in with an excuse?"

"Yeah. Head cold."

"Uh-huh." I went over and cracked the window that looks down toward the rear end of the Federal Building on

Golden Gate. Cold wind and drizzle were preferable to lethal tobacco smoke. "What else did you find out from Rivas?"

"Doesn't seem to be anything thick between him and Pendarves. He claims they haven't said more than fifty words to each other the past week, and none at all in two days."

"You think there's any chance he's the third witness?"

"Next to none."

"Another bust, then."

"Not exactly. I did pry something out of him on Containers, Inc.—something Rivas admits he let slip to Pendarves once."

"And that is?"

"The Lujacks are running an illegal shop."

"Illegal? Meaning what?"

"Most of their labor force is undocumented aliens," he said. "Out of the drive-by hiring halls in the Mission."

"The hell."

"Puts a whole new slant on things, doesn't it."

It did that, if it was true. Somewhere around a million illegal aliens from Mexico and Central America now live in California, thousands of them in San Francisco's Mission District and in Daly City farther west; many have no jobs and no way of getting legitimate work without green cards from the Immigration and Naturalization Service. So the drive-by halls were born, and have flourished in the city and throughout the state.

On a dozen or more street corners in the Mission, illegals congregate early every morning, like cattle in pens, waiting for employers on the prowl for cheap labor to come driving along. A painting contractor, for instance, goes to a drive-by hall that specializes in illegals with painting skills; picks as many men as he needs for a particular job, or series of jobs, and hauls them to and from the sites; and pays them wages far below union scale—in cash, always, so there is no record of their employment. If the employer is a plumbing contractor, or runs a gardening business, or owns a factory that makes containers and requires the services of multipurpose workers, he goes to the street corner where his particular brand of illicit labor has assembled.

The police can't do much about the drive-by halls except to disperse crowds of men that sometimes become unruly; they don't have the jurisdiction. The INS has enacted a law carrying stiff penalties for employers caught hiring illegals, but they're too understaffed and overworked to effectively enforce it. So both the illegals and the cheap-labor bosses make out fine: One side avoids the need for applications, interviews, union cards, and green cards; the other side avoids paying union wages, as well as withholding tax and FICA to the state and federal governments. But the big loser isn't the IRS or the Franchise Tax Board or the INS. It's the citizen and legitimate union worker, no matter what his race or job skill, who can't find work to support *his* family because the positions have all been filled by illegals.

The real villains are the greedy employers. So far, after two meetings with Thomas Lujack and three weeks of work on his defense team, I had maintained a neutral attitude toward him; I neither liked nor disliked him, neither believed nor disbelieved in his innocence. If he was employing illegals, it tipped my feelings over onto the negative side. But it didn't make any difference in how we handled his case; didn't make him guilty of vehicular homicide or attempted vehicular homicide.

I asked, "How long have they been using illegals?"

"A long time, according to Rivas," Eberhardt said. "Years."

"How come you didn't pick up a whisper of it before this? Hell, how come the Daly City cops didn't when they were investigating Hanauer's death?"

"The Lujacks have got it covered up pretty well, for one thing. You'd have to go deep into the company books to get a real smell of it. There's never been a complaint to the INS, evidently."

"How'd Rivas find out about it?"

"How do you think? He's Mexican and lives in the Mission."

"Has *he* got a green card?"

"Oh, yeah. He showed it to me."

"If he told Pendarves and you," I said, "he must have told others. You'd think somebody would've let it slip."

"Who's going to blab a thing like that to the cops, get himself branded as a snitch? I had to practically threaten it out of Rivas, poor bastard. And I had to promise him we'd keep shut about where the information came from. At that, I don't think I got the full story."

"What do you think he held back?"

"Beats me."

After a few seconds I said, "Now I'm wondering if this has anything to do with Hanauer's murder."

"Same here. But I don't see how."

"Neither do I. And even if it did, why wouldn't Thomas himself have come out with it to save his own hide? Hiring illegal aliens is a minor offense compared to second-degree homicide."

"I can think of one reason," Eberhardt said.

"Yeah. He's guilty as hell on all counts. But that still doesn't explain how the illegals thing could have triggered the hit-and-run."

"Some sort of fight about it, maybe. One of them wanted to keep hiring illegals, the other one didn't."

"That's not much of a motive for murder. Did Rivas know which of the Lujacks does the actual hiring? Or was it Hanauer, maybe?"

"None of them. Shop foreman named Vega, Rafael Vega."

"You know this Vega?"

"Talked to him briefly a couple of weeks ago. Didn't leave much of an impression one way or the other. But Rivas seems to be afraid of him."

"He give you any idea why?"

"No. Wouldn't talk about it." Eberhardt's pipe had gone

out; he paused to relight it. "So what do you think? Should I have a talk with Vega?"

"Let's both have a talk with him. Coleman Lujack too."

"Now or later?"

"Now," I said. "It beats sitting around here waiting for Glickman to call."

INDUSTRIAL WAY angles off Bayshore Boulevard just beyond where Bayshore crosses the southwestern boundary line between San Francisco and Daly City. It's an odd, grim little pocket of light industry, low-income housing, and urban squalor. Here you have the desolate, 440-acre ruins of Southern Pacific's Bayshore Yards; and nearby, the predominantly black Sunnydale Housing Projects, overrun with poverty, drugs, and drug-related gang violence—the same projects that had "terrified" a touring HUD official in the Reagan Administration a few years ago, even though he had visited them in the company of a police escort. Not far away, crowning the low Daly City hills, are saggy rows of the "ticky-tacky" houses ridiculed by Malvina Reynolds in her protest song "Little Boxes." Within a two-mile radius are two of the city's major sports and recreation centers, Candlestick Park and the Cow Palace; Highway 101, the main arterial leading down the Peninsula; the rugged San Bruno Mountains and the upscale hillside community of Brisbane.

An odd little street, Industrial Way, within the odd little pocket—a three-block-long dead end lined with small manufacturing and warehousing companies, an auto-body shop, an outfit that makes statuary for gardens and cemeteries, and one big land-ocean freight-forwarding operation. There is no other industry in the immediate area; Industrial Way and its tenants sit alone, flanked on one side by Bayshore Boulevard climbing toward Brisbane, and on the other side by the abandoned railroad yards.

It was a little before two when I turned onto Industrial. Eberhardt and I had flipped a coin to see who would drive and I'd lost. The morning drizzle had evolved into a misty rain, with dark low-hanging clouds. The weather gave the ravaged yards an even gloomier aspect: war zone after a recent cease-fire. The property had been this way for several years now, steadily worsening since a fire of dubious origin destroyed one of the main buildings and Southern Pacific decided to phase out operations here. Before that, for nearly seventy years, the Bayshore Yards had been one of the line's main repair centers for locomotives and cars: miles of track, a big roundhouse, warehouses, other facilities. Now most of the track had been taken up, the buildings were just burned-out shells, parts of which had collapsed during the recent earthquake, and the only reminders of what the acreage had once been used for were the rusting corpses of a water tower, some hoists, a few discarded boxcars, flats, and tankers. Those, and SP's one remaining operational facility here: their freight claims department on Sunnydale at the far end of the property.

Beside me, Eberhardt said, "This place depresses me every time I come out here. You know what I mean?"

"Too well."

"I used to go into the Bayshore Yards when I was a kid," he said. "One of the wipers in the roundhouse was a friend of my old man's and he'd let me hang around sometimes, watch the work that was going on. I had a thing about trains in those days. Wanted to be a gandy dancer."

"Track worker? You?"

"Yeah, well, I was a kid. Eleven or twelve. Go out on a handcar, swing a nine-pound sledge like John Henry, repair track . . . hell, it seemed like a pretty exciting life."

"Sure. Hard work, low pay, and a high risk factor."

"Just like being a cop," he said wryly.

"You made the right choice, Eb."

"I suppose. But man, the yards were really something in those days. Now look. Nothing left but rats and weeds and junkies wandering in to shoot up. Vandals don't even bother with it anymore. It's a crying shame the SP doesn't do something about it."

"Seems I heard they're trying to sell the property."

"Who to?"

"Anybody who'll buy it, I guess."

"You'd think the city would be interested. Or San Mateo County. Or both together. They could clean it out, put in a park maybe. Cheap housing, if nothing else."

"The city's deeper in debt than the federal government," I said. "San Mateo County too, for all I know."

"Yeah," he said. "Shit," he said.

Containers, Inc., was at the far end of Industrial Way—a large corrugated-iron building that housed the manufacturing plant and shipping facilities, with a much smaller structure built onto the near side for the office staff. From a distance, the whole thing had the appearance of a squared-off metal igloo. There was no fence around it, but at night the grounds were lighted by sodium-vapor arc lights, and the entire building was protected by an alarm system; a private security patrol also cruised the area after dark. It was that kind of area.

Opposite the office wing was a small parking lot, jammed now with a couple of dozen vehicles. I pulled in there, found an empty slot and filled it.

The death of Frank Hanauer, the murder charge against Thomas Lujack, and all the publicity surrounding the affair did not seem to have had any adverse effect on the factory's business. Over on the far side, where the loading docks were, trucks jockeyed around and men and forklifts worked busily; the steady thrum of machinery came from inside the big building. Not that the activity surprised me at all. Nothing much interferes with the grinding wheels of industry these days, not where a product-in-demand is concerned. Everybody needs boxes to put things in, commercial establishments in particular; and in a consumer society, the product is all that matters. Who cares who makes the boxes—illegal aliens, space aliens, even murderers—just so long as they get made.

We went into the main office, a good-sized room divided in half lengthwise by a waist-high counter. On our side were some uncomfortable-looking visitors' chairs and a closed door; on the other side were four desks occupied by three women and one man, two of the women working computer terminals, the man talking on the telephone. The third woman, whose desk was nearest the counter, didn't seem to be doing much of anything; and she evidently didn't want to be disturbed while she was not doing it. I had to call to her twice before she deigned to acknowledge our presence.

Her name, according to one of those little wood-and-brass identifiers, was Teresa Melendez. She was young and dark and buxom and ripe-looking, the kind of woman who would weigh two hundred pounds someday if she was not careful about her diet. She said, "What can I do for you?" in a bored monotone with not too much accent. This was the first time I'd been here, but Eberhardt had paid a couple of previous visits; if she recognized him, she gave no indication of it.

"We'd like to see Thomas Lujack," I said.

"He's not here."

"Has he been in today?"

"No."

"How about Coleman Lujack?"

"You have an appointment?"

"I think he'll see us without one."

I gave her one of the agency cards with both Eberhardt's and my name on it. Ms. Melendez didn't even glance at it. She put her back to us and went away through a doorway, not hurrying, showing off her hips under a tight leather skirt. Eberhardt watched with considerable interest, until I said, "And you engaged to be married soon, you old lecher." Then he scowled and looked at a spot on the wall, pretending he didn't know what I was talking about.

Ms. Melendez came back pretty soon and said that Mr. Lujack would be right out, why didn't we have a seat. So we each had a seat. The chairs were as uncomfortable as they looked. "Right out" translated to five minutes; then the near inner door opened and Coleman Lujack favored us with his presence.

He was not much to look at—a drab, rabbity version of

his brother, who by most standards qualified as dapper and handsome. Coleman was in his early forties, a couple of years older than Thomas; slight of build, sparse of hair the noncolor of lint. His brown suit didn't quite fit him properly, his blue shirt was wrinkled, and the knot in his tie was crooked. If he'd had ink-stained fingers, you would have sworn he was a minor company clerk.

He greeted us diffidently, put dampness on my hand when he shook it, and ushered us inside to his private office. It was small and windowless, and as disheveled as he was. Judging from a couple of sporty prints on the walls, and a carved and painted mallard decoy on one corner of his desk, shooting ducks was what he liked to do in his spare time. Trying to shoot ducks, anyway. As nervous as he was, I would have put my money on the ducks. I would also have been afraid to hunker down in a blind with him and a loaded shotgun.

Coleman removed catalogs from one of the two visitors' chairs, mates of the ones out front, and plunked them down on top of a boxy piece of furniture that pretended to be a solid-block table but was actually a common variety of floor safe. He said, "Sit down, sit down," and then went behind his desk and did the same himself. He lit a cigarette before he said, "Why are you both here? You find out something to help clear Tom?"

I said, "No, not yet."

He waited for me to go on, and when I didn't he asked in his nervous way, "Well, then? What can I do for you?"

"Your brother didn't come in today. Why?"

"He had an outside appointment."

"Who with?"

"One of our suppliers in Emeryville."

"What time was the appointment?"

"Eleven this morning, with lunch afterward."

"You talk to him today?"

"No, not since last night. Why are you—"

"You saw him last night, after work?"

"At my home, yes."

"Social occasion?"

"We had business matters to go over."

"What time did he arrive?"

"Around seven—I don't remember exactly."

"How long did he stay?"

"Until nine."

"You're sure it was nine? Not eight or eight thirty?"

"It was nine. He mentioned the time, said he'd better be getting home. He called Eileen to tell her he was on his way."

"Was anyone else there?"

"Working with us, you mean? No. But my wife was home."

"Did she see your brother? Can she verify that he didn't leave until nine?"

"Yes, sure," Coleman said, frowning. A long ash broke loose from his cigarette and fragmented on the desk; he brushed it off agitatedly. "Why are you asking so many questions? Has something happened?"

"Well, for one thing," Eberhardt said, "Nick Pendarves was almost run down and killed last night. Outside the bar he frequents. He says your brother was driving the car."

Coleman gaped at him. "You . . . are you serious?"

"Don't we look serious, Mr. Lujack?"

"But my God! You can't believe that Tom . . ."

"Not if he was with you at nine o'clock."

"He was. I told you he was. Pendarves didn't tell the police Tom tried to kill him . . . ?"

"Not as far as we know," I said. "What he did do was make some veiled threats. I was there; I heard him."

"Threats? What kind of threats?"

"The nonspecific kind."

"Christ. He wouldn't do anything violent, would he?"

"Let's hope not."

"Tom . . . does he know about this?"

"I tried to call him last night. From what you tell us, he was at your home. I told his attorney about it this morning."

Coleman shook his head. "You're sure Pendarves is telling the truth? He really was almost run down?"

"Yes."

"Does he claim he actually saw the driver of the car? If he does, then it proves he's an unreliable witness—"

"He doesn't. He's assuming it was Thomas."

"The same sort of assumption he made three weeks ago," Coleman said bitterly. "Damn the man. Damn him."

Eberhardt said, "That's not the only reason we're here, Mr. Lujack. There's another little matter we're interested in."

"I don't . . . what matter?"

"Illegal aliens."

There was a silence. From the factory came the steady hum and whine of machinery, a voice yelling something in Spanish; in here, the only sound was the quickened rasp of Coleman's breathing. He had quit looking at Eberhardt and me. His eyes followed the movement of his fingers as he removed another cigarette from the pack, lit it from the butt of the one he had burning. The office was already thick with smoke, and what he added to it now made me cough. I swatted at a drift of the pale death, sent some of it back his way.

"Well, Mr. Lujack?"

"What about illegal aliens?" he said to his hands.

"You or your brother should have told us you were employing them."

"Why? It has nothing to do with your investigation."

"Maybe it does," I said. "It's a can of worms anyway—one Pendarves might just open up on you."

"What do you mean by that?"

"Something he said last night. He knows you've got a factory full of undocumented workers, and he's got a mad-on against your brother. He might decide to blow the whistle to the INS."

"Christ! As if Tom and I don't have enough problems . . ."

Eberhardt said, "Nobody forced you to hire illegals."

Coleman spread his hands defensively. "A lot of small businessmen do it these days. It's a matter of economics—"

"It's also against the law."

"I know that. But companies like ours *have* to cut costs to stay in business. Our profit margin—"

"We're not interested in your profit margin or your excuses," Eberhardt said. "All we're interested in is how it affects the job we were hired to do. *Somebody* killed Frank Hanauer, and that somebody had to have a reason."

"It couldn't possibly have anything to do with our hiring practices."

"No? What makes you so sure?"

"It just couldn't, that's all."

"Did Hanauer approve of employing illegals?"

"Of course he approved."

"No trouble between him and your brother about it?"

"No. None."

"Trouble between Hanauer and an illegal?"

"Not that I know about."

"Your brother and an illegal?"

"No. I told you before—Frank got along with everyone and so does Tom. Neither of them had any enemies here."

"Hanauer had one somewhere," I said.

"Well, it wasn't Tom."

"Big turnover rate among the illegals, is there?"

"They come and go."

"But some stay on. Some have been here a while."

"We always try to keep good workers."

"Rafael Vega one of them?"

"Rafael? He isn't an illegal."

"But he is in charge of hiring them?"

". . . Yes."

"You give him carte blanche on who and when and how many?"

"Mostly. He's the shop foreman. And he knows those people; he lives among them."

Those people. "So maybe he also knows something you don't—something that'll help clear your brother."

"He doesn't," Coleman said. "If he did he would've come forward by now."

"Unless he doesn't know he knows it," Eberhardt said. "Maybe nobody asked him the right questions. How about if you send for him and we'll see what kind of answers he gives us."

"He isn't here."

"Off work today, you mean?"

"Yes."

"Called in sick?"

"I don't think so, no."

"Uh-huh. Lot of people off work today. Your brother, Vega, Pendarves."

"Coincidence. You can't make anything out of that."

"Maybe not. Tell us about Vega."

"Tell you what? He's an excellent worker, very dependable."

"Except for today."

Coleman didn't say anything.

"How long's he been working for you?"

"Seven years."

"How does he get along with the undocumented workers?"

"Very well. How many times do I have to tell you that we've never had any trouble here at the factory?"

"Just one big happy family," Eberhardt said sardonically. "You wouldn't mind letting us have Vega's home address, would you?"

Coleman crushed out what was left of his second cancer stick, nibbled at his lower lip like a rabbit working on a piece of celery. "I'll tell Ms. Melendez to give it to you," he said, and reached for the telephone, and then paused with his hand on the receiver. "Is that all? If there's nothing else, I have work to do."

"Another good worker," Eberhardt said. "No, there's nothing else. Not right now, anyway."

We got on our feet. Coleman said, "*You* don't intend to report us to the INS, do you? I mean, it would do Tom more harm than good. . . ."

"That all depends, Mr. Lujack."

"On what?"

"On what we find out about Frank Hanauer's death. But by then it might not matter. By then Pendarves may have already turned you in."

Out front, Ms. Melendez stopped doing nothing much long enough to provide Rafael Vega's home address. That was all she gave us; no smile, no good-bye. None of the other office staff did any smiling, either. Working at Containers, Inc., was a bundle of fun, all right.

On the way through the misty rain to the car, Eberhardt said, "Coleman's some piece of work."

"Yeah. He grows on you—like mold."

"I wouldn't trust him as far as I could throw him. Could be he wasn't as chummy with Hanauer as he'd like us to think. Could be *he* had a reason to want Hanauer dead."

"It's buried deep, if so."

Eberhardt grunted. "Kind of a bust, talking to him. But at least we know Thomas is all right."

"Not necessarily in the clear, though. Family alibis aren't worth a damn. Let's see if Glickman's made contact with him yet."

We got into the car. While I was punching out Glickman's number on the mobile phone, Eb said thoughtfully, "Funny that both Pendarves and Rafael Vega didn't show up for work today. Might be a coincidence, like Coleman said. Might also be some connection between those two, huh?"

"We'll go over to the Mission and ask Vega. Or one of us will if Glickman and Thomas are ready to talk."

They were, it turned out. Eb and I tossed a coin to see which of us would go where. He got the Mission, I got Glickman's office downtown.

Chapter 5

BACK IN THE BARBARY COAST DAYS, before and for a while after the 1906 quake, the block of Pacific Avenue between Kearny and Montgomery was known as Terrific Street. There were twenty-four saloons and dance halls in that one block, among them the Criterion, the So-Different, the Golden City, and Spider Kelly's notorious watering hole on the first floor of the Seattle Hotel. On Terrific Street in those days you could buy just about anything in the way of sinful pleasure, from opium dreams to "specialty" prostitutes from the four corners of the globe.

The saloons and dance halls are generations gone, victims of the Red Light Abatement Act of 1914, but most of the original squat brick buildings are still standing today—survivors of the '89 quake as well. Their outward appearance hasn't changed much since the post-1906 reconstruction. Despite the cars in the street and the high rises towering on all sides, you can almost feel their history—a sense of what it must have been like on the Barbary Coast a century ago.

Nowadays, the Terrific Street buildings house offices, many of which are vacant. There is an overabundance of downtown office space, particularly in the modern Financial District to the immediate north, and as a result the owners of these venerables have been reluctant to make improvements or lease concessions demanded by current and prospective tenants. Some of the owners were being forced into making repairs because of structural weakening after the recent quake; but the buildings' age and brick construction still make them undesirable now that everyone's earthquake consciousness has been raised. If it weren't for the fact that they're a part of the Jackson Square Historic District, they might have been sold long ago and razed in favor of high rises. One of the country's most flamboyant criminal attorneys, Melvin Belli, still has his offices in one of them and makes a practice of sitting in his window and sneering at tourists who come to gawk. Less well known, if no less competent, attorneys— criminal and otherwise—also have their offices on Terrific Street. Paul Glickman is one of them.

I entered his building, across the street and down the block from Belli's, at three twenty. Glickman and his partner, Elston Crandall, occupied the entire second floor. Their reception room was far more sedate than Belli's, which I had had occasion to visit once; in fact, about the only thing they had in common were high ceilings, windows facing Pacific, and outside window boxes full of flowers. I gave my name to the male receptionist and was shown into Glickman's private sanctum right away.

He was alone when I entered, seated behind a broad walnut desk that faced his own row of windows overlooking Terrific Street. Thomas Lujack wasn't due until a quarter of four. I'd wanted a few minutes alone with Glickman first; he had had a client with him when I called from Containers, Inc., and we had spoken just briefly. He stood to shake my hand, then waved me to a chair upholstered in tan cloth. Tan and walnut-brown were the dominant colors here—all very tasteful and dignified, so as to inspire confidence in his clients, no doubt. *He* inspired confidence too: in his early fifties, trim, with salt-and-pepper hair, calm eyes that looked at you steadily from beneath bushy brows, and a quiet take-charge manner. If I ever had the misfortune to find myself charged with a felony, he was the man I would want to defend me.

He had a habit of steepling his fingers when he talked from a seated position; he did that now. Without preamble he said, "It appears Nick Pendarves was in error last night. Mr. Lujack claims he was at his brother's home in Burlingame until nine o'clock."

"Coleman confirms it," I said. "Eberhardt and I talked to him an hour ago."

"So. If Pendarves was wrong once in making a 'positive' identification, he could just as easily be wrong twice."

"It's a nice legal point, anyway."

"Mmm. It almost makes me wish Pendarves had filed a police report. Which he hasn't yet, or I would have heard about it."

"You don't really want it in the public record, do you?"

"Only if it can be proven beyond a doubt that there wasn't a deliberate attempt on Pendarves's life. I find it hard to believe that Mr. Lujack would hire someone to run down Pendarves with a car, but a jury might not. Juries are unpredictable, especially in a homicide trial."

"I don't see any way of proving it now," I said.

"No, neither do I."

"I take it Pendarves hasn't tried to contact Thomas since last night?"

"No."

"With any luck, he won't. What was Thomas's reaction when you told him about the incident?"

"Shock, dismay, anger. He sounded genuinely upset."

"*He* won't do anything rash, will he?"

"I warned him against it."

"Then Pendarves is the only one we have to worry about. He may just let the whole thing slide, but I wouldn't want to bet on it."

"Would it do any good for you to talk to him?"

"I doubt it. But I'll give it a try tonight." I glanced at my watch; it was twenty of four. "There's something you should know before Thomas gets here," I said, "something Eberhardt found out today from a coworker of Pendarves's named Antonio Rivas. I don't know that it has anything to do with Frank Hanauer's murder, but it's a possibility." I went on to tell him about the illegals situation at Containers, Inc.

Glickman had one of those unreadable courtroom faces, an attribute that helped make him a good trial attorney, but I could tell from the clipped way he said "Mr. Lujack should have seen fit to tell us that himself" that he didn't like the news any better than I did.

"His brother claims they kept quiet because it couldn't have any bearing on Hanauer's murder. The real reason is they were afraid it would leak out to the INS."

"If it becomes a matter of public record now, it could have a prejudicial effect on our case."

"Unless it relates to the homicide in a way that proves Thomas innocent."

"Do you think it might?"

"Too soon for me to say. How would you've handled the illegals thing if the Lujacks had owned up in the beginning?"

"Advised them to turn themselves in immediately," Glickman said. "And to issue a statement to the media that they were doing so voluntarily, as an act of contrition. The public approves of voluntary confessions of minor sins, if they're done at the right time for the right reasons; it would have helped Thomas's credibility. Going public at this late date would have the opposite effect, I'm afraid. The prosecution would see to it if the case does go to trial."

"So how do you handle it now?"

"That depends. On what Mr. Lujack has to tell us, and whether or not you can establish a link between the illegals matter and the death of Frank Hanauer."

Thomas Lujack showed up ten minutes late and full of apologies. "Traffic's snarled on the Bay Bridge," he said. "People drive like idiots in bad weather." He pumped my hand, pumped Glickman's, hung his damp London Fog trench coat on an antique clothes tree, and plunked himself down on another of the visitors' chairs.

He was a couple of years younger than his brother, and far more stylish in his appearance and dress. Longish fox-brown hair, swept back on both sides in thick wings; silky-looking mustache that partially concealed a weak mouth. Wearing a Harris tweed sport coat today, over a mint-green shirt and designer jeans, with a couple of flashy gold chains looped around his neck. He made me feel rumpled and out-moded by comparison. He even managed to make Glickman look stuffy and bourgeois, like a Capitol Hill Republican.

Usually he had an easy, breezy way about him that may have been natural and may have been calculated for effect. The past couple of times I'd seen him, though, he'd been as fidgety as his brother. Today he couldn't seem to keep his hands still; they plucked at the creases in his trousers, touched his face, touched his hair, drummed at the arms of the chair, fiddled with the gold chains.

He said to me, "I guess Paul's told you I was at Coleman's until nine last night."

"He told me," I said. "So did Coleman."

"Ah? You talked to him? Well, good, good. Then you know I had nothing to do with what happened to Pendarves. *If* anything happened. I doubt it, myself."

"You go straight home after you left Coleman's?"

"Sure. Straight home."

"I called your house at a quarter of ten. There was no answer."

"Quarter of ten last night? That was about when I got there. You must have just missed me."

"Uh-huh. Where was your wife? Coleman said you called her before you left his place."

"At a friend's. I picked her up on the way. I've been using her car since . . . well, since December fifth. She's got a rental but she doesn't like to drive much."

I watched his hands dip and flutter. The nervousness didn't have to mean anything. Hell, if I were facing one vehicular homicide rap, and had just been accused of another by the star witness in the first case, I wouldn't be sitting still either.

I said, "You have any contact with Pendarves in the past three weeks? Any kind at all?"

"Christ, no. You think I want anything to do with that schmuck?"

"You might have tried to talk to him, see if you could convince him he was wrong about what he saw."

"Uh-uh. No way. Paul warned me against that."

"Suppose Pendarves tries to talk to you about last night. How do you handle him?"

"I don't," Thomas said. "I steer clear of him."

"And if he makes any overt threat or action?"

"I report it to Paul immediately."

Glickman's hard steady gaze was fixed on his client. After a few seconds he said, "Now then, Mr. Lujack. We'll discuss your practice of hiring illegal aliens."

Thomas sat still for a couple of beats, showing no reaction. Then his hands began to move restlessly again, and he smiled in a wry and self-deprecating way. "So you found out about that."

"Did you think we wouldn't?"

"Well, I hoped not. It's not something I'm proud of."

"Why didn't you confide in me?"

"I didn't see any reason to. Neither did Coleman. Why open up a can of worms if you don't have to?"

"If it's opened publicly now," Glickman said, "it won't help you in court."

"I know. But it's not going to get opened publicly, not if we keep it among ourselves."

I said, "What makes you so sure?"

"The INS hasn't tumbled in six years. Why should they now?"

"Is that how long you've been employing illegals? Six years?"

"About."

"Whose bright idea was it in the first place?"

"Does that matter?"

"It might. It ever occur to you that maybe there's a connection between the illegals and Hanauer's murder?"

"Oh, come on. What possible connection could there be?"

"You tell us, Mr. Lujack."

"None. None at all."

"Was it Hanauer's idea?"

"To hire illegals? No. It was Coleman's."

"You and Hanauer approve it right away?"

"More or less. We were still on shaky financial ground in those days and it was a way to save ourselves thousands of dollars a year. Hell, like it or not, undocumented workers have become a common business option—"

"You or Hanauer ever have trouble with your workers? Somebody you had to fire, for instance?"

"I know I didn't. Frank would have mentioned it if he had. Besides, neither of us hires or fires the factory workers. Our shop foreman takes care of that."

"Rafael Vega."

"Right."

"Did Vega have trouble with any of the illegals during the past year?"

"Nothing he reported . . ." Thomas's voice trailed off, and he frowned. At length he said, "Well, there was one clash between him and Frank. But it was so minor I'd forgotten all about it."

"What kind of clash?"

"Words, that's all. A couple of months ago."

"Were you there at the time?"

"Yeah. It got a little heated."

"What did they have words about?"

"Production. We had a rush order for a hundred gross of number ten singlewalls, one that Frank brought in personally, and we were behind schedule. He blamed Vega for the delay."

"You said the exchange got heated. How heated?"

"Oh, they did some shouting at each other. Vega threatened to quit, but that was just chili-pepper talk."

"That all he threatened to do?"

"You mean did he make any threats against Frank? No, it wasn't like that. Nothing personal. Just one of those workplace flare-ups, that's all. The next day it was like it never happened."

"How did Hanauer and Vega get along otherwise?"

". . . All right. No problems."

"You sound a little hesitant."

"I'm just trying to remember. To be honest, I don't think Frank liked Vega much. And the feeling was probably mutual. But again, it wasn't personal."

"What was it, then?"

"I guess you'd call it bigotry," Thomas said. "Frank didn't care for Mexicans. Didn't actively hate them, you understand—just didn't much care for them as a race. He thought they were lazy."

"Uh-huh. And Vega knew or sensed this."

"I wouldn't be surprised."

"How about you? What's your opinion of Latinos?"

"I'm no bigot, if that's what you mean. I like Mexicans just fine."

Sure you do, I thought. That's why you hire illegal aliens and pay them starvation wages without any benefits. That's why you use phrases like "chili-pepper talk."

I said, "You and Vega get along all right?"

"Sure. Fine."

"You pay him well?"

"Damn well. He's never had a kick coming on that score."

"So he has no reason to hate or dislike you."

"Not unless *he's* a bigot."

"You think he might be?"

"He keeps it to himself, if he is."

"Tell me about him."

Thomas shrugged. "Good worker, keeps his people hopping. We never have to worry about the manufacturing end with him on the job. He can be hard-nosed sometimes—fiery. You know how those Mexicans are. The Latin temperament."

"Meaning he sometimes flies off the handle?"

"Sometimes." Thomas smiled his self-deprecating smile. "He's got my kind of pop-off temper. Especially after he's been drinking."

"He drinks on the job?"

"No, no. I mean when he's hung over, after a wet night."

"That happen often?"

"Not often, no. I don't think he's a heavy boozer. Once or twice a month he'll come in and you can tell he was shitfaced the night before. That's about it."

Glickman had been sitting quietly all this time, listening to my Q & A with Thomas. Now he stirred and said to his client, "It's possible, whether you think so or not, that this man Vega has motive to want to harm both you and your late partner. If you'd been completely honest with us from the beginning . . ."

He didn't need to finish the sentence; Thomas got the point. "Okay, I was wrong and I apologize. What else can I say?"

"Is there anything else you've neglected to tell us?"

"No. Absolutely not."

"However small it might be."

"I swear it—nothing."

"Because if there is," Glickman said, "and I find out about it, I'll resign immediately as your defense attorney. And I'll be obliged to pass on my reasons to whomever you get to replace me."

I said, "That goes for me too."

Thomas bobbed his head and said that he understood. He looked innocent and eager to please; but there was sweat on him now and he seemed even more nervous. *Had* he been honest, or was he trying to con us by deflecting suspicion elsewhere? Was he what he appeared to be, an unethical but basically decent businessman caught in a web of circumstance, or was he in fact a cold-blooded murderer?

I just could not make up my mind, one way or the other.

Chapter **6**

FROM TERRIFIC STREET, I drove back to O'Farrell and the office. Eberhardt wasn't there, but the answering machine had a message from him.

"Vega wasn't home," his voice said. "Nobody else was, either. One of the neighbors told me Mrs. Vega works too, cooks in some restaurant in South San Francisco, doesn't get home until after six. There's also a son living with them; neighbor didn't know where I could find him or his father. I'd go back out there after six but I've got an early date with Bobbie Jean in San Rafael. Vega can wait until tomorrow, no? Let me know how it went with Glickman and Thomas. I'll be home until five forty-five or so."

No, dammit, I thought, Vega can't wait until tomorrow. But my annoyance didn't last long. There was no sense in blaming him for not being a workaholic. Detective work is just a job to him—nine-to-five and on to more important things. Hell, he was getting married in a few months. I couldn't expect him to put extra hours into a muddled and maybe futile case like this one, just because it was frustrating the hell out of *me.*

I called him at home and told him how things had gone with Glickman and Thomas Lujack. Then I told him I'd do the follow-up on Rafael Vega myself, tonight.

He said, "You trying to make me feel guilty?"

"No. I don't have anything better to do."

"You sure?"

"I'm sure. Give my love to Bobbie Jean."

I locked up for the night and walked to Van Ness and ate an early dinner at Zim's. It was just six when I came back and got the car out of the parking garage near the office, and six fifteen when I turned off Mission Street onto Sixteenth.

On a dreary weekday evening like this one, at the tag end of rush hour, the Mission looks like any other crowded ethnic neighborhood of older buildings and graffiti-scabbed walls; you need a hot summer Saturday to appreciate its full ambiance and flavor. The people hurrying along the wet sidewalks and the types and names of the business establishments told you that the population here was heavily Latin. But this was far more than a barrio. It was a place where old cultures clashed with new; where you could sample the pleasures of yesterday's world and the probable horrors of tomorrow's; where the good and the bad and the ugly coexisted and cohabited in a tolerant, dynamic, and too often deadly disharmony.

When I was a kid growing up a few miles from here, in the Outer Mission, this neighborhood had been solidly working-class, populated mostly by Irish immigrants, and dominated by two-hundred-year-old Mission Dolores and its newer, ornate basilica. The district's metamorphosis had been gradual at first, radical in the past decade or so. It was still solidly working-class, at least at its residential core, and still one of the poorer neighborhoods in the city, but Mission Dolores was no longer its spiritual hub—a fact you might find surprising, given the strong Latin emphasis on religion, if you weren't aware of all the other factors that had gone into making it what it was today. It had no hub, no focal point now; it was a kind of mutant, neither one thing nor another, neither bad nor good, just a teeming, formless entity that writhed this

way and that and went nowhere at all. And it was still mutat-
ing—into what was anybody's guess.

The Latinos were partly responsible for its present state,
in particular the disillusioned young and the steady influx of
frustrated and sometimes desperate illegals. So was the heavy
concentration of drug dealers and cocaine, heroin, crack, and
methamphetamine addicts in the four-block area around Sixteenth and Mission that has been dubbed the Devil's
Quadrangle. So was its floating population of drunks, hook-
ers, misfits, drifters, and homeless citizens. So were the impoverished elderly, forced into the area's shabby residential
hotels by redevelopment projects in other parts of the city. So
were the predators who preyed on the unfortunate and the
unwary, and seemed to take periodic delight in setting fire to
buildings both abandoned and occupied. So were the neighborhood activists, who had brought about small cosmetic and
public-service improvements and who continued to lobby long
and loud for major ones. And most recently, so were the New
Bohemians, once entrenched in North Beach and then in the
Haight-Ashbury, who had been drawn to the Mission by its
still-affordable rents; who had opened repertory theaters,
avant-garde art galleries, funky cafes where you could listen
to poetry readings while you sipped espresso, bookstores new
and used that specialized in radical political and feminist literature, and legitimate nightclubs as well as the bandit variety
that operated without business permits. You could buy or do
or see just about anything in the Mission these days, from the
simple to the depraved. You could also lose your money or
your life if you weren't careful—and not just after nightfall.

I drove up Sixteenth past Mission Dolores. Some of the
older wood-frame homes and gingerbread-adorned apartment
houses in this area had been damaged by the October quake,
especially along Shotwell a few blocks east; but the structures
flanking Albert Alley, the narrow little side street on which
Rafael Vega lived, seemed to have survived with a minimum
of harm. Parking on Albert or in its immediate vicinity was
impossible; finding a space within walking distance took me

fifteen minutes of circuitous driving. The rain had quit for the time being, but the wind still blew cold and damp. I was chilled by the time I completed a vigilant five-block walk and located Vega's address.

He and his family occupied the lower flat in a well-maintained two-unit Italianate Victorian, set back behind a gated fence and a nice little garden. By Inner Mission standards, it was a pretty affluent residence. The Vegas had cut themselves a slice of the American Dream, and never mind that it was at least partially at the expense of their Latino brethren.

Lights glowed behind a drawn shade in one of the front windows, so somebody was home. Huddled on the porch, I rang the Vegas's bell. Almost immediately, hurrying footsteps sounded inside. A porch light flicked on, locks clicked, and chains rattled, and then the door jerked inward—all as if the woman who stood there had been waiting eagerly for a caller. She was in her mid-forties, plump without being fat, with coffee-dark skin and black hair pulled into a tight bun. One hand came up to her mouth when she saw me. The worried look in her eyes staggered over the edge into fear.

"*Sí?* Yes? What do you want?" Her English was heavily accented, her voice a little thick—the kind of thickness that comes from alcohol. I could smell the wine on her breath.

"Mrs. Vega?"

A convulsive nod. "*¿Es él mi esposo? Dios mia,* my husband?"

"He's why I'm here, yes, but I—"

"What has happened to him? Where is he?"

"Mrs. Vega, I'm here to see your husband, not to tell you anything about him."

She stared at me for two or three beats. Then the fearshine in her eyes dulled and she sagged a little against the door, crossing herself. Relief seemed to have clogged her throat; she had to clear it before she could speak again.

"Who are you? What do you want with Rafael?"

"Just to talk to him."

"You are not from the—" She bit off the rest of the sentence: "police," maybe, or "Immigration Service."

"I'm here on my own," I said. I told her my name, but not what I did for a living. "Your husband and I work for the same man—Thomas Lujack."

"Ah," she said, but it was just a sound without meaning.

"May I come in, Mrs. Vega?"

She hesitated. "Rafael . . . you know he is not here."

"I'll talk to you instead, if that's all right. It won't take long. *Con su permiso.*"

Again she hesitated, longer this time. Finally she made a motion with one hand, almost of resignation, and drew the door wider. "Come in."

I followed her across a short hall and through a doorway on the left. She was steady enough on her feet, but slow and deliberate in her movements: not drunk yet but working on it. Alcoholic? Her appearance said no. Her face was free of the blotchiness and doughy laxity of the habitual drinker, and her hair and her brown wool skirt and white blouse were in neat array.

The room she led me into was a high-ceilinged front parlor. It was overstuffed with a hodgepodge of good quality but mismatched furniture, and dominated by religious paintings and a large statue of the Virgin Mary on the mantel above a walled-up fireplace. Two odors lingered on the too warm air: scented candle wax and red wine. There was a bottle of burgundy and a half-filled glass on the table next to a Mexican rocker.

"You will have some wine?"

"No, thank you," I said. "Nothing for me."

We both sat down, her on the rocker and me on a carved rosewood settee. She looked at her glass but didn't pick it up. Instead she plucked at her skirt as if removing invisible flecks of lint. I noticed then that her hands were remarkably young and delicate—the hands of a woman half her age.

"Mrs. Vega, will you tell me why you're so worried about your husband?"

"He . . . since last night he has not been home. Always before he tells me first before he goes away, but this time . . ." She shook her head and sighed and said, *"Ay de mí,"* as if in supplication.

"You have no idea where he might be?"

"No one has seen him, no one knows. Paco has gone to ask others, friends of my husband. . . ."

"Paco?"

"My son. He believes . . . ah, no. No."

"He believes what, Mrs. Vega?"

"Nada. No es importante."

"What time did you last see your husband?"

"Half past ten. Here, in this room."

"Did he say where he was going when he left?"

"No. He said nothing."

"Why would he go out at that hour?"

"The telephone call . . . it must have been."

"Someone called him right before he went out?"

"Sí."

"Do you know who it was?"

"No. He talked in the kitchen . . . not long."

"How did he act after the call?"

"Act? *¿Que quiere decir?*"

"Was he upset, angry, excited?"

"Upset . . . *disconcerto? Sí, disconcerto.*"

"Who might he have gone to meet? Someone from his work, maybe? Or a close friend?"

I thought I saw her wince before she said, "Rafael knows many people. Many people . . ." She shook her head again; reached for the glass of burgundy and took a small swallow and then held the glass in both hands, as though they were cold and the wine radiated warmth.

"You said he always tells you when he's going away. Did you mean away on a trip?"

"Sí."

"Does he take many trips?"

"No. Not many."

"How often?"

"Two times, three times each year."

"For how many years now?"

She made a vague gesture.

"Where does he go on these trips?"

"San Diego sometimes. Mexico sometimes."

"Where in Mexico?"

Another vague gesture.

"Does he have friends in San Diego? Relatives?"

No answer. Again she drank from her glass, a larger swallow this time.

"Does he go alone on these trips, *señora*?"

"*Sí*, alone," she said. Firmly and positively, the way you do when you're not at all sure of something and trying to convince yourself it's so.

"So you think he might have gone to Mexico or San Diego this time?"

"Only last month he was away," she said.

"For how long."

"Four days."

"What do you think he does when he's away?"

No answer.

"Is it part of his job to go on these trips?"

No answer.

"Mrs. Vega, I know your husband hires illegals for Containers, Inc. Is that why he—"

"What the hell's the big idea, pancho?"

He was standing in the hall doorway, a beefy kid who walked soft for his size: I hadn't heard him come into the house and apparently neither had Mrs. Vega. He was about twenty, wearing a thick down jacket and a pair of Levi's jeans; his bandit's mustache would give him a ferocious look even when he wasn't angry. He was angry now. His eyes blazed, the cords in his neck bulged, and he stood with his feet apart and his hands fisted on his hips. There was nothing belligerent in the pose. His anger struck me as the protective variety.

"What you bothering my mother for?" he said. "Asking so damn many questions?"

"Are you Paco?"

"Yeah, I'm Paco." He took a couple of steps into the parlor. "Who're *you,* man? INS green-carder?"

"No."

"You sure talk like one."

I stood up, doing it slowly so he wouldn't get any wrong ideas. "I'm a private investigator," I said. "Working on behalf of your father's employer, Thomas Lujack. I'll show you my ID if you want to see it."

". . . You trying to get Lujack off? The murder charge?"

"That's right."

"Well, you're wasting your time. That *marrano* is guilty as hell. I hope they stick his ass in the gas chamber."

Mrs. Vega said, "Paco!" in a thick-sharp voice.

"Sure, Mama, I know—you don't like that kind of talk in your house. Well, I don't like you drinking so much wine either. What good's that stuff gonna do? Bring him back, make things better?"

"Paco," she said, and this time it was like a moan. Softly she began to cry.

He said, "Christ," but he went over and put his hand gently on her shoulder, leaned down to whisper something in Spanish. The words didn't make her stop crying, but they did make her put her glass on the table and then reach up to clutch at his hand.

"Why do you think Thomas Lujack is guilty?" I asked Paco.

"What I think is my business."

"Why don't you like him, then? Something to do with your father?"

"Look, man, why don't you get out of here? There's nothing for you in this house."

"You have any idea where your father is?"

"No. I wouldn't tell you if I did."

"Why not? You wouldn't be afraid he had something to do with Frank Hanauer's murder, would you?"

"What? Man, you're crazy. Get out of here."

"Why does he go to San Diego, Paco? Why to Mexico?"

He pulled away from his mother, stood flat-footed again with his hands curled into fists. "I'm not gonna tell you again. Out, right now, or I throw you out."

He meant it; it was in his eyes. I had pushed him as far as you could push a man in his own home. I raised my own hands, slowly, and held them palms outward as I said, "I'm going. I didn't come here to make trouble. All I'm after is the truth."

"You got everything you're gonna get out of us. So don't come back. Understand?"

Without answering I moved over to the doorway. Paco stood watching until I passed through into the hall; then he turned back to his mother. She was still sobbing quietly. Just before I opened the front door, I heard him speak to her in Spanish. He didn't know that I had a working knowledge of the language, so he didn't bother to lower his voice. The words were as clear as they were bitter.

"Hush, Mama," he said. "He's not worth your tears."

He didn't mean me. He was talking about his father.

WHEN I GOT BACK to my car I found that somebody had broken into it. The passenger door had been jimmied open, snapping the lock so that I ended up having to tie the door shut with a piece of wire. The only thing of real value, the mobile phone unit, was intact and undamaged, which meant that the thief hadn't had the right tools or was scared off or was just some poor desperate junkie looking for cash or small valuables. In any case the glove compartment had been hurriedly rifled.

An old clunker like mine, I thought. Parked on the street for little more than an hour, nothing in it worth stealing except a difficult-to-remove cellular phone, and it had still been an instant target.

Life in the Mission at the beginning of the nineties.

Life in the goddamn city.

Chapter 7

NICK PENDARVES was not in the Hideaway when I got there. I took the same stool I had occupied on my last visit and asked Max, the laconic bartender, if Pendarves had come and gone. He said no. I tried to get him to talk about the incident last night, but he wasn't having any. Pulling words out of him was like trying to pull wood splinters out of your own behind: slow, frustrating, and ultimately futile.

Most of the regulars were there, in their customary places. One who wasn't in his customary place was shy Douglas Mikan, who was usually engaged in a chess match with Harry Briggs, the retired civil servant, in a back-wall booth. There was no sign of Briggs tonight and Mikan was sitting at the bar, one stool removed from mine, with his nose aimed downward into a glass of draft beer. As always, he wore a suit and tie—the only one of the regulars who dressed formally. His mother's influence, I supposed. Her name had been Grace, according to the bar gossip I'd picked up, and she had also been a regular until her death a couple of years ago.

Tonight there was a remote look on Douglas's chubby moon face, as if he had ridden his thoughts to some faraway place—a pleasant enough place, because he didn't look un-happy. Dreamer, I thought; wanderer in an imaginary world, maybe, that was far kinder to him than the one he lived in.

"How come no chess tonight, Douglas?" I asked him.

He mumbled something that sounded like, "Harry didn't come in," without looking at me.

"Well, how about a game with me?" It was better than just sitting here at the bar, doing nothing while I waited. "I won't give you much competition but I'll try like hell."

The invitation seemed to please him. He accepted, asked Max for the chess set, which was kept behind the bar, and we went to one of the booths and set up a game. I tried to draw him out about Pendarves's troubles while we played, but he was as reticent as Max. Between moves he sat staring at the board, as if I weren't even there. So I sat quiet, too, and brooded about Rafael Vega.

Who had called Vega at ten thirty last night? And why? The call could have had something to do with the alleged attempt on Pendarves's life; the timing was about right. But if there was a connection, what was it? And why hadn't he come home last night or shown up at work today? There were a lot of other questions I wanted answered too: Had Vega had any-thing to do with Frank Hanauer's murder? Why did he make periodic trips to San Diego and Mexico? Why did his wife drink too much wine and react so strongly to what was, after all, only a twenty-four-hour absence? Why did his son think he was unworthy? And why did Paco dislike Thomas Lujack so much?

Douglas beat me quickly and badly, twice, and then mut-tered something about having things to do at home. I was no challenge to his abilities; I wouldn't have wanted to keep play-ing me either. He thanked me politely and waddled off, and I went back to sit at the bar with what was left of my beer.

After a while Peter Vandermeer came up next to me to order a fresh drink. He was the elderly amateur historian who had staked a claim to the other back booth, where he pored over his books and pamphlets. We exchanged hellos, and he proceeded to tell me an amusing anecdote about Emperor Norton, one of San Francisco's legendary characters, who in the 1870s had proclaimed himself Emperor of the United States and Defender of Mexico. The anecdote was good enough so that I bought his drink for him. He gave me a wink and a sly smile along with his thank-you; he seemed pleased with himself, as if he'd done something clever. Hell, he probably had. I'd paid for his drink, hadn't I?

I watched him resettle himself in the booth and open a thick battered old volume bound in buckram. Almost eighty and as sharp as a tack, with more curiosity and enthusiasm than most people half his age. Unlike Cybil Wade, he had grown old only in body, not in mind. And yet, until recently Cybil had been every bit as sharp-witted and young-spirited as Vandermeer. Genetics had a great deal to do with it; Alzheimer's, for instance, had been proven to be a genetic disease. But there were intangibles too—environment, health, interests, attitudes. In the long run, I thought, it's a crapshoot. If you survive, you grow old—that's a given. But *how* you grow old is as unpredictable as world politics, as unknowable in advance as the existence of an afterlife.

If I lived to be seventy-five or eighty, what would my life be like? I could no longer work, at least not actively, and work had always been my prime motivation. I had no family, no one close to me except Kerry and Eberhardt . . . and what if, in the great perverse scheme of things, I outlived both of them? What if I then fell ill or became incapacitated in some way and was no longer able to care for myself? I could no more live in a nursing home than Cybil could. It might not be so bad if I developed a disease like Alzheimer's, because for the most part I wouldn't know what was happening to me; but if I retained my faculties, then it would be hell existing in that kind of closed-in, waiting-for-the-end environment.

Being old would be tolerable if your mind and body both cooperated; if you turned out like Peter Vandermeer over there. But even then, it couldn't be any bed of roses. Society was controlled by the young, geared toward the young . . .

and the young wanted little enough to do with the old, because they did not care to be reminded of their own vulnerability and mortality. So society shunned the elderly, pushed them off into "acceptable" corners—homes, retirement communities, pensioners' hotels, senior citizens' activities, sad little "social clubs" like the one I was sitting in right now.

I'm fifty-eight, I thought. If I live another twenty years, I'll *be* Peter Vandermeer . . . if I'm lucky.

The thought was chilling.

I went into the men's cubicle and used the urinal and then washed my hands and splashed a little water on my face. When I came back out again I felt better. But I did not look at Peter Vandermeer anymore. And I didn't think about him anymore, either, at least in part because Ed McBee came in and created a distraction.

McBee, a former longshoreman, was something of a film buff; and he liked nothing better than to express outrageous opinions that would get a rise out of his drinking companions. As soon as Max made him a bourbon and water, he started a conversation about movie comedy teams and which of them was the best. The consensus seemed to be evenly divided between Laurel and Hardy, which would have been my choice, and the Marx Brothers. McBee held out for the Three Stooges.

To support his claim he produced a newspaper clipping, which he said was a translation of part of a long, scholarly article on the Three Stooges by an eminent French film critic, and commenced to read it aloud.

" 'With the exception of the tragic comedian Jerry Lewis, no one in cinema has captured the human dilemma so movingly and eloquently as have Larry, Moe, and Curly—Les Trois Imbeciles. The impressive body of film work left by Les Trois Imbeciles resounds with a single transcendent theme. It is the Jungian notion of the male's painful struggle to come to grips with his own unconscious, specifically with the deeply repressed feminine side of his nature—' "

Bob Johnson made a snorting sound. Somebody whose name I didn't know said, "Horse manure!"

Undaunted, McBee continued. " 'This struggle, so essential in man's search for wholeness, is exemplified in such acknowledged film classics as the epic *The Three Stooges Go Around the World in a Daze* and of course, *The Three Stooges Meet Hercules.* ' "

Annie Stanhope choked on her sherry.

" 'Interpreting these works,' " McBee read, " 'the film connoisseur must regard Larry, Moe, and Curly as a trinity, three parts of a single entity. In Moe, one senses man mired in his conscious state. Curly is man's feminine unconscious, the embodiment of youth and innocence, the very qualities that man must recapture to come full circle in his life's journey. Larry is perhaps the most complex recurring character in the history of American film. He represents man in transition, caught between the polarities of Moe and Curly. He is, one could say, a work in progress.' "

"Gawd," Frank Parigli said, not without reverence.

" 'In short, Moe must become Curly, by way of Larry, to achieve his full human potentiality. That profound pilgrimage is not without pain—even deep scars and bruises. Indeed, Les Trois Imbeciles display their particular genius when they give symbolic physical expression to the difficulties of the metamorphosis. Each precisely choreographed punch in the nose and each graceful poke in the ribs reverberates with meaning. Observe that it is Moe who metes out these blows, Moe whose psyche is characterized by repression and denial, Moe who utilizes violence to mute the imploring call to growth coming from his unconscious. *C'est tragique!* But there is no denying the plaintive urgency of the call *nyuk! nyuk! nyuk!* voiced by Curly. To ignore it is to convict oneself forever to the half-life of the unconscious.' "

There was more, but the other regulars hooted it down. A half-serious, half-satirical debate ensued, with McBee holding his own against the rest of them. Most of it was amusing, but my attention kept wandering from the backbar clock to the street door and back to the clock. Coming up on eight forty-five and still no Pendarves. Maybe his brush with death had spooked him into staying clear of the Hideaway for a while . . . except that that sort of ostrich reaction didn't jibe with my reading of him. Whatever else he might be, I felt pretty sure he was neither a coward nor a timid soul.

The Three Stooges debate ended and the table conversation broke up into individual exchanges. I finished my beer, ordered another even though I didn't want it, and tried not to fidget while the clock ticked away more empty minutes. Nine. Nine fifteen. Nine thirty. Still no Pendarves.

The hell with it, I thought. I paid my tab and got out of there.

THERE WAS A LIGHT on in the rear of Pendarves's house, in what I thought might be the kitchen. The rest of the place was dark; I drove around onto 47th Avenue to make sure.

At the end of the block I turned around, came back slowly, crossed the Rivera intersection, and parked near the corner. The Plymouth Fury was neither on the street nor in his driveway, but he could have put it away in the detached garage; the garage door was shut. So was he home, or was that light in the back just a burglar light?

I'd already decided not to try talking to him at his house; even with the best of pretexts, my showing up there was liable to arouse his suspicions. But I still wanted him to be home. For him to go anywhere other than the Hideaway this late was unusual enough to arouse *my* suspicions. So I switched off the engine, turned my overcoat collar up, put my gloves back on, and went to find out one way or the other.

The wind off the ocean was cold enough to burn where it touched the skin; and even though it wasn't raining, the fog was so thick with moisture it functioned as a drizzle. Walking alone in heavy fog always gives me a remote, dreamlike feeling: blurred lights, oddly distorted shapes, sounds so muffled I could not even hear my own steps. In silence I crossed the empty street, went down the sidewalk alongside Pendarves's house, and then past the hedge that separated his side yard from the weedy lot on which the garage had been built.

Ahead, then, I could see puffs of vapor down low to the ground, at the bottom of the lowered garage door. At first I thought it was ground mist. But the puffs were too thinly pulsate, like steam escaping through a valve—

Christ!

I broke into a hard run, off the sidewalk and through the wet weeds onto the drive. Then I could hear the steady throb of the engine inside the garage; the fog and wind kept the sound of it from carrying more than a few yards. Then, too, I could smell—faint out here but unmistakable—the acrid stench of exhaust fumes.

There was a handle on the weather-warped wood of the garage door, but nothing happened when I turned and then yanked on it. It must have had some kind of snap-lock inside: You could pull it down to engage the lock from out here but you couldn't open it without a key. I ran around on the side nearest the house. An access door was set into the wall toward the back, the upper part of it glass. I caught the knob but it was locked too. Without thinking about it I turned sideways and drove my elbow against the glass; the wind took the sound of it shattering and broke that up into fragments too. Clouds of carbon monoxide came pouring out at me. I ducked my head away, reached through the jagged opening, managed to find the inside knob and free the push-button lock without cutting myself, and dragged the door open.

The interior was so thick with fumes I couldn't see the car. I plunged in blindly, holding my breath, narrowing my eyes to slits; struck metal almost instantly, barking my knee, then clawed along the car's side until I located the handle on the passenger door. It was unlocked. I got the door open, bent my body inside. Despite the dull furry glow from the dome light I could barely see; the monoxide burned my eyes, made them run with tears. I had to rely on my groping hand to determine that the driver's seat was empty.

I fumbled for the ignition, twisted the key; the steady wheezing rhythm of the engine cut off. Smoke had filtered into my lungs by this time and it tore the air out of them in a series of explosive coughs. I levered up and over the seat back, just long enough to sweep one hand across a rear seat as empty as the front buckets; then I pulled back out of the car. By the time I staggered outside through the open doorway, my knees were rubbery and I was choking on the fumes.

Ten paces from the door, I braced myself against the garage wall. It took minutes for the icy night air to clear the poison out of my lungs so I could breathe normally again without hacking. My eyes quit shedding tears but the fire in them lessened only a little. The taste of sickness was on the back of my tongue.

Nobody came to help or hinder me, drawn by the escaping smoke or by the sounds I'd made. Both Rivera and 47th remained deserted. For the time being, this little drama was going to keep on being a one-man show.

I let another two or three minutes go by, to make sure that the monoxide had thinned enough so it wouldn't do any more damage to my lungs. I no longer felt any sense of urgency. As dense as those trapped fumes were, the car's engine had been running a long time—much too long for anybody in there to have survived.

When I finally did go back in I put my handkerchief over my mouth, something I should have thought to do the first time. A pace inside, I felt along the wall next to the door. An old-fashioned knob-style light switch was mounted there; when I twisted it, a low-wattage bulb came on above a workbench along the back wall. Dull saffron light glinted off the metal surfaces of the car.

It wasn't Pendarves's old Plymouth Fury. It was a newish —and unfamiliar—silver-gray BMW.

What the hell?

I made sure the dozen feet of rough-concrete floor between the BMW's front end and the bench was empty, then went to the passenger door and leaned inside for a better look at the interior. Empty seats, empty floorboards in the rear. I backed out. There was still enough smoke to keep the fires burning in my eyes and chest; I found the latch on the garage door, released it, hoisted the door about halfway. Wind blew in, gusting, and dried the fresh layer of sweat on my face. I spent ten seconds sucking at the cold air. Then I moved over to where I could see along the driver's side.

That was where he was, sprawled face downward in close to the front tire, arms and legs outflung. On the back of his head was a smear of blood, dark and coagulated but still wet enough to glisten in the shadow-edged light. But that wasn't what caught and held my attention, what caused the top of my scalp to prickle and contract. It was the shape of him, and the clothes he was wearing.

On one knee beside him, I took hold of his limp shoulder and lifted him part way onto his side. Just enough so that I could look into the empty staring eyes, the lean face mottled a shiny cherry-red color.

Not Pendarves's car, and not Pendarves.

The dead man was Thomas Lujack.

I KNELT THERE for a time, stunned and confused, trying to come to grips with what I'd found. What in God's name was Lujack doing here, dead, in Pendarves's garage? The only thing I could think of was that he'd come to talk, even though he'd been warned to stay clear of Pendarves, the confrontation had turned ugly, and he had lost the punch-up. But why here in the garage? Why was he dead of carbon monoxide from the BMW he must have been driving? And where was Pendarves?

A car hissed by on Rivera without slowing; the sound of its passage brought me out of myself. I took a closer look at the blood smear on Thomas's head. Under his thick mat of hair, just above the occipital bone, the skin was split and looked darkly bruised. But there was nothing distinctive about the wound; it could have been made by just about anything, including the concrete floor. I lifted and turned the body again. He was wearing the same Harris tweed jacket, mint-green shirt, and designer jeans, and they looked the same as they had in Glickman's office: no tears or blood spatters or stains of any kind. I peered at his face, then paid some attention to his hands. No marks on his flesh, either. If he'd been in a fight, he had been struck only in the body and hadn't landed any solid blows himself—which seemed unlikely. He could have been thrown down in a struggle and banged his head on the concrete, but it was a better bet that he'd been clubbed from behind. The closed garage, the running engine, the presence of both Thomas and his car ruled out freak accident and suicide. This was homicide, plain and simple. Cold-blooded, premeditated murder.

Why?

Dammit, why would Pendarves kill him this way?

My stomach had begun to act up, as it always did when I was this close to violent death. I was not breathing well, either, but that was mostly the fault of the carbon monoxide. Quickly I patted Thomas's coat and pants pockets: he wasn't carrying a gun or any other kind of weapon. On my feet again, I went over by the door and sucked again at the night air until my stomach settled and I had better breath control. Then I was ready to get on with it.

Nothing on the floor near Thomas or anywhere else on that side of the BMW. I got down and looked under the car. Nothing there, either, as near as I could tell without a flashlight. I opened the driver's door, being careful not to smudge any prints that might be there, and poked through the glove box and found the registration slip. The owner of the car was Thomas's wife, Eileen. I sifted among the other items in the compartment. No gun, no other kind of weapon, and nothing that told me anything I didn't already know. The rest of the car's interior was just as barren.

I'd been in that damned garage long enough. I went back outside, shutting the light off on the way. Raining again; the wind had died down but the night seemed even colder. I looked up toward the house. The one light still burned, and it was still the only one on. He's not there, I thought. No sign of his car, and I've been here long enough to attract his attention if he was hanging around waiting for the monoxide to do its work. But why would he go off and leave the BMW pumping away in the garage? Where's the sense in that, in any of this?

The gate into the rear yard was latched but not locked. I went through it and across a section of weedy grass, skirted some bushes, and came to a flight of stairs that led up to where the lighted window was. Under the stairs was a door; the way the house had been built, it would give into a basement. It was sure to be locked tight but I tried it anyway. Yeah. I moved over and climbed the stairs, warily but not trying to be sneaky about it.

At the top was a little platform porch railed on the two sides. The door into the house was as tight-locked as the one into the basement. On the jamb was a doorbell, something you find occasionally on the backsides of older houses. I thought it over for a few seconds and then pushed the bell. Inside, the thing made a low, flat, buzzing sound. I stood with my ear against the door, listening for footsteps. All I heard was silence.

After half a minute I leaned out over the railing for a look through the lighted window. Kitchen, all right. I could see about half of it, including the sink and drainboard, the refrigerator, part of a stove, part of a Formica-topped table and two chairs. Everything was immaculate, gleamingly so, like a fifties-style remodeler's showroom. That surprised me a little; Pendarves hadn't impressed me as an orderly man. Just the opposite, in fact—he was pretty careless about his appearance. But then, maybe he had somebody come in and clean for him, and what I was seeing was the result of a recent tidying.

I straightened, put my hand on the doorknob, took it away again. No real point in my trying to get inside the house. Pendarves wasn't here; and if there was anything to find on the premises, it was the cops' job to find it.

Descending the stairs, I hurried across the yard and through the gate and alongside the garage. Except for the fog-smeared streetlights and nearby house lights, there was nothing to see; I was still alone on the property. I crossed the empty expanse of Rivera to where my car was parked. Got in and stripped off my gloves and sat for half a minute to let my breathing even out again; my lungs still weren't working right.

I was lifting the receiver on the mobile phone when the night went red behind me.

The redness brightened swiftly, making the fog look as though it were drizzling blood. I sat unmoving, watching in the rearview mirror as a black-and-white prowl car came into sight, heading west on Rivera. It was moving at a pretty good clip, its dome light slashing at the wet dark, until it passed through the intersection; then the driver braked abruptly and swerved over to the curb in front of Pendarves's garage.

A brace of patrolmen piled out. Both carried flashlights, switched them on at the same time; the beams burned bright tunnels through the red-splashed drifts of fog. They stopped together at the garage door, as if they were surprised to find it half open and the car engine shut off inside. They seemed to hold a hurried conference, after which they drew their sidearms in unison. One of them eased the door up a little farther and ducked under it; the other went into a shooter's crouch and swept the interior with his light. After a few seconds the crouching one straightened again, turned away and moved along the near-side wall, out of my range of vision.

I put the phone receiver back in its cradle, thinking: Somebody beat me to it. One of the neighbors, who spotted me poking around? But then why were the cops surprised at what they found over there? Sure, the call could have been made before I opened the door, but that had been at least twenty minutes ago. Prowler calls in this neighborhood, with the Taraval precinct station only a little over a mile away, were routinely answered in half that time.

As I watched, the garage door went up all the way. Then the patrolman inside turned his flash on Thomas Lujack's corpse, held it there until his partner came in through the access door and joined him. Both of them still had their weapons drawn. If they'd caught me on the premises, as they would have if they'd arrived five minutes sooner, they'd have hassled me pretty good.

The way it was now, I wouldn't get much more than the fish-eye. All I had to do was go on over there, nice and slow, and then tell them the exact truth. I could give them enough bare facts to save time and trouble when the homicide inspectors arrived. Besides, it was the law-abiding and the smart thing to do.

I didn't do it.

Up until a year ago, I would have—without hesitation. But I was neither the man nor the detective I had been a year ago. There was a wrongness about the whole scenario over there; I had felt it as soon as I realized who the dead man was, and the arrival of the prowl car had shoved it up close to the surface. Thomas Lujack's death hadn't ended my involvement with him, or with Nick Pendarves; I felt that, too, just as strongly. It seemed imperative to keep my name out of the official report, to not blow my cover at the Hideaway.

I waited until one of the patrolmen radioed in and the two of them together drifted into the shadows toward the house. Then I started the car and went away from there, running dark like a thief in the night.

BAD NIGHT all around.

I couldn't sleep, couldn't even get into a doze. My lungs ached and my head felt clogged with too many random thoughts, like a pressure building up. After a while the unease came, crimping at the edges of my mind. Then the claustrophobia, as if the darkness was contracting around me—outside pressure added to the pressure within. Even when I turned on the light the sensation of being squeezed and suffocated did not lessen any. Anxiety attack, the first in three months.

The clock said one thirty when I got up. I paced from room to room but it did no good; the trapped, fearful feeling seemed to worsen. There was nothing for it then but to get out and away. I dressed quickly and left the building and put my

car around me again and began to drive with the window
rolled down and the wind blowing icy mist against my face.

I drove here and there, going nowhere. Wet shiny streets,
mostly deserted, reflecting splinters of light that stabbed into
my eyes and made them burn again. Over in the Tenderloin,
the night people were out alone or in little shadowy groups—
pimps, whores, pushers, muggers; drunks and addicts and
flesh-hungry johns. The predators and their prey, even more
voracious in bad weather because it made tempers short and
patience thin. On Marina Boulevard, the empty Green looked
like a barren graveyard, the tall bobbing masts of the boats in
the yacht harbor like skeletons performing a *danse macabre*.
Along the fringes of the Presidio it was as if I were passing
through a tropical rain forest—trees and bushes dripping,
dripping, making me think of acid rain eating away unseen at
leaves and roots so that one day there would be nothing left
but blighted gray vegetable matter . . . seen one dead tree,
you've seen them all. At Cliff House and Ocean Beach, wind-
driven surf boiled foaming over the rocks and raged at the
shore, and there was no peace in that, either—there can never
be peace in the presence of raw violence. At 47th and Rivera,
where raw violence had taken place earlier, there was the
illusion of peace because the police were gone and the dead
man was gone and the house was dark . . . but the illusion
was worse than the violence itself; an illusion is a lie and a lie
is always worse than the truth. . . .

I drove some more, another half hour or so—here and
there, going nowhere. At last I could feel the fatigue taking
over, and with it came the beginnings of ease both physical
and mental. The night felt less ominous, less tragic; it was
merely lonely, the way even good nights are. I knew I could
go home then, that when I got there the flat would no longer
be a tightening snare. And I was right.

I slept immediately and dreamlessly, for a little more than
four hours. When I awoke at 8:00 A.M., to face the dull gray
of another day, I was all right again.

Chapter **9**

THE TELEPHONE RANG at eight thirty, as I was getting dressed. Eberhardt or Paul Glickman, I thought. It was Eberhardt.

"You hear the news yet?" he said.

"What news?"

"I figured," he said. "Why the hell don't you read the newspapers? Or listen to the damn radio?"

"My life is depressing enough without wallowing in other people's misery. What's up?"

"Thomas Lujack is dead, that's what's up. Murdered last night. Way it looks, Nick Pendarves killed him."

I feigned astonishment. There would be no use in confiding in Eb; he would only raise a fuss. He has been a conservative, law-loving man all his life, except for one foolish slip a few years ago; ever since that slip, he has become even more rock-ribbed in his outlook. Besides, I had no satisfactory explanation to give him for my actions last night—or at least none that would satisfy him.

Thomas Lujack's death had made page two of the *Chronicle,* not because of the circumstances but because of the tie-in to the Hanauer thing. The details were sketchy, so Eb had thought to call one of his cronies at the Hall of Justice for a complete rundown.

His account contained two pieces of information that I paid particular attention to. One was the fact that the call alerting the police had been anonymous: male voice saying that something funny was going on at Pendarves's address, the garage door was shut and a car engine was running inside. That explained the reactions of the two patrolmen. It also added to my feeling of wrongness about the whole business. The other piece of information gave me pause, though, because it tended to support the circumstantial evidence: Pendarves had disappeared. His Plymouth Fury had been found abandoned near Stow Lake in Golden Gate Park at six this morning.

I asked, "What's the official theory?"

"Either Thomas went to see Pendarves on his own hook or Pendarves asked him to come. Depending on which, there was some kind of fight or Pendarves deliberately cold-cocked Thomas; then he finished the job. One way it's first-degree, the other way maybe it's second-degree. Up to him and his lawyer to convince a jury."

"You buy all that?"

"Any reason I shouldn't?"

"For one thing, why would they meet in the garage?"

"That's where Pendarves was when Thomas showed up. Or Thomas was knocked out somewhere else and Pendarves carried him into the garage afterward."

"All right. But why kill him with carbon monoxide?"

"Some screwy idea that jumped into Pendarves's head, maybe on account of it was also a good way to get Thomas's car off the street and buy himself some time. Who knows why people do crazy things? They don't know themselves, half the time."

"Were his fingerprints on the BMW?"

"No. Which doesn't mean diddly and you know it."

"Yeah. Gloves." The same reason they hadn't found *my*

prints on the BMW. "So Pendarves set up the monoxide thing and then just took off, huh?"

"Panicked and took off, right."

"Why didn't he just hang around and wait for the monoxide to do its job and then get rid of both the car and the body? He'd be in the clear that way."

"Like I said, he panicked. It happens."

"Inspectors find any evidence that he went on the run? Suitcases and clothing missing?"

"No," Eberhardt said, "but so what? He could have packed light; you can't always tell. There isn't anything in the house that's worth much."

"Why would he abandon his car?"

"Throw the law off his scent. Called a cab or somebody he knew and had himself picked up in the park and driven to Greyhound or the airport or any one of a hundred places. Takes time to check all the possibilities." He paused. "Listen, you got a reason for being so doubtful?"

"No specific reason," I said. "I'm playing devil's advocate, that's all. But doesn't it seem a little off-the-wall to you?"

"A little, I guess," he admitted. "What're you thinking? That it might tie into the Hanauer case? Same person who ran down Hanauer killed Thomas?"

"Possible, isn't it?"

"Anything's possible. But hell, why? Why frame Pendarves? Where's the sense in that?"

"Where's the sense in Hanauer's murder or any of the rest of it? I want the answers, Eb. Don't you?"

"Sure. Thomas's wife and brother probably will too. Don't let's get ahead of ourselves."

"Yeah. Either of them able to shed any light on what happened?"

"No. Coleman told the cops he hadn't talked to Thomas since yesterday afternoon and then it was about business. The wife said he stayed in the city after the conference with you and Glickman. Called her and told her he had some things to take care of and he'd be home late, but he didn't say what the things were."

"Okay," I said. "I'll talk to Glickman. Then we'll see how things stand."

We rang off. And as I finished dressing I thought: I don't care about the circumstantial evidence or what anybody says —it didn't happen the way it looks. It's a phony, a setup. Nick Pendarves damned well did not kill Thomas Lujack.

GLICKMAN SAID, "The family hasn't decided if they want you men to continue your investigation. They're still in shock."

"You talk to both the wife and brother?" Eberhardt asked.

"Yes."

"Separately?"

"Yes."

"And they both said the same thing?"

"More or less. It's not surprising that they should be indecisive at this point—"

"It is to me," I said. "Why would they need to think about it? Pendarves may or may not have killed Thomas, but he didn't run down Frank Hanauer. And Thomas probably didn't either. Don't they want his name cleared?"

"I should hope so."

"And while they're making up their minds? What are we supposed to do? Sit around on hold?"

"Legally there is nothing any of us can do until the family makes a decision."

"Which could take days."

"Yes. But I doubt it'll be more than twenty-four hours."

I glanced at Eb, who shrugged. Eberhardt the philosophical; *Que sarà sarà.* There were times when I wished I could adopt his detached professional attitude, but this wasn't one of them. I fidgeted on Glickman's upholstered visitor's chair. We were in his private office on Terrific Street, and the antique ship's clock on one wall said that it was already five minutes before noon.

To Glickman I said, "Did you tell them there's some doubt Pendarves is guilty? That Thomas's murder may in fact be tied directly to Hanauer's?"

"I told them you expressed that concern, yes. Coleman asked if there was any evidence to support it. I had to tell him no."

"That's part of the reason for us staying on the job. To find evidence to support it."

"I told him that too. He said he would think about it."

"Yeah," Eberhardt said. "Think about it."

"Will you talk to them again?" I asked Glickman. "Try to use your influence?"

"Certainly. But you must understand, I'm in a touchy legal position here. I can only go so far."

Strict letter of the law, I thought. Well, good for you, Paul. I hope nothing happens to turn *your* head. I hope you keep on being one of the lucky ones.

EBERHARDT WENT to finish up a routine background investigation and I went back to the office, where I dug Thomas Lujack's home telephone number out of the file. Ten rings, no answer. We hadn't been given Coleman's home number, but I knew that he lived in Burlingame; and even though the number was unlisted, it took me all of ten minutes to get it. And all of five seconds to reach his answering machine. I hung up without leaving a message. If I was going to talk to him, I wanted it to be in person.

The next call I made was to Containers, Inc. A bored female voice—Teresa Melendez, no doubt—informed me that Mr. Coleman Lujack was not in the office today because there had been a death in the family. She didn't seem to care much that a second of her three employers had died by violence. But that might say more about the Lujacks and the climate at Containers, Inc., than it did about her personally.

I asked, "How about Rafael Vega? He come in today?"

"No," she said. "He's still sick with the flu."

WHEN KERRY ARRIVED for our four o'clock date I was in the bedroom straightening up. She made a small joke about being honored by clean sheets and the absence of dust mice, but neither of us laughed much. She asked for a glass of wine, and I had a Diet Pepsi so she wouldn't have to drink alone. We sat in the living room and made conversation for a few minutes, none of it about Cybil. There was a small awkwardness between us, as between new lovers, that we could not seem to banish. It was there even when we went to bed.

We needed each other now more than ever, but for me, at least, our lovemaking was no better than it had been the last time. Part of it was the circumstances; part of it was that Kerry's passion was tainted with a kind of desperation, as if she were trying too hard to please both of us, too hard to feel good and carefree again . . . and failing on all counts. All she got out of it, and all I got out of it, was physical release. And we both knew it.

For a long while we didn't speak. It was a dark silence, as dark as the dying day outside.

"It's hurting us, isn't it," she said finally. Statement, not question.

"We'll get through it, babe."

"Not this way. Not with Cybil living with me and shutting you out, not with us sneaking around and screwing in the afternoon like a couple of high-school kids. I hate this, damn it. I *hate* it."

"Don't blame Cybil—"

"I don't, any more than I blame Ivan for dying. It's the situation that's intolerable. I'm going to see somebody, right away . . . no more waffling."

"Geriatric specialist?"

"Somebody like that. I'll check into it first thing tomorrow."

"You want me to come along when you go?"

"No. It's something I'd better do alone."

"Well, if you need me, for any reason . . ."

"I know," she said.

She burrowed closer to me. And pretty soon I felt wetness against my arm and chest: She was crying without sound.

"Why?" she asked then, as a child might—rhetorically and with great sadness. "Why do people have to get *old*?"

AT THE HIDEAWAY that night, there was plenty of lip service paid to Thomas Lujack's murder and Nick Pendarves's disappearance. Even Max was stirred up enough to offer a comment now and then. In the lives of most if not all of the regulars, it was the most exciting and shocking thing to happen in years, and they were having a ghoulish fling with it.

They did not want to believe Pendarves was guilty, but that was because he was one of them. It made them uncomfortable to think that a man capable of cold-blooded murder might have been part of their close-knit little group. More importantly, it constituted a threat to their sanctuary and, by implication, to each of them individually. If Pendarves had killed a stranger, he might just as well have decided, to their way of thinking, to dispose of one of *them*. And if they weren't safe here in the Hideaway, then they weren't safe anywhere.

The irony in that was their willingness to talk freely in my presence, as if circumstances had made *me* one of them now. The truth was, they didn't know me any more than they knew Nick Pendarves . . . than they knew each other. Does anybody ever really know another person, even someone close? No, but we need to believe that we do. That's one of the necessary illusions we live by: that we are always safe in the company of friends and loved ones.

So I sat observing the regulars work like busy spiders at repairing the torn strands of their illusion. Nick Pendarves a murderer? Ridiculous! Why, there had to be some mistake, some other explanation. Somebody else must have murdered that bum Thomas Lujack. Or else it was some kind of crazy accident. Either way, Nick had gotten scared and run off. Hell, who wouldn't run? Cops would say he did it, he'd known that. Damn cops. They'd as soon railroad an innocent man as go out and hunt down the guilty one. . . .

There was only one mildly dissenting voice—Bob Johnson's—and it didn't take much to get him to relent and come around to the group position. At first he said, "Well, I don't know . . . Nick *could* have done it. He's got a temper, you know that."

"You ever see him raise a hand to anybody?" Kate Johnson asked.

"No, I never did. But I heard him yell plenty of times. . . ."

"I've heard *you* yell plenty of times, Bob Johnson. You never raised a hand to me or anybody else."

"Me and Nick are two different people."

"Not so different."

"What about that wife of his? What's her name?"

"Jenna," somebody said.

"Yeah, Jenna. She divorced him for abuse, didn't she?"

"*She* said he abused her. Nick said it was BS."

"Well, sure. What'd you expect him to say?"

"Nick doesn't seem like the sort to beat up a woman," I said.

"Didn't beat her up," Ed McBee said. "Wasn't that kind of abuse. She claimed he bullied her, threatened her, made her do for him all the time like a slave. Claimed she didn't have a life of her own."

Annie Stanhope snorted, aimed one of her knitting needles at McBee. "Jellyfish, that's what Jenna is. No backbone. Let him wear the pants for years, did everything he told her without a whimper, and then decided she was tired of it and wanted a divorce. It was that high-hat sister of hers talked her into it. The one in Chico she went to live with."

"That sister's a real ballbuster, all right," Charlie Neale

said. "Came in here once, made some smart remark about my crippled leg. Right to my face."

"What'd you do about it?" McBee asked.

"Showed her my crutch. Said if she made another smart remark, she'd need a proctologist to remove it from her backside."

"The hell you did."

"The hell I didn't. *You* know a good proctologist, Ed?"

Everybody laughed. And that was the end of the dissent.

A little later I managed to steer the conversation to possible places Pendarves might have gone to hole up. There were plenty of opinions but none that had any basis in fact. He didn't have any relatives that the regulars knew about. Nor friends out of state or even out of the city. Nor property other than his house. Nor special places that he liked to visit; he didn't fish or hunt and when he took his yearly vacation, McBee said, all he ever did was putter around his house or sit here in the Hideaway drinking beer.

I asked if he was seeing a particular woman, or if he had seen one at any time since his divorce. Frank Parigli said, "Nah, he was all through with women after Jenna," which prompted Lyda Isherwood to laugh her big, booming laugh.

"That's what you think," she said.

"What's that supposed to mean, Lyda?"

"What do you think it means?"

"Whores?" Parigli was incredulous. "You trying to tell us he *paid* for it?"

"Plenty of men do. Haven't you, Frank?"

"No, by God."

"Not even once in your life?"

"No!"

"Well, Nick did. More than once."

"How in hell do you know?"

"He told me so."

"Bull."

"Maybe he paid Lyda for it," Neale said slyly.

"Not me," she said. "When I retired from the business I retired for good."

"You ought to retire that madam story," McBee said. "You never ran a house in Nevada or anywheres else. Only thing you ever ran besides your mouth was that lunchroom down at China Basin."

Unruffled, Lyda winked at him. "That's what *you* think, honey."

"What kind of hooker did Nick go for?" I asked her.

"Call-girl kind. Not the cheapies, either. Hundred-dollar girls."

"Same one each time?"

"He didn't say."

McBee gave me a squinty look. "You don't think some call girl would let him hole up with her, do you?"

"Depends on the girl," I said. "How well he knew her, how much money he had to offer."

"Bah. I don't believe it."

"Neither do I," Parigli said. "And I don't care what Lyda says, I don't believe Nick's been paying for it. He's not that sort."

"Every man's that sort," Lyda said, "at least until he gets too damn old to care. Deprive a horny male long enough and he'll mortgage the house for a night with a circus fat lady."

I stayed until almost ten. By then the regulars had had enough alcohol and enough group reinforcement to gloss over Pendarves's faults and foibles and elevate him to the status of martyr. The web of illusionary safety had been repaired, made strong again. I didn't blame them. Take away an elderly person's sense of security, and he's left feeling naked and helpless. It is the last and most vital of all our necessary illusions; without it, life can become unbearably hopeless.

As I walked through the wet night to my car, I thought with sudden insight: Isn't that what's happening to Cybil right now? Isn't Kerry and Kerry's apartment *her* last illusion of safety, and isn't she terrified that without that sanctuary *her* life will become unbearably hopeless?

Chapter 10

THURSDAY MORNING.

From the office I called Paul Glickman. He had nothing to tell me; he hadn't been able to get back in touch with either Coleman Lujack or Thomas Lujack's widow.

Nick Pendarves was still among the missing.

Eberhardt was late again. And there had been no messages on the answering machine.

Status quo.

I scribbled a note to Eberhardt, left it on his desk, locked the office, picked up my car, and headed south across the city to Highway 280.

THE HOUSE owned by Thomas and Eileen Lujack was high in the hills above San Carlos, at the end of a twisty little street ludicrously named Sweet William Lane. It was similar to most of the others in the neighborhood—big ranch-style place not more than twenty years old, built of wood and field-stone, with plenty of glass to take advantage of what, on a clear day, would be a miles-wide view of the bay from near San Francisco on the north to near San Jose on the south.

Low, dark clouds obscured most of the view today, though at least it wasn't raining here just now. The lot was big for this area, about two acres, the grounds well landscaped with lawn and shrubbery and flower beds; a gnarly old oak and a couple of acacias would provide shade in the summer. Scattered on the lawn and under the trees, peeping out here and there from among the vegetation, were at least twenty gaudily painted, three-foot-tall cast-iron gnomes, each one with a different facial expression ranging from weepy to lusty-leer. The gnomes gave the place a whimsical aspect, like some sort of Disney exhibit. Cute kitsch.

At a conservative estimate I put the value of the property at half a million dollars. Pretty fancy digs for the part-owner of a box factory that grossed around three million a year. But then, Thomas and his wife may have bought it before 1975, when Bay Area real estate prices began the steep ascent to their present dizzying heights. Back then, you could have bought all of this for under $100,000.

Sweet William Lane widened into a turnaround in front of the house, like a bulb at the end of a crooked thermometer. I parked near the driveway and went in along a fieldstone walk. One of the gnomes scowled at me as I passed; I scowled back at him. The front porch was half hidden by wisteria bushes, and the front door had a knocker in the shape of a smiling gnome's head. More cute kitsch. I found a doorbell and used that instead.

The door opened pretty soon, to reveal a thirtyish, ash-blond woman dressed in a black suit and a gray blouse. She frowned and blinked and said, "Oh. You're not the taxi."

"No, ma'am."

"I mean, you're not the taxi driver."

"Yes, ma'am. Are you Eileen Lujack?"

"That's right. Who are you?"

I let her have my name and one of my business cards.

"Oh," she said, "yes, Tom mentioned you. I think your partner came to see me once, didn't he? Elkhart or Eisenhardt or something like that?"

"Eberhardt."

"Eberhardt, yes. You should have called first."

"Ma'am?"

"Before you came all the way down here to see me."

"I tried to call a couple of times yesterday—"

"I was so upset, I didn't want to talk to anybody. So I turned the bell on the phone all the way down. That way I couldn't hear it when it rang."

"I'm sorry about your husband, Mrs. Lujack."

"Thank you. You're very kind."

"Would you mind talking today? There are a few things I—"

"Well, I can't," she said. "Not now. I'm going to be late as it is." She looked at a platinum-gold wristwatch and then past me, down Sweet William Lane. "He should have been here by now. The taxi. I *told* them I had an eleven thirty appointment with the funeral people and they said they'd send somebody right away. That was forty minutes ago."

"If you'd rather not wait," I said, "I could drive you."

"Oh, would you? You wouldn't mind?"

"Not at all. We can talk on the way. Where is it you need to go?"

"Just into town. San Carlos. Saxon and Jeffrey—that's the name of the funeral home. But what about the taxi?"

"Ma'am?"

"Well, he'll come eventually and I won't be here. The taxi company won't like that. They might not come at all the next time I need them."

"You can call and cancel on the way. I have a phone in my car."

"You do? Oh, good. We'd better hurry then."

She went and got her purse, locked the door, and set the burglar alarm. While I waited I remembered what Eberhardt had told me after his talk with the lady. "She's kind of a ditz," he'd said. "Not quite as bad as your typical Hollywood dumb blonde, but close. Thomas didn't marry her for her IQ, that's for sure." Eb can be a sexist sometimes, if a benign one, and at the time I'd put the description down to his piggy tendencies. But now that I had spent five minutes in Eileen Lujack's company, I decided he'd been speaking the nonsexist truth. She was a tall, leggy, chesty, blue-eyed, clear-skinned, gnome-loving ditz. And if she had spent any of the last thirty-six hours grieving over her husband, you couldn't tell it by looking at her.

When we got to the car she gave it a wary look, as if she were afraid it might fold up around her like one of those comic jobs in a Mack Sennett two-reeler. She said, "What happened to your door?"

"Somebody broke in a couple of nights ago. I haven't had a chance to get the lock fixed."

Her expression said she was wondering why anybody in his right mind would break into a wreck like this, but she had the grace not to put the thought into words. I helped her in through the driver's door, made an effort not to look at her legs as she scooted across the seat and swung them over the cellular phone unit, and then took my place under the wheel.

"I guess you have trouble with cars too," she said.

"Well, not usually."

"We never used to. Not until that awful thing with Tom's car and poor Frank Hanauer. Now the police have my car too. They . . . what's the word when they keep your property?"

"Impound."

"That's right. They impounded it. Tom got me a rental when he started using mine but I don't like driving it. I don't like driving at all, really, and today I just couldn't. I should have called one of my friends but I didn't think about it in time. . . ." She sighed heavily. "Are you sure you don't mind driving me?"

"Positive. I'm glad to help."

She directed me downhill through a warren of little streets and onto Alameda de las Pulgas. On the way I called the local cab company and let her cancel her order. Afterward she sat stiff and erect, not too close to the wired-shut door, and folded her hands tightly around her purse.

"I can't believe Tom's gone," she said. "I mean, I know he is but I just . . . I can't believe it. You understand?"

"I think so, yes."

"We had such a nice life until a month ago. Such a lovely life. And now . . . it's all come apart, it's all over. How can it happen like that, so suddenly?"

People make it happen, I thought. People and all their shortcomings, all their big and little evils. But I was not about to get into that with Eileen Lujack. I gave her the standard: "I don't know."

"So suddenly," she said again, with a kind of awe in her voice.

I said, "The last time you talked to your husband was when he called from San Francisco Tuesday afternoon?"

"What?" She was still thinking about her lovely life and how it had so suddenly come apart. "Oh . . . yes."

"What time was that?"

"I don't remember exactly. About five."

"He said he was staying in the city because he had something to do?"

"Yes."

"Did he give you any idea what it was?"

"Just business, that's all."

"What did he have to say about Nick Pendarves?"

"*That* man." She shuddered. "Tom didn't say anything about him."

"Nothing at all? He didn't tell you that Pendarves was almost run down and killed on Monday night? The threats Pendarves made afterward?"

"No. I didn't find out about any of that until Coleman told me yesterday."

"Why do you think he kept quiet about it?"

"He didn't want to worry me, I guess. He never talked much about things like that. You know, the trouble he was in —Frank Hanauer getting killed with Tom's car."

"Did he ever mention Pendarves to you?"

"Not that I remember. His name was in the papers . . . Pendarves's name, I mean. That's how I knew who he was."

We were approaching the intersection with San Carlos Avenue. Mrs. Lujack told me to turn right on San Carlos, and as I followed instructions I asked, "Was your husband in the habit of discussing business matters with you?"

"Hardly ever. I don't have a very good head for business."

Yeah, I thought.

"But Tom did," she said. "Coleman too. I never thought they'd make so much money from the factory, not after the way it started out. But they did." She laughed—a small, odd, puzzled sound. "He was right about the coyotes, I guess."

"Ma'am?"

"Oh, just something Tom said once."

"About coyotes?"

" 'The coyotes are going to make us rich.' That's what he said. I asked him what he meant but he said it was just a joke and it wasn't worth explaining. You don't know what he meant, do you?"

"No," I said. "You're sure he said the word 'coyotes'?"

"Well, it sounded like coyotes."

"When was that, do you remember?"

"Oh . . . at least five years ago. Before we bought the new house."

"The house you live in now, you mean?"

"Yes."

"You've owned that property just five years?"

"Almost five, yes."

"Must have set you back quite a bit."

"Oh, it did. Over four hundred thousand. I didn't think we could afford it, but Tom said we could. That was when Containers, Inc., really started to do well."

I ruminated on that while we waited at a red light. When the light changed I asked her, "Do you know Rafael Vega, Mrs. Lujack?"

"Who?"

"Rafael Vega. The shop foreman at Containers, Inc."

"Oh. I don't know anybody who works at the factory. Well, except Coleman, of course. I've only been there a couple of times. It's really not a very nice neighborhood."

We were coming into downtown San Carlos now. I made another turn at her instruction, and then said carefully, "There's a reason I've been asking all these questions. I think it's possible Nick Pendarves may not be the person who murdered your husband. Did Paul Glickman mention that to you?"

"No. No, he didn't." It took her a couple of seconds to get a firm grasp on the idea. "But . . . I don't understand. Tom was found in Pendarves's garage. Who else *could* have done it?"

"The same person who ran down Frank Hanauer, maybe."

". . . You have some idea who that is?"

"Not yet. But with a little more time I think I can find out."

"You mean you want to keep investigating?"

"With your permission."

There was a little silence before she said, "I don't know. You've been investigating ever since Frank was killed, you and your partner, and you haven't found out who was responsible. Coleman doesn't think we need you anymore. He says the police are doing everything that can be done."

"When did you talk to him about it?"

"Yesterday. He came to the house."

"Well, he's wrong, Mrs. Lujack. The police are convinced Pendarves is guilty of murdering your husband. And they think your husband was guilty of running down Hanauer. They're not going to look in the same places Eberhardt and I will be looking."

"I don't know," she said again. "Now that Tom's gone, maybe the best thing is for us to just put the whole ugly business behind us and go on with our lives."

Not her words, I thought. "Is that what Coleman said?"

"Yes."

"And you feel that way too?"

"I . . . I'm not sure what I feel right now."

"You don't believe your husband killed Hanauer?"

"Oh no. Of course not."

"And you do want to see his name cleared?"

"Yes, but . . . you could go on investigating for months and months and it would cost us thousands of dollars and the chances are you still wouldn't find out anything."

Coleman again. He seemed to be trying to manipulate her, which meant he was either a callous bastard or he had reasons for wanting Eberhardt and me out of the picture, the truth buried along with his brother.

I said, "I'm not trying to drag things out for a bigger fee. Believe that, Mrs. Lujack. All I want is the truth, and another week or so to get at it. If Eberhardt and I don't come up with something definite after that, we'll quit and bill you for expenses only—no other fees. I'll put that in writing, if you like."

"Well . . ."

"Will you think it over? Talk to Paul Glickman about it?"

"Yes, all right. But I'll have to talk to Coleman too."

"By all means." And so will I, I thought. "I'll call you tonight and you can let me know then."

We rounded another corner, and there was the Saxon and Jeffrey Funeral Home—white pillars, brick and glass, a circular drive in front, and a side drive with a hearse parked under a porte cochere. It looked like a cross between a neo-colonial home and a suburban savings-and-loan. I pulled into the drive and stopped in front.

Mrs. Lujack said, "Thank you again for driving me."

I told her she was welcome, and got out and leaned back in to give her a hand. But she didn't seem to want to leave the car just yet. She sat staring through the side window at the funeral home.

"Mrs. Lujack?"

Her head jerked, and when she looked at me her eyes

were moist. "Oh," she said. Then she said, "I don't want to go in there and talk about Tom's coffin, Tom's funeral. I really don't." And softly she began to cry.

She loved him, I thought then. She did love him.

I realized something else, too, in that moment: Eileen Lujack may not have a high IQ, but she was neither shallow nor frivolous. Eberhardt and I had both been wrong. She wasn't a ditz at all.

Chapter **11**

IT WAS RAINING again when I got back to the city—a hard rain, wind-driven into diagonal sweeps. Close to a week straight now of this kind of weather, and no immediate relief in sight. It began to get to you when it went on this long; a damp gray began to form inside you, too, like a kind of parasitic mold. Nice thought. What a gloomy old fart I was turning into. I laughed at myself, wryly, as I turned off 101 onto Bayshore Boulevard. Look on the bright side, pal. With all this rain, maybe there won't be any more dire rumblings about drought and water rationing come summer, and the water company won't have an excuse to raise its rates again.

The way it looked, Thomas Lujack's recent death hadn't done any more to slacken activity at Containers, Inc., than had Frank Hanauer's. The wheels of industry keep right on grinding, all right, through thick and thin; dead bosses have about as much effect as a ten-minute coffee break. I parked in the lot and hustled inside through the rain, laughing at myself again. Mr. Metaphor: Second-Rate Philosophy at Cut-Rate Prices.

Teresa Melendez wasn't at her usual station; this time I

got to talk to a tight-lipped guy in a corduroy jacket who seemed annoyed at having to work the switchboard. Yes, Mr. Coleman Lujack was in today but he wasn't seeing anybody. I gave my name and said my business was urgent and asked him to please request ten minutes of Mr. Lujack's time. Reluctantly, he used the intercom; talked and listened for ten seconds, disconnected, and said in I-told-you-so tones, "Mr. Lujack is sorry, he isn't seeing *anybody* today."

Especially not me, I thought.

I said, "Rafael Vega. He come back to work?"

"No. And he still hasn't called in. Now if that's all, I have work to do."

"Me too," I said to myself on the way out. "But nobody seems to want to help me do it."

THE OFFICE was locked up tight; Eberhardt still hadn't put in an appearance. There was only one message on the answering machine, and it made me swear out loud. It was from a screwball Hollywood TV producer named Bruce Littlejohn, who had latched onto me after the publicity surrounding my abduction and escape. He was bound and determined that he was going to make a TV movie about my life; I was bound and determined he wasn't. I'd told him so the last time we talked, not mincing words. That had been over a month ago, and I'd dared to believe that he had finally gone away. Fat chance. He was like malaria or herpes: Once you were exposed to him, you couldn't seem to get rid of him.

I didn't listen to his message; as soon as I heard his voice I flipped the switch to rewind. While some old coffee reheated on the hot plate, I took care of my mail and got no answer on a call to Rafael Vega's home number. The coffee tasted stale, and the sandwich I'd bought on the way from Containers, Inc., wasn't much better. I was forcing down the last of each when Eberhardt showed up.

He came in blowing and shivering and smacking his gloved hands together. "Christ, it's cold out there. Windchill factor must be zero. Some damn weather."

"Yeah," I said. "Makes you want to stick a feather up your ass and fly south for the winter."

He stared at me for a beat and then laughed. "That's pretty good," he said. "You make that up or what?"

"Heard it from Bob Hope."

"Huh?"

"Never mind." It was something my old man used to say on days like this. I hadn't thought about it in two decades or more. Why it should have popped into my mind today was a question I didn't want to have answered, either by Eb or myself. The less I dwelt on my old man, the better.

While Eberhardt poured himself a cup of coffee, I told him about my conversation with Eileen Lujack. He said, " 'The coyotes are going to make us rich.' What the hell is that supposed to mean?"

"Something to do with illegals, maybe. Seems to me I've heard the word before, in that context."

He shrugged. "You think it's important?"

"It might be. The money angle is, that's for sure."

"Yeah. Thomas couldn't have afforded a four-hundred-thousand-dollar piece of property five years ago, not on his annual draw and what the company was worth back then. We should have dug deeper into his background, I guess. But hell, he was our client; we weren't trying to get anything on him."

"Or Coleman."

"Or Coleman. So what do you think? They're mixed up in something a lot shadier than hiring undocumented aliens?"

"That's how it adds up. And if they are, Hanauer had to know about it too. It's got to be the hidden motive in both murders."

"You really think Pendarves was framed, huh?"

"More so all the time."

"But why? It just doesn't make sense with Thomas the victim."

"Maybe Pendarves has some idea. And that's another thing that keeps bothering me: Why haven't the police found a trace of him since Tuesday night?"

"He picked a hole somewhere and pulled it in after him."

"I hope that's it."

"What other explanation is there?"

"He could be dead," I said.

"Dead?"

"Murdered, just like Thomas. Can you think of a better way to cement a frame against him?"

"Christ. Killed the same night as Thomas, you mean?"

"Before or after, and his body dumped somewhere. That could be the reason his car was found abandoned in Golden Gate Park."

He thought about it. "I like the other theory better."

"So do I . . . for now. If Pendarves *is* alive and holed up somewhere, it figures to be right here in the city. And that probably means somebody's hiding him."

"One of his pals from the Hideaway?"

"Or one of his pals from work. Antonio Rivas, for instance."

"No way," Eberhardt said. "I told you, they weren't close."

"You also told me Rivas was holding something back. Maybe it involves Pendarves."

"Rivas as the third witness? I thought we ruled that out."

"We did. As a matter of fact, I'm inclined to rule out the third-witness angle entirely."

"That makes two of us."

"What I'm thinking," I said, "is that maybe Rivas knows something more about the Lujacks and their tie-in with the illegals. And that maybe he also let that something slip to Pendarves."

"So you want me to have another talk with him."

"Wouldn't hurt. Wouldn't hurt for you to check into Coleman's background and life-style either . . . see if *he's* been spending more money the past five years than he should have been."

"Now? I thought we were still on hold until Thomas's widow makes up her mind."

"She'll come through. Why waste time?"

"Uh-huh. All right, what the hell—I want answers as much as you do." He drained his cup as I got to my feet. "So what're you gonna be doing while I tackle Coleman and Rivas?"

"Finding out what happened to Rafael Vega," I said.

LA MODERNA MARKET was on Howard Street, half a block off Sixteenth in the heart of the Mission. A display window full of fresh fish and hanging strands of chorizo flanked the entrance on the left; on the right under an awning were open bins of vegetables and green and red chilis. There were customers inside but the place wasn't crowded; it was a little after three and still raining hard. The butcher shop and meat counter ran the bodega's full length and was staffed by two men in blood-spattered aprons. One of them, using a cleaver to whack a chunk of beef into soup meat, was Paco Vega.

Finding him hadn't been difficult. Eberhardt had neglected to ask the Vegas' talkative neighbor where Paco worked, but when I'd looked her up twenty minutes ago, she'd given me the information without any prodding. While I was in Albert Alley I'd rung the doorbell at the Vega flat, on the chance that Mrs. Vega was home. There had been no answer.

Paco was intent on his work and didn't see me right away. The other butcher was telling a heavyset woman in black that they didn't have any *sesos* today; she didn't seem to want to believe him. I stood alone at the counter, watching Paco wield the cleaver. He did it with short, clean, professional strokes, but the strokes were harder than necessary; there was a dark, set expression on his face, and each time the blade thumped down, white muscle-knots appeared at the corners of his mouth. Paco Vega was an angry young man.

He got even angrier when he finished and looked up and saw me. His eyes blazed for a couple of seconds; then he slammed the cleaver into the block, burying the upper edge a good two inches deep, and walked hard to where I was.

"What the hell you doing here, man?" he said in a low, strained voice. "I thought I told you to stay away from me."

"Your mother, you said, not you."

"Yeah, well, it goes for me too."

"We need to talk, Paco."

"I got nothing to say to you."

"Now. In private."

"I just told you . . ."

"About your father."

". . . What about him?"

"He's in trouble and you know it."

"You're full of shit, pancho."

"Am I? Then he's no longer missing? Everything's fine at your house again?"

"That's none of your business."

"I think it is," I said. "It might also be police business. Now do we go someplace private and talk?"

We locked gazes for about five seconds. But worry or fear had taken the edge off his anger; his eyes flicked away from mine and he licked his lips. "Through the door in back, near the coolers," he said, and walked off that way himself.

The door in back was actually two—swing doors with a sign on one of them that said *No Entrada.* I pushed through into a storeroom piled with crates and boxes, some full and some empty. Paco came through another swing door from the butcher shop, and without looking at me or saying anything he moved along an aisleway past the meat storage locker. I followed him out through a door at the rear, onto a short, narrow, L-shaped loading dock. There was an alley back there, and a space just wide enough for a medium-sized truck to pull in alongside the dock and then to back up to the short arm of the L for unloading. The space and the dock and the rain-swept alley were all deserted now.

Paco moved away from the door by several paces, in close

to the building where the wind wasn't quite as sharp, then stopped and turned to face me. "So?" he said.

I said, "Where's your father?"

"Oh come on, man. You think I know? He's been gone four days now, no word, no nothing. My mother cares but I don't. The hell with him."

"Suppose he's been hurt or worse?"

"Yeah, sure. That's what she thinks. Not me."

"What do you think?"

"Uh-uh. I came out here because of what *you* think."

"He's involved in hiring illegals," I said. "Has been for years. I don't think that; I know it."

"Big deal. So're a couple thousand others in this city, Hispanics and Anglos both. Go call the INS. You think they care? They don't care, not about small-timers like my old man."

"Maybe he's not such a small-timer."

"What's that supposed to mean?"

"Coyotes, Paco. The coyotes."

It was a pretty good blind shot. He went tight; you could see him drawing in on himself. "I don't know what you're talking about, pancho."

"No, huh?"

"No. What's coyotes got to do with anything?"

"You tell me."

"I already told you." He shook his head. "Man, you must think I'm some kind of dumb spick."

"On the contrary. I think you're a pretty smart Latino."

"Yeah? Then why'd you mention the cops inside? So I'd come out here and tell you all I know about my old man and the wetbacks, right? Like I'm so stupid I don't know the city cops can't mess in INS business."

"They can if there's homicide involved," I said.

Magic word. He repeated it, blinking: "Homicide?"

"Two of your father's employers in the past month. First Frank Hanauer and now Thomas Lujack."

"So? Some guy named Pendarves took Lujack out."

"Did he? I don't think so."

Paco ran the back of his hand over the bandit's mustache, rubbed the palm down over the front of his bloody apron. "What're you trying to say? My old man was mixed up in murder?"

"Maybe."

"Bullshit. He didn't have nothing to do with either killing."

"How do you know he didn't?"

"You got proof he did? Show me some proof."

"Why'd he disappear if he's not guilty of anything?"

"Quit pushing me. I told you, I don't know why."

"But you've got some idea. Maybe your mother has too. If I have to go talk to her again, I will."

That was the wrong thing to say; all it did was stir up his machismo. The white muscle showed again at the corners of his mouth. "Stay away from her," he said. "I'm warning you, man—stay away from my mother!"

He punctuated the words by delivering a flat-palmed punch to the fleshy part of my chest, above the heart. There was enough force behind it, and he caught me unawares enough, so that I was driven backward into the building wall. I hit it hard with my shoulders and spine—hard enough to unfocus my eyes for a second. Any harder and there might have been some damage to my backbone.

Anger kindled bright and hot. I came off the wall sideways, like a ball bouncing crooked, and caught one handful of his apron and another handful of his hair and spun him around and slammed *him* up against the building. I had an urge to hit him, hurt him; managed to fight it off. He grunted, struggled, tried to punch my kidneys, but I had him pinned tight, with my hip and leg hard into his crotch so he couldn't use his feet. The blows he struck were short-armed and didn't hurt.

It wasn't long before he quit trying to fight. He said between his teeth, "Anglo bastard!"

"Easy now. Unless you want to keep things rough."

His mouth cramped up; he would have spit in my face if I hadn't had his head turned at an off angle.

"Where's your father?" I asked him.

"Fuck you."

I pulled his hair, not gently. "Talk to me, Paco."

"I don't know where he is!"

"Tell me what he's into, then."

". . . All right! You want to know what he's into? He's into young pussy, all the young pussy he can get!"

I was silent. There was nothing for me to say just yet.

"Why you think my mother drinks? Him and his young pussy." It had been bottled up inside him for a long time; now that he'd let some of it out, the rest came spewing forth like vomit purge. "She knows he's gonna leave someday, known it for years, but she pretends he won't—keeps right on pretending we're a big happy family. Well, now she's got to face it and she can't. Four days means he's not coming back this time but she still can't face it so she drinks herself sick and prays for him to come home the whole damn time. He's a pig, he treats her like shit, and all she does is drink and pray for him to come home."

I let go of him and backed up a step, all in one motion. But he was not going to make any more trouble with me; it was his old man he hated, his old man he wanted to hurt. He leaned against the wall and hit it with his fist—three times, hard, hurting only himself.

I asked, soft, "Who is she? The woman you think he ran off with?"

"Who knows? Some young Latina with big tits, you can bet on that."

"You don't have any idea who she is?"

"No." He smoothed his hair and then spat on the dock, but not in my direction. "He didn't brag to anybody like he usually does. Not this time."

"Would he leave the city with her? Go back to Mexico, maybe?"

"Depends on how much *dinero* he had put away. What's

to keep him here? Not my mother, not me, not any of his scams."

"What scams?" I said.

"Huh?"

"His scams, you said. What scams?"

"You already called it, man. Wetbacks."

"Just hiring them? Or is it more than that, like smuggling them across the border? Is that the reason for his trips to San Diego and Mexico?"

Paco watched me for a clutch of seconds. His hard facade was back in place; the code of machismo would never let it crack for long. "Uh-uh," he said through a tight, bitter smile. "I'm not gonna do your work for you. Not when it comes to my people."

"You want your father punished, don't you?"

"For what he's done to my mother. But that's *my* job— mine and a good lawyer's. The other thing . . . no. You want him for that, you go get him on your own. You and the fuckin INS."

He shoved along the wall toward the door. I didn't try to stop him. When he got there he stopped and half-turned and said, "I meant what I said about staying away from my mother. She's had enough crap. You bother her again, you'll be damn sorry."

And then he was gone.

He's still sick with the flu.

The memory fragment came to me just after I exited the alley onto Howard, on my way to where the car was parked. I'd been walking fast because of the rain; now I walked even faster, remembering.

On Tuesday Coleman Lujack had told Eberhardt and me that Rafael hadn't called in to explain his absence. Today, the tight-lipped office worker had claimed Vega still hadn't called in. But yesterday, Teresa Melendez had told me on the phone that Vega was "still sick with the flu." And now *she* was off the job too.

Some young Latina with big tits, Paco had said.

Teresa Melendez?

Chapter **12**

THE MALE VOICE on the line said, "Containers, Inc. Good afternoon." You can never be sure about voices on the telephone but it sounded like the tight-lipped guy I'd dealt with earlier.

"Containers, Inc.," I repeated, roughening my own voice, making it a little deeper. "Some kind of business outfit, are you?"

". . . Yes?"

"Teresa Melendez work there?"

"Yes, she does, but she's not here today."

"You know where I can reach her?"

"I suppose at her home. Who's this, please?"

"Officer Walter Keene, San Francisco Police. Badge number seven-three-nine-nine-two."

"The police?"

"That's right. Mind telling me if Ms. Melendez is married?"

"Married? I don't understand . . ."

"We're holding a man who claims to be her husband. Assault and battery, drunk and disorderly. He busted up a bar in the Mission. He can't hardly talk, he's so sozzled; all we could get out of him is he's married to this Teresa Melendez. He had your telephone number on a piece of paper in his pocket."

"Oh," the guy said. "Well, it might be her ex-husband. Is his name Arturo?"

"That's it. She divorced him, huh?"

"Last year."

"Well, he thinks he's still married and he keeps yelling for her. What's her address and telephone number?"

There was a silence.

"Hello?" I said. I didn't have to work at sounding annoyed. "You there?"

"Yes. I'm not sure I ought to give out that information. . . ."

"This is the police department, for Christ's sake. What's your name, mister?"

That convinced him; citizens don't like angry-sounding cops to have their names. He cleared his throat and said meekly, "If you'll hold the line just a minute . . ."

"Hurry it up, all right?"

He went away. The phone booth smelled of somebody's cheap cigar; I opened the door all the way. This was a dark, Western-style neighborhood tavern on Geneva, not far off Mission, that wasn't doing much business at four o'clock on a rainy workday afternoon. Half a dozen customers hunched like sullen vultures over the bar and the jukebox was silent. I'd come in here to make the call because car phones sound like just what they are—they don't filter out traffic noises— and everybody knows police vehicles aren't equipped with cellular phones. If you're going to run a bluff, you'd better run a good one.

It was a minute or so before the guy came back on. "Officer Keene?" I grunted, and he said, "Sorry to be so long. Teresa Melendez lives at eight-oh-six Atlanta Street in Daly City. Her telephone number . . ." and he went on to give me that.

"Got it," I said. "Thanks."

"Glad to be of help, officer."

He was a good citizen, he was.

IN THE CAR I called Harry Fletcher at the Department of Motor Vehicles and asked him to run Teresa Melendez's name through the computer, let me know what kind of car she drove and its license number. I could have called Harry in the first place, after I'd determined that she wasn't listed in the San Francisco phone book (which includes Daly City) under either Teresa or T. Melendez; but for all I knew there were fifty Teresa Melendezes living in the Bay Area. Even if there were only two or three, it would have taken too much time to sift out the right one.

I asked Harry to get me the same information on Rafael Vega's vehicle. If Vega *was* shacked up with Teresa Melendez, his car would be somewhere in the vicinity of her home; and if I spotted it, then I'd know for sure without having to knock on her door blind.

IT WAS FOUR FORTY when I turned off Industrial Way into the parking lot at Containers, Inc. Dusk was already settling, like thick soot drifting down through gray water, and the outside lights—widely spaced sodium-vapor arcs on metal poles—were on. When it got to be full dark, the arcs would put a greenish tinge on the night and create pockets of deep shadow where the light didn't quite reach.

I drove slowly past the parked cars. I had no idea what kind Coleman Lujack drove, but whatever it was, it figured to be expensive. There was only one expensive model slotted among the compacts and junkers—a new Chrysler Imperial— and that was his, all right. It had a personalized license plate that read COLE L.

I backed into a space near it, midway between two of the sodium-vapor lights. From there I could watch the office entrance, but I was in shadows and at enough of an off angle so that the staff inside couldn't see me from their desks. I maneuvered myself into a comfortable position and settled down to wait.

After ten minutes the mobile phone interrupted the monotonous beat of the rain. Harry Fletcher. Teresa Melendez, he said, drove a five-year-old Honda Civic, license number 1BTQ 176; the vehicle registered to Rafael Vega was a Buick Skylark, vintage 1987, license number 1MXX 989. My memory isn't what it once was, so I wrote all of that down in my notebook.

A little after five, people began to file out of both the office and the factory. None of them was Coleman Lujack. I spied the tight-lipped guy but he didn't notice me; his transportation was on the opposite side of the lot. I got glances from a couple of the workers who passed near my car, but they weren't interested enough to ask me what I was doing there. Hard rain and long workdays dampen curiosity as well as spirits.

The lot was mostly empty by five thirty—just Coleman's Imperial and three other cars. It was cold in my clunker by then, with the wind and dampness seeping in through cracks around the wired-shut passenger door, and I was cramped and getting hungry and running out of patience. Come on, Coleman, I thought. Shag ass. Don't you have a hot toddy or something to go home to?

If he did he wasn't in a hurry to get it. It was almost six before he finally showed. He was wrapped in a gray trench coat and carrying an umbrella that he left furled as he crossed the lot; the rain had let up into a fine mist. He was one of those people who look straight ahead when they walk, as if they're peering down the length of a piece of three-inch pipe, so he didn't see me until he was at the door of his Chrysler and I was already out of my car. Then he came to stiff attention and stared as I approached him, his head making little involuntary bobbing movements, like a bird watching an oncoming cat.

"What are you doing here?" he said. He sounded nervous

and put out, with an undercurrent of something that might have been fear.

"Waiting for you."

"Why? We don't have anything to discuss. If we had I would have seen you earlier."

"There are some questions I want to ask you."

"What questions?"

"Why don't we go inside? Or sit in your car where it's dry?"

"No," he said, "I can't take the time. I have an appointment."

"It won't take long."

He hesitated, as if weighing the idea, then shook his head and bent to unlock the driver's door.

"Rafael Vega," I said. "Illegal aliens. Coyotes."

His reaction was like watching a piece of badly edited film: freeze frame for three or four seconds, followed by jerky action in which he finished the unlocking process and yanked the door open. He said without looking at me, "I don't know what you're talking about."

"Okay. Try this: Nick Pendarves didn't kill your brother."

"Nonsense."

"Is it, Mr. Lujack?"

I thought for a second that he was going to dive into the car to avoid both me and the issues I'd just raised; but he didn't do it. He straightened slowly, faced me again. The greenish effect of the nearest arc light gave his skin an unhealthy cast.

He said, "Of course Pendarves is guilty. All the evidence—"

"Evidence can be faked."

"You have proof that it was?"

"Not yet. But I'm working on it."

"On whose authority?"

I didn't answer that.

"I see," he said. "So I suppose you expect me to pay you."

I didn't answer that either.

"How long will it take? Another month or two—or six? And at what, two or three hundred dollars a day?"

I had my hands in my overcoat pockets and I kept them there so I wouldn't be tempted to hit him. I hurt him with my eyes, though; I must have because he winced and fastened his own gaze on my mouth.

"Why are you afraid of the truth, Mr. Lujack?"

"I'm not afraid of the truth. I know the truth."

"Do you? All right, who killed Frank Hanauer? Your brother?"

"Of course not."

"Well, Pendarves didn't do it. So who did?"

"I doubt if we'll ever know, now."

"Because Thomas is dead? That doesn't necessarily follow. Don't you want his name cleared?"

"If possible, yes. But you haven't been able to do it in a month and neither have the police."

"I still can, if you cooperate."

"I've given you all the cooperation I'm going to."

"It wouldn't be the INS you're worried about, would it?"

"Damn the INS," he said. "All I'm worried about is my sanity. I've taken all the grief and anguish I can stand; so has Tom's widow. As far as we're concerned, it's over now, finished. Let the dead alone and the living go on living."

Nice little kiss-off speech—emotional, forceful, sincere. I didn't buy a word of it. But there was nothing I could do about it. I just stood there while he folded himself into the front seat, looked up at me long enough to say, "Please don't bother me or Eileen again. If you do . . ." Then he slammed the door, as if to emphasize the implied threat. I heard the lock click an instant before he ground the starter.

I backed off a couple of steps, holding my anger in check, as he drove off. He thought he'd handled me just right. He thought this was the end of my nosing around in his and his brother's private affairs. He thought that whatever he was hiding was going to stay hidden.

He thought wrong.

ACCORDING TO MY MAP, Atlanta Street was in a narrow little section of Daly City flanked by the western slopes of the San Bruno Mountains, Colma's Olivet Memorial Park and Serbian Cemetery, and the Cypress Hills Golf Course. For some reason known only to its developers, there being no body of water within miles, most of the streets had been given nautical-type names: Harbor, Dockside, Windjammer, Frigate, Pirate Cove. Maybe it had to do with the fact that the section resembled a short peninsula jutting out from the Daly City mainland. More likely, the names had nothing to do with anything except fledgling cleverness. Just another variety of cute kitsch, after the fashion of the gnomes in Eileen Lujack's gardens.

As the crow flies, only a few miles separated Teresa Melendez's home from Containers, Inc. But the crow would have had to fly straight up over the San Brunos, just as I had to drive up over them on Guadalupe Canyon Parkway, and that increased the distance considerably. Guadalupe Canyon was where the end of the notorious car chase in *Bullitt* was filmed—the one that inspired the endless, mindless succession of TV-show car chases and cinematic demolition derbies that continue to offend the senses. But that was more than twenty years ago, before the road underwent improvements and its daily traffic load was still light. Nowadays they couldn't have closed it off for a couple of days as they did back then; it had become a well-traveled commuter thoroughfare and the animals in the rush-hour zoo would have rioted at the inconvenience.

I turned off Guadalupe onto Orange Street, made a wrong turn, and discovered that most of the little peninsula—the part with the nautical street names—was hidden away behind a high rustic retaining wall that extended east-west for several blocks. The only through street had a guardhouse and guard at the entrance, and when I passed by I could see acres of trailers on landscaped lots. So the landlocked peninsula was mostly a fancy trailer park bounded by brown hillsides and a couple of cemeteries and made up of streets called Frigate and Pirate Cove. I didn't even try to figure it out. There are some things that defy deductive reasoning.

I found Atlanta Street finally; it dead-ended at the street along which the retaining wall ran. Ninety-eight percent of the residences in this part were the standard Daly City variety dubbed "little boxes" by Malvina Reynolds—squarish row houses standing shoulder to shoulder with their neighbors, built close to the sidewalk, garage below and living quarters above, narrow entranceways between with staircases leading up to the front doors. The other two percent, scattered here and there, were newish detached houses and older cottage-style dwellings that looked uncomfortably out of place, like liberals that had wandered by mistake into a stadium full of right-wing fundamentalists. Eight-oh-six Atlanta turned out to be one of the cottages, small and white-frame and not too well kept up, with a little front garden behind a low fence and a carport instead of a garage on one side. Lights burned behind drawn curtains, and there was one vehicle parked under the carport, so somebody was home.

The parked car was a brownish compact. I couldn't make out the license plate as I drove past, but I was pretty sure the make was Honda and the model Civic. The curb in front was empty; so were the curb spaces before another cottage on one flank and row houses on the other. An empty white van waited at an angle across the way; it was the only street-parked vehicle in the immediate vicinity.

I circled the next block and came back on Atlanta. No sign of Rafael Vega's Buick anywhere along there. I tried the cross streets, taking it slow. That didn't buy me anything either.

So maybe I was wrong about Vega and Teresa Melendez. And maybe I was right and he was out buying groceries or liquor or condoms, or doing any one of a hundred other things.

I drove over to Mission and stopped at the first restaurant I saw, a Mexican place that specialized in Yucatan dishes. I ate a burrito with prawns and mushrooms and cilantro; I drank three cups of coffee; I sat and thought about things and didn't have any brainstorms. At eight o'clock I put myself back in the car and returned to Atlanta Street.

The lights were still on in Teresa Melendez's cottage. The Honda Civic was still parked under the carport. And there still wasn't any sign of Rafael Vega or his Buick Skylark.

Behind the parked van was curb room for another car, as well as some shadow from an overhanging pepper tree. I thought I could sit there for a while without attracting attention. I made a U-turn, parked, drifted low on the seat, and waited.

Seconds crawled and minutes crept, the way they had in the parking lot at Containers, Inc., the way they always do on a stakeout. God, how I hated stakeouts—short or long, it didn't make any difference. The passive waiting, the boredom, the slow, slow passage of dead time. How many did this make in the past thirty-odd years? How many empty, wasted, lost hours? Too damn many. The physical discomfort was also becoming less tolerable, especially on nights like this, with the rain stopping and starting, stopping and starting, and the wind and the cold sneaking into the car and conspiring to numb my feet. Nights like this, I felt every one of my years. Nights like this, I understood why old men wrap themselves in sweaters and shawls and then sit close to heaters, stoves, blazing fires.

Nine o'clock. Nothing happened at 806, except that the light in the front window went out. But there was still a light on at the rear; I could see the faint glow of it against the wet dark.

If he was out somewhere and coming back, I thought, wouldn't she put the front porch light on for him? No, hell, not necessarily . . . not if he was going to park under the carport too and go in through the rear door. For all I knew, that glow over there was the *back* porch light.

Nine thirty. And that was all I could take—of the cold, of the waiting, of the boredom. Besides, the later it got and the longer I sat here, the shorter the odds that somebody would notice me and call the cops. I wasn't even sure why I'd sat here this long, put myself through the discomfort. If Vega *was* shacking up with Teresa Melendez, what did it matter if I braced him tomorrow instead of tonight? I'd put almost a month into this investigation; another few hours hardly mattered much.

I wondered if I was becoming an obsessive-compulsive where my work was concerned. I'd always had that tendency, always been able to control it before it got out of hand. But now? The earthquake had something to do with intensifying it, but mostly the cause was those three desperate months in the mountain cabin. Another little legacy of change. And something else for me to worry about in my spare time.

I MADE MYSELF go home, instead of out to Taraval and the Hideaway. It would have been after ten by the time I got there, and some of the regulars would already have left. If I was ever going to find out anything from them, which at this point seemed unlikely, it wouldn't be tonight.

There was one message waiting for me. From Eileen Lujack. She said she'd decided to call me because she was going to spend the evening with a friend. She said my home number was on the business card I'd given her, as if she were telling me something I didn't know. She said, "I thought about what you said today and I just don't think it's a good idea for you to keep investigating. I really don't. I think the best thing for everybody is if we just let the dead alone and the living go on living."

Coleman Lujack's phrase, word for word.

Chapter **13**

THE SAN FRANCISCO BRANCH of the Immigration and Naturalization Service is downtown on Sansome, in the U.S. Customs complex. I got there at nine thirty on Friday morning, found the office open for business, and talked my way into an audience with a deputy district director named Clement Orloff.

Orloff was young, officious, conservative in attitude and appearance, and a hard-line INS loyalist. He didn't want to tell me anything until I told him exactly what I was working on, complete with names and addresses. I said I wasn't there to turn anybody in; I said I needed more time and information before I could make any direct accusations; I said I wasn't trying to hide anything or I wouldn't have come to see him in the first place, would I? We argued a little, and I stonewalled him, and finally his zealousness got the better of him and he agreed to answer my questions. But I'll be damned if he didn't insist on taping the conversation.

"Tell me about the coyotes," I said.

"Smugglers," Orloff said promptly. "Also known as

'travel agents.' Scum, as far as we're concerned. They prey on their own kind."

"Smuggle illegals across the border, is that it?"

"No. To U.S. points after the illegals have found their way across."

"I'm not sure I understand."

"For a fee, the coyotes arrange and provide transportation from border areas to cities up north—areas where other illegals congregate and where they can find work."

"The coyotes operate down around San Diego, then?"

"Thick as flies," Orloff said. "The illegals need them to get past the San Onofre checkpoint."

"What's that?"

"The last Border Patrol checkpoint, on Highway Five sixty-seven miles from the border—our last defense against illegal immigration into Southern California. If an illegal gets safely past San Onofre, there's not much to stop him from reaching the L.A. area and then migrating elsewhere."

"Are the coyotes organized?"

"Some are, some aren't."

"But there are large rings?"

"Certainly."

"Big money in that type of smuggling, right?"

"Lord, yes. Illegals come over the border in droves. We caught well over a million last year, and that is no more than twenty-five percent of the estimated total influx. Most of the ones that are caught and sent back try again until they make it."

"Looking for the promised land," I said.

"Mmm. Of course, IRCA has been a major deterrent. Otherwise the situation would be much worse."

"IRCA. That's the immigration reform law passed a few years ago?"

"Yes. The Immigration Reform and Control Act of 'Eighty-Six. It provides amnesty for qualified families, and penalizes employers for hiring illegals and requires them to file documents verifying that their foreign workers are authorized to be in this country. An excellent program."

"Seems to me I've heard rumblings that it isn't working as well as expected."

"Of course it's working," Orloff said defensively. "More than four million illegals have achieved amnesty so far. But that's not enough for La Raza Centro Legal and the other liberal groups."

"What's their position?"

"Oh, that IRCA hasn't eliminated the basic economic incentive for immigrants to come here, and that it hasn't really slowed the influx of illegals because a lot of the amnesty people are providing an established network to bring in impoverished friends and relatives. They want all sorts of additional reforms."

"Sounds reasonable."

"Doesn't it, though."

I was not about to argue the point with him; trying to argue with a loyal bureaucrat is a job for other zealots and masochists. I said, "Let's get back to the coyotes. How do they operate?"

"Well, the organized rings have brokers who work both sides of the border. Mexicans with valid U.S. visas that allow them to travel back and forth undisturbed. On U.S. soil they congregate where the illegals do after crossing. In San Ysidro, for instance, there's a supermarket ten blocks from the border that is a coyote hotbed."

"If you know about these places, why can't you shut them down?"

"We try, God knows. Agents from Brown Field—that's the main Border Patrol station down there—raid them periodically. And undercover agents from our antismuggling unit do what they can to infiltrate the gangs. But there are too many illegals, too many coyotes, and too few of our people. . . ." He made a frustrated gesture.

I asked, "What happens once the deals are set and money changes hands?"

"The illegals are loaded into cabs and driven to safe areas," Orloff said. "Then they're transferred to private vehicles—trucks of different sizes, passenger cars. The coyotes pack them in like sardines for the runs north. Illegals have been found under the hood and crammed into the trunk, sucking on hoses for air. More than a few have died en route."

Christ. "What's the going rate per person?"

"Depends on the final destination. Seventy-five dollars to Santa Ana, one hundred dollars to L.A. Some of the freelance coyotes charge more. They're even worse scum; they've been known to abandon passengers after being paid."

"The organized rings need financing to get started, don't they? So they can hire brokers and drivers, buy vehicles if needed?"

"That's right."

"Where does the money come from? Strictly from Mexican interests, or are there Anglos who play dark angels?"

"There are Anglos," Orloff said. Not without reluctance, as if he didn't like to admit that some of his own countrymen could also be scum. "Is *that* the reason you're here? You know someone, an Anglo, who might be involved with the coyotes?"

"Maybe, maybe not. As I told you, I'm not sure of my facts just yet."

"If you have knowledge of felony activity involving the federal government, it's your duty—"

"Let's not start that again, Mr. Orloff. I know my duty—to the federal government, and to my profession, my clients, and myself. When there's anything definite to report, I'll report it. You have my word on that."

"I hope your word is your bond," he said sententiously, and made a little production of switching off his tape recorder.

We both got on our feet. He didn't offer to shake hands before I went out; neither did I. Each of us had our reason. He didn't want to touch a private detective of questionable moral fiber and possible liberal cant. I didn't want to touch an asshole.

THE SKY HAD QUIT its copious leaking during the night, and this new day wasn't as gray or damp as the past several had been. There were patches of blue here and there in the overcast, through which a pale winter sun kept trying to shine. Hallelujah. The wind was still gusty and chill, but then you couldn't expect too much sudden improvement in the weather at this time of year. I took advantage of the dry air and pale sun by walking over to the building where Bates and Carpenter had its offices, three blocks from the INS encampment. I thought that since I was in the neighborhood, I'd take a little of my time and a little of Kerry's to see how she was bearing up.

But she hadn't come in today. Her secretary, Ellen Stilwell, didn't know exactly why—just that Kerry had called to say she had some "personal business" to attend to.

"Did she mention her mother?" I asked.

"No. No, she didn't."

Downstairs in the lobby I shut myself inside a public telephone booth and called Kerry's home number. The line burred to itself eight or nine times, and I was about to hang up when Cybil's frail voice said, "Hello?"

I cleared my throat. "May I speak to Kerry, please."

". . . She's at work."

"Oh, of course. What time did she—"

"Who is this?"

I said my name. "Cybil, I hope you're feeling—"

She hung up on me. Fast and hard.

IT WAS FOGGY in Daly City. But then, it is almost always foggy in Daly City, no matter what the weather happens to be in San Francisco and other parts of the Bay Area. Something to do with proximity to the ocean and wind currents. Wisps of the stuff crawled along the rooflines of Teresa Melendez's white-frame cottage, blew down into the empty carport. The Honda Civic wasn't anywhere on the street either. Nor was Rafael Vega's Buick Skylark.

Another impasse.

Well?

EBERHARDT WAS AT HIS DESK when I came into the office, reading what looked to be magazine tear sheets with an expression of mildly horrified fascination. He put the sheets down in a hurry when he saw me, as if I'd caught him doing something not quite wholesome.

"Oh," he said, "it's you."

"Who'd you think it might be? The vice squad?"

"Huh?"

"What've you got there? Dirty pictures?"

"This? Nah."

"What then? You were pretty engrossed."

"Yeah, well . . . never mind. Where you been all morning?"

"Working. How about you?"

"Yeah," he said. "Waiting for a call right now. You talk to Glickman?"

"No. Did you?"

"Little while ago. One guess what he had to say."

"Coleman Lujack fired him, and us by extension."

"Right. We're to keep our noses out of Coleman's business from now on. That's a direct quote from Coleman."

"The hell with him. You have a chance to do much digging into his finances yet?"

"Some. Provocative stuff but none of it conclusive."

"Same here. Provocative and nasty."

I told him about my talks with Coleman and Paco Vega, my so-far uncorroborated guess about Rafael Vega and Teresa Melendez, and what I'd learned from Orloff about the coyotes. He agreed that it was a good bet the Lujacks had gotten themselves mixed up in the "travel agenting" of illegal aliens, probably through Vega and his contacts, and probably by financing one of the coyote rings. Eb's check on Coleman had turned up a situation parallel to his brother's: He, too, appeared to be living a little too high off the hog for his share of the Containers, Inc., profits. At a conservative guess, each of them had to be raking in around fifty thousand dollars annually as their share of the scam.

"But there's no hard proof of any of it," Eberhardt said. "And we still don't know who killed Hanauer and why. And if you're right about Thomas, who killed *him* and why."

"I'll lay you odds Coleman and Vega had a hand in at least one of those murders and probably both."

"His own brother?"

"Why not? Cain killed Abel, didn't he?"

"Who? Oh, the Bible . . . yeah."

"Vega's the key," I said. "Find him, we find the answers and the proof we need."

"He's in Mexico by now. Why else would he have disappeared?"

"I'm not so sure, Eb. I think maybe he's still around."

"Because of what Paco said about him shacking up with some bimbo? Hell, the kid could be wrong. So could you about Teresa Melendez."

"I'll find out by tonight, one way or another."

"You intend to keep working on this, huh? Even though we've been canned?"

"Sure. Don't you?"

He gave me his long-suffering look. "We're on shaky ground and you know it. Coleman and the widow could make big trouble for us—harrassment, invasion of privacy. We could lose our licenses."

"Not if we bust the whole thing wide open."

"Big if. I say play it smart and back off. Turn what we have over to that INS guy—what's his name, Orloff?—and let him handle it."

"No," I said.

"Why the hell not?"

"We were hired to prove Thomas didn't kill his partner. We haven't proved it yet."

"Ahh. His hands were dirty whether he ran Hanauer down or not. Just as dirty as Coleman's and Vega's. What difference does it make if he was guilty of homicide or not?"

"It makes a difference," I said. "You want to give up on the case, go ahead. But I'm going to see it through."

He shook his head. "You are one stubborn wop, you know that?"

"So you keep telling me. Anything new on Pendarves?"

"Well, he's not hiding out at Antonio Rivas's place, I can tell you that. There wouldn't be room. In addition to Rivas there's his wife, three kids, mother-in-law, and pregnant seventeen-year-old unmarried niece—all in five rooms on Bryant Street."

"What about the information Rivas was holding back?"

"I couldn't get it out of him. I doubt if has anything to do with Pendarves anyway."

"The coyote angle?"

"That's my guess," he said. "Rivas got a whiff of it, but he's not talking on account of he's afraid of Vega."

I asked if he'd checked with the Hall of Justice for an update on the police search for Pendarves. He had, and there were no new developments. And no leads at all on how Pendarves might have gotten out of the city and the Bay Area, if he *had* gotten out. One of the people they'd contacted was Pendarves's ex-wife, Jenna, in Chico; her comment was that she hadn't had any dealings with him since the divorce and that she hoped he rotted in hell. Her sister was even more outspoken. If he showed up around there, she said, she'd blow his head off with her shotgun.

"Maybe somebody already did," I said. "Blow his head off, I mean."

"Are you back on that kick again?"

"If he isn't dead—dead since last Tuesday night—why hasn't there been a trace of him since?"

"I can think of ten reasons—"

His telephone bell cut him off and put an end to the argument.

While he took the call I glanced through my mail, discarded all but a small check I'd been expecting, and then dealt with my one phone message. It was from Barney Rivera, an old friend and chief claims adjuster for Great Western Insurance's local office. Periodically he tossed bones our way, little ones that the company's small investigative staff was too busy to bury on its own, and I caught another one when I called him back—a home-accident claim in which fraud was a possibility.

As I hung up I saw that Eberhardt was reading the magazine tear sheets again, with the same expression of mild horror that he'd worn earlier. I said, "What *is* that you keep reading?"

He blinked, put the sheets down. There was a silence; then he sighed and said, "Article from some magazine. Bobbie Jean found it."

"Article about what?"

"She thinks it's the funniest thing she ever read." He scowled. "I don't think it's a damn bit funny," he said.

"Well, what's it about?"

"Private parts."

". . . Say that again?"

"You heard me. Private parts."

"Whose private parts?"

"Men's. The, uh, dingus."

"Dingus," I said.

"Yeah. You think it's possible for a guy to break it?"

"Break it?"

"His dingus. You think it could happen?"

"What do you mean, break it?"

"Just what I said. You know what 'break' means."

"Impotency? Is that what you're—"

"No, goddamn it. *Break* it. Fracture it like a bone."

I stared at him "You mean while it's erect?"

"No, while it's dangling like a piece of linguine! Sure I mean while it's erect!"

"I don't believe we're having this conversation," I said.

"All right then, forget it. Just forget it."

Neither of us said anything for a time. Eberhardt sat fiddling with one of his pipes, his shaggy brows pulled down in a glower. His face was red.

"Eb," I said finally, "let me see the article." He didn't object, so I got up and went over and read it standing beside his desk.

The title was "You Broke Your *What*?" and it was written in a wryly humorous style. But it contained quite a few anatomical facts and medical case histories that made it seem all too authentic. It said that in the penis there are two tubelike masses of tissue called the *corpora cavernosa,* which become filled with blood during sexual arousal and thus cause an erection. Each of these tubes is covered with a fibrous sheath that stretches thin—so thin that in certain freak instances it can be made to rupture. Also at danger, in even rarer cases, are the outer sheath of the penis and the urethra.

There have been close to two hundred documented cases of penile fracture, the article said. In about half of them, the fracture occurred during intercourse or attempted intercourse —a freak accident, what the French call a *faux pas de coit,* in which the man either "missed the introitus" and hit a solid portion of his partner's anatomy, or rammed his member into a mattress or other object disassociated from his partner, or performed so vigorously and "in such an unusual position" that the penis literally cracked as if it were made of glass. In other reported cases, the victim had caused fracture by means of careless masturbation, catching his organ in his pajamas, falling out of a tree, and swatting his erect member with his hand so he wouldn't have to get out of bed and urinate. One man had even done the damage, so the article said, in a corral on a horse ranch; facts on this case history were mercifully vague.

On the one hand, all of this was painful to read about and to contemplate; on the other hand, it was pretty amusing stuff and I couldn't help smiling a little and chuckling a couple of times. This only increased Eberhardt's glower. When I finished reading and handed the tear sheets back to him, he said, "You think it's funny too, huh?"

"No, not really. Still, some of those cases . . ."

"Yeah, I know. How the hell could you miss the target? Or ram your dingus into the mattress?"

"I guess it all depends on the circumstances," I said.

He quit scowling and gave me an anxious look instead. "You don't think it's all a hoax? You think it could really happen?"

"Sounds plausible to me."

"Jeez," he said. Then he said, "What do you suppose they do in a case like that?"

"Who?"

"Doctors. Don't be dense."

"How should I know?"

"Well, I mean, do they treat it like they would a busted arm? You know, put it in some kind of cast?"

The image that conjured up brought another chuckle out of me. "Sure," I said, "a great big one. So the guy can impress his friends, have everybody sign it."

"Ha ha," he said sourly. "Big joke. How would you like it if it happened to you, wise guy?"

"I wouldn't, but there's not much chance it will. You worried it might happen to *you*?"

"Hell, no. What makes you think I'm worried?"

"You sound worried."

"Bullshit. It's just . . . I can't think of anything more humiliating, that's all. You'd never live it down if anybody found out. And what if the damage was permanent? What if you could never have sex again?"

"That's a pretty sobering thought, all right."

"Break your dingus," he said. "What'll we find out next?"

Chapter 14

AFTER A LATE LUNCH at Zim's I drove out to foggy Daly
City for another check on Teresa Melendez's house. Still no
Buick Skylark in the vicinity. And at first, no Honda Civic.
But when I circled the block and came back for a final drive-
by, there it was, laboring uphill on Atlanta Street, farting
smoke through a defective exhaust.

I slowed, and so did the Civic to make the turn into the
cottage's driveway. La Melendez was the woman behind the
wheel. As near as I could tell from a distance, she was alone
in the car.

I pulled over in front of the house and got out and walked
fast up the drive. I was fed up with all the skulking around
and the game of *Is she Rafael Vega's girlfriend or isn't she?*
The time had come for a direct approach. If the answer was
yes and Vega got told I was on his tail and why, maybe it
would bring him out into the open where I could get at him.
And if the answer was no, then I could quit sniffing around
Teresa Melendez and do my hunting elsewhere.

She was leaning into the Honda's backseat when she
heard me coming. She backed out in a hurry, clutching a bag

of groceries in the crook of one arm, and gave me a tense, wary look. There was no immediate recognition in it; maybe she was afraid I was a rapist, or at least a dirty old man. She was wearing a belted raincoat and a scarf over her black hair. Her lipstick was too red; it made her mouth look like a bloody slash.

"Afternoon, Ms. Melendez," I said. "Remember me?"

"No," she said, but now she did; I could see it in her eyes. I could also see that she liked having me there about as much as she would have liked confronting a rapist. She remained tense, wary. Her other persona—the bored, aloof sexpot—was nowhere to be seen.

"Sure you do. The private detective. My partner and I were at the factory the other day, to see your boss."

"Oh . . . yeah. What you want here?"

"Talk to you."

"Why?"

"I think you know the answers to some questions."

"I don't know nothing. And you don't work for Mr. Lujack no more."

"He tell you that?"

She licked her mouth, made it glisten like freshly spilled blood. A sudden frown pulled the corners of it down, giving her a pouty look. Some men would think she was hot stuff, but I didn't happen to be one of them.

"How'd you find out where I live?" she demanded.

"Finding things out is what I do for a living."

"You're the one called up yesterday. Pretending to be a cop . . . all that crap about Arturo."

"Did I?" I smiled at her. "I don't remember."

"*¿Que pasa?* I told you, I don't know nothing."

"You know Rafael Vega."

". . . What's he got to do with anything?"

"He's mixed up in Thomas Lujack's murder."

"Rafael? You're crazy. . . ."

"That's not the only thing he's mixed up in either."

"What're you talking about?"

"Coyotes, Teresa. You know what they are, don't you?"

She knew. Little worms of fear crawled in her eyes now. She couldn't quite hold my gaze; hers kept dancing away, coming back, dancing away. "Crazy," she said again, but it came out weak and strained this time. "*Demente,* that's what you are."

"Where is he, Teresa?"

"Who?"

"Rafael Vega."

"How should I know?"

"You're good friends, aren't you?"

"Pah. He's just somebody I work with."

"Never dated him or anything like that?"

"He's married."

"Uh-huh. When did you see him last?"

"Last week. This week he didn't show up for work."

"How come?"

Shrug. "Maybe he's sick."

"With the flu?"

"Who knows? He didn't call in."

"Then why'd you tell me he was sick with the flu?"

". . . What? I never told you that."

"Sure you did. On the phone two days ago."

She shook her head; shook it again. Despite the cold, there was a thin film of sweat on her upper lip. "Listen, why you bothering *me*? Huh? Why don't you go talk to his family?"

"I already have. His son thinks he's been seeing another woman. Been shacking up with her."

"Me? He says it's me?"

"No. I do."

"Well, you know what? You're full of shit."

"Why didn't you go to work yesterday, Teresa? Why aren't you working now?"

"I don't have to tell you why I do anything. I don't have to talk to you no more. Get out of here, leave me alone."

"No reason you shouldn't talk to me, if you've got nothing to hide."

"I mean it—leave me alone. You want me to call the cops? You want me to start screaming?"

"All right," I said. "But when you see Rafael, give him a message from me. Tell him I'm looking for him. Tell him I know all about the coyotes—"

She spun away from me, so abruptly that she lost her grip on the bag of groceries. The sack fell at her feet, broke open, spilled out a loaf of bread and a six-pack of Stroh's and half a dozen other items. She was rattled enough, and wanted clear of me badly enough, not to care. Without even hesitating she plowed through the strewn groceries and then through a gate in the fence and was gone around the rear of the cottage.

I stayed where I was until I heard the door slam. I hadn't been wrong, I was thinking, hadn't been wasting my time. She was Rafael Vega's mistress, all right. She knew what he was mixed up in—some of it, anyway—and where he was or how to reach him. She would deliver my message. And when she did, things were going to happen.

Good or bad, things were going to happen.

I HUNG AROUND the neighborhood for the better part of an hour, driving a little, parking in different locations where I could keep an eye on her house. But she didn't leave again, and nobody came to see her. Finally, at three thirty, I gave it up and went on my way.

Snagging Rafael Vega wasn't going to be *that* easy.

BACK TO THE OFFICE. Eberhardt was gone, and there were no messages. I considered doing some work on the home-accident case for Barney Rivera, but I was too restless for routine business; it could wait until Monday. I locked up and went away again almost immediately.

Four thirty on a Friday afternoon; a long, lonely weekend stretching out ahead of me. Unless Kerry could get away, which wasn't likely. Cybil demanded all of her free time. I wondered again where she'd been today, if she'd consulted a geriatric specialist and what she'd been advised. Well, she'd call when she had something to tell me.

I held an image of her up in front of my mind's eye. And as always, I felt the old sweet ache start up. A man shouldn't love a woman as much as I loved Kerry; that much emotional attachment isn't healthy, because there is too much dependency tied up in it. Somebody in my line of work needs to be independent. Loners don't get distracted; loners have total focus on the job at hand; loners make the best detectives.

Loners die lonely, I thought.

The hell with that, I thought. I'm emotional and dependent. . . . So what? I'm also too damned analytical for my own good. Sentimental slob and deep-thinker—how's that for an epitaph?

In the car again, I started home to my flat. And then changed my mind on the way up Pine and kept going past my turnoff at Laguna. I was in no frame of mind for a passive evening at home. When I felt like this I needed to keep moving, keep doing things, keep working.

Out There at the Beach was where I went, even though it was too early for the Hideaway. For no particular reason I drove by Nick Pendarves's house. On the property next to the garage where Thomas Lujack had died, a man was out working busily in his garden. As soon as I saw him I pulled over to the curb. The police would have talked to him by now, without much result, but there was no reason I shouldn't have a few words with him myself. Better that than just driving aimlessly.

Fog banks were piled up over the ocean, spilling landward, but overhead the sky was still partly clear and turning a sooty gray-black. There was maybe twenty minutes of light left, and the neighbor was making the most of it. He was in his sixties, lean and spry, wearing old clothes and gardening gloves and a Giants baseball cap. An array of tools was spread out among shrubs and flower beds and climbing-plant trellises, and he was using a pair of clippers to shape some kind of bush that looked pretty shapely already. A gardener—the manic type. The past few days of rain and soggy ground would have been hell for him. And who knew but what it would start raining again tomorrow.

I leaned on a low grape-stake fence and hailed him. A much higher board fence, along which a geometrically trimmed hedge grew, separated his property from Pendarves's. That fence was why he probably hadn't seen or heard much the night of Thomas Lujack's death.

He came over with a certain amount of reluctance. But his curiosity got the better of his passion for gardening when I told him I was a detective investigating the murder next door. He assumed I meant police detective; I didn't correct the assumption. His name was Anderson, Lloyd P. Anderson. He hadn't ever told his wife what the *P* stood for, he said, so he wasn't about to tell me.

"Told the other officers everything I know," he went on, "which ain't much. Hell, it ain't anything. The wife and me missed all the excitement. Watched a damn crime movie on TV that night, while a real crime was going on right under our noses. Makes you think, don't it?"

"It does that."

"Nick Pendarves . . . it's still hard to believe. Oh, sure, he's got a temper, but murder? You never figure somebody you know, somebody living right next door, is capable of a thing like that."

"How well do you know him, Mr. Anderson?"

"Hardly at all, considering we been neighbors twelve years. He kept to himself. Not that there's anything unusual about that. Most of us do, out here. Value our privacy more than your average city dweller."

"So you wouldn't have any idea where he might have gone."

Anderson shook his head. "Still haven't found a trace of him, eh?"

"Not yet. Do you know any of his friends? Anybody who came around to see him regularly?"

"Nope. Didn't seem to have many friends or visitors, not since his wife left him. But like I said, we value our privacy out here. He minded his business and I minded mine. Except for the one little run-in we had two years ago, but that didn't amount to much."

"What run-in was that?"

"Oh, just a disagreement," Anderson said. "That's how come I know about his temper. In the middle of it I thought he was going to haul off and smack me one." He grinned wryly. "I'd of sued the pants off him if he had. I know my rights."

"What was the disagreement about?"

"Weeds."

"Sir?"

"Weeds," Anderson said. "His property was full of 'em. Weeds and high grass, dry grass, growing right up alongside our boundary fence there. All up around that tinderbox garage of his too. Fire hazard. I told him that, told him he better cut 'em down."

"And he refused?"

"At first. What was I worrying about fire for, he said, when we live in the fogbelt. I finally offered to pay part of the cost. Figured it might shame him and it did, up to a point. He gave in and had the weeds and grass cut, but damned if he didn't present me with a bill for half the charges. He didn't try to stick me for having his junk carted way at the same time, though. I'd of drawn the line at that and I guess he knew it."

"Junk?"

"Out behind his garage. Old tires, rusty pipe, all sorts of crap. He'd of let any more pile up and it'd been worse than an eyesore. We'd of had rats, sure as hell."

"He sounds like the careless type," I said.

"Careless? Hell, he's a pure slob. You been inside his house? That's where I talked to him; I went over there and he invited me in. Regular pigsty."

I thought of the immaculate kitchen I had glimpsed

through the window on Tuesday night. "You wouldn't happen to know if he had somebody come and clean for him recently?"

"Nope. Why'd you ask that?"

"I saw his kitchen. It's spotless."

"That so?" Anderson was surprised. "Don't seem like him, hiring a woman to clean up his mess. Might marry one, get himself a legal maid, but pay for housekeeping? Not Nick Pendarves."

"Maybe he didn't hire it done."

"Well, he didn't do it himself," Anderson said. "Not if that kitchen is spotless. I'd bet money on that."

So would I. What I was thinking now was that maybe Lyda Isherwood was wrong about Pendarves's love life being confined to occasional sessions with a call girl. Maybe he had a lady friend after all. And if I found her, maybe I would also find him.

THE ATMOSPHERE in the Hideaway that night was more subdued than usual, as if the thing with Pendarves, still unresolved as it was, was starting to weigh heavy on his drinking companions. It was not that they were beginning to doubt his innocence; believing in that was too important to them. It was just that it had gone on too long. What they wanted now was to put the whole unpleasant business behind them so they could begin to forget it had ever happened.

There were none of the animated group exchanges of my last visit—not much talk at all. I heard laughter only twice while I was there, brief spurts of it that had a strained, hollow quality, like nervous chuckles at a wake. Several of the regulars sat alone: Harry Briggs in one of the droplit booths, playing chess by himself because Douglas Mikan was absent; Peter Vandermeer in the adjoining booth, absorbed as usual in a book; Ed McBee at the bar and Lyda Isherwood at one of the tables. The rest were in small clusters of two and three.

I sat for a time with Lyda. At first she was reluctant to talk, which was a good indicator of how low her spirits were;

the loud bantering voice and booming laugh were just memories tonight. She was a little drunk, too, on brandy old-fashioneds. She finished one just after I sat down, and I bought her another. That loosened her up enough to answer my questions.

"A girlfriend? Nick? Nah," she said, "not him. He's been paying for it since his wife quit him. Call girls, you know? *I* know all about that racket. I used to run a whorehouse outside Carson City during the war. World War II. You believe it?"

"I believe it."

She waved one of her thick arms. "Most of 'em in here don't. But it's the gospel truth. Big fancy whorehouse outside Carson City. Red plush furniture, four-poster beds, silk sheets. Silk sheets, by Christ. Then it burned down. Right to the damn ground and I was out of business. I couldn't afford to open another place, not unless I wanted to do it cheap and I'm not cheap. Never a cheap lay, never a cheap madam."

"Lyda, about Nick—"

"What about Nick?"

"Isn't it possible he's seeing somebody here? On the sly?"

"You serious, Art? Your name's Art, right?"

"Right."

"You serious, Art? Why'd he want to do that?"

"Maybe the woman's married," I said.

"Nah, no way." Lyda gave a loose-lipped, humorless grin. "No woman here is that stupid, married or otherwise."

"Why would a woman have to be stupid to take up with Nick?"

"He's a user, that's why. Male chauvinist pig."

"He abuses women, you mean? Like he abused his wife?"

"Abuses anybody that'll let him," Lyda said. "He had a dog, he'd run that dog's legs off just for a pat on the head. That's the way he is. Everybody knows it and don't let 'em tell you any different."

"Where do you think he is, Lyda? Who'd hide him out?"

"Nobody that didn't like to be used," she said.

I gravitated to the company of several of the other regulars, but none of them had any more to tell me than Lyda had. If Pendarves *was* seeing a woman, Hideaway denizen or not, he'd been doing it with a covert secrecy the CIA would have envied. Either that, or the people here knew all about it and for one reason or another were keeping it strictly among themselves.

I gave it up at ten o'clock. The edge was off my restlessness, and the prospect of being alone in my flat had grown more appealing than the company here. More than on any other night since I'd been coming to the Hideaway, the place and its patrons depressed me.

Outside, the fog had rolled in thick and sinuous—a great woolly blanket of it that deadened all sounds except the fretful warnings of the foghorns, fuzzed lights and obscured objects more than a few feet away. The sidewalks, as usual, were deserted. A car whispered by on 48th Avenue, another over on the Great Highway that looked as though it were plowing through drifts of dirty snow. The beach beyond was totally hidden, as if behind a rippling wall.

I crossed 47th, went past a couple of parked cars to where mine waited in midblock. I got my keys out as I cut around the front end to the driver's door. Most of my attention was on the door lock; the fog was clammy and the wind chill and I was in a hurry to get inside, put the heater on. Stupid lapse in caution. I didn't see him until he came gliding around from the rear, crouched low. Or hear him until he said, "Don't move, man, don't move!" in a rough voice shaking with tension, the English a little broken and Mexican-accented.

Rafael Vega, sure as hell.

With a gun in his hand.

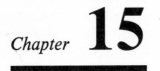

Chapter **15**

IT WAS TOO CLOSE to the way in which I had been kidnapped, the beginning of those three months of hell. Dark night, empty streets, me on the way to my car and home, him lurking in the shadows and catching me off guard and throwing down on me. Maybe that was why I did it. Or maybe it was that the new, dark side of me seized momentary control. I'll never know for sure. There was no conscious thought involved, and therefore no memory later.

Frozen tableau for a span of time that might have been as few as two seconds or as many as ten. Vega at a standstill a couple of paces away, holding the handgun at arm's length; me just as motionless, still bent forward at the waist—seeing him with a tremendous clarity as if he were on a brightly lit stage instead of a dark city street. Medium height, wiry, somewhere around 160 pounds; thick black hair blown wild by the wind; angular face all pinched up, lips wet and rubbery-looking; eyes wide and full of fear and death. All of that so clear, so sharply detailed, and then in the next instant obliterated by a black tide of fury that seemed to swell through my head.

And I did what I had no notion of doing, what I would never have done before my abduction.

I reached out and tore the gun from his hand.

He neither pulled the trigger in reflex nor reacted in any other way. One second he was pointing the weapon at me; the next I had my hand on it and was ripping it free of his fingers. But I did not have a tight grip and I couldn't hold on to it. It fell clattering; kicked under my car without going off. Vega made an astonished bleating sound, staggered backward with his eyes popping. I remember that plainly: His eyes seemed enormous, great bulbous staring things ready to burst from his skull. I think I made a noise myself, a kind of crazy roaring.

He turned tail and ran.

I would have caught him in the first twenty yards but I slipped on the wet pavement, ricocheted off a parked car and down to one knee. By the time I got my feet under me again he had opened up a thirty-yard lead. He ran in a loose-jointed zigzag fueled by terror, throwing wild looks over his shoulder as he pounded across the streetcar tracks and out onto 48th. Beyond, on the Great Highway, the vague lights of an oncoming car sliced through the fog from the north. If Vega saw the lights he misjudged the nearness of the car; he barreled up across the landscaped median strip between 48th and the highway, kept right on going under the furry red DON'T WALK signal.

Squeal of brakes, long angry horn blast, the headlights pinning him for a second, then veering away as the car swerved. The front bumper hit him, but the car was almost stopped by then and it didn't knock him down. He bounced off in a kind of lurching pirouette, stayed on his feet, and plunged upward along the wide sandy path that led to Ocean Beach.

I lost sight of him for a few seconds; the fog had him in a tight gray embrace. As I pelted across the median strip, the car frog-hopped ahead through the crosswalk and stalled. I ran around behind it. The engine roared just as I cleared the fender, and the pavement took a skin of rubber off screaming tires; the driver did not want any part of Vega or me or our trouble.

When I came up onto the sandy trail I saw Vega again through rents in the mist, slogging upward less than twenty yards away. The sand was wet but not hard-packed and he couldn't generate any speed. Neither could I, after another few strides along the path. But I seemed to be gaining on him anyway.

Over the pound of blood in my head I could hear the breakers for the first time—a dull muffled roar punctuated by the rasp of my breathing and the whisper and grind of my shoes digging into the sand. Years since I'd been to this section of Ocean Beach, before the sewer project began, but they couldn't have widened or altered the shape of it much: low dunes flanking the trail here, stretching out parallel to the Great Highway; from the dunes to the waterline, fifty yards of flat, sandy beach . . . nothing on it but driftwood and sand dollars, dog crap and human litter. There was no place for him to go or hide out there. If I didn't lose him in the fog . . .

Now he was up to where the trail crested and then dropped down to the flat part of the beach. The mist was thick here, eddying close to the ground and as wet as rain; I had to keep swiping at my eyes to clear moisture out of them. At that I saw him only in disjointed glimpses, as if he were a figure in one of those flickery early silent films.

Ten yards separated us now. He threw another look over his shoulder, and when he saw how close I was, panic drove him sideways over the waist-high chain link fence that bordered the path. On hands and knees he scrambled through ice plant and tule grass, up the side of the nearest dune.

I vaulted the fence in an awkward twisting motion, came down wrong and sprawled out on my face in a clump of ice plant. Its slick, wet, swollen leaves had the feel of a dead man's fingers. I clawed up through it, getting my legs under me. Vega was almost to the top of the dune, but when he caught hold of a clump of grass to pull himself the rest of the way, it tore free in his hand and he slid partway back down. That gave me just enough time to get a hand on his ankle. He flailed wildly with his feet, kicked free, managed to pitch his body over the top of the dune. But I was still right behind him, digging hard into the sand. When I came up over the top he was scrabbling through a shallow depression to the base of the next dune. He wasn't going to have enough time to climb that one and he knew it; he twisted around so that he was on his back, facing me with his legs and arms up like a cat in fighting position.

I threw myself at him. One of his knees dug into my belly, made me grunt in pain, and he shoved me off with enough force to roll me over. Wet sand got into my open mouth, down into my throat; I gagged, spat, shook my head as I scraped back onto my knees. He was right there, trying awkwardly to kick me in the head. I went at him again, knocked him backward. But I could not get my body on his, could not find enough leverage for a solid blow.

We punched at each other, squirming and sliding around. Neither of us did any damage. He kept screaming at me the entire time, garbled Mexican obscenities in a gasping voice soaked in fear. He thought he was fighting for his life. Maybe he was. The rage in me was as black and merciless as death.

The skirmish seemed to go on and on, like that dream where you're trying to run away from something, or toward something, and you can't move your arms and legs except in a dragging way that is savagely frustrating. It couldn't have lasted more than a minute; it seemed ten times that long. We might have kept it up to the point of exhaustion if I hadn't failed to protect my head after a wild swing. A handful of flung sand caught me full in the face and for a few seconds I went blind.

I reared away, pulling in on myself like a turtle while I struggled to clear my vision. But he didn't press his advantage. Instead I heard him going away from me . . . flight, not fight. Through stinging eyes I looked for him, didn't see him. But I could hear him—down now, not up. Then I knew where he was.

I scrambled across the width of the depression, came up at the edge of the slope that dropped off to the flat part of the beach. Fog roiled around down at the bottom, making Vega seem two-dimensional, wraithlike, as he got his feet under him. He looked up once to where I was and then began to run toward the hidden surf.

I threw myself over the edge, half-slid and half-rolled down the incline. By the time I fetched up at the bottom, he had disappeared. I ran staggering in the direction he'd gone. Ran blindly, waving my arms in front of me in a witless effort to tear away more of the mist. There was pain in my chest now and I couldn't seem to take in enough air.

The ocean's thunder grew louder, the sand underfoot a little more firmly packed: I was nearing the waterline. Icy wind, thick with the smell and taste of salt, burned my cheeks and numbed my bare hands. Another ten feet and the fog parted enough so that I could make out the surf foaming up white over the sand, the waves riding high and angry before they broke. Vega wasn't anywhere in the fifteen-yard stretch visible ahead.

Which way, left or right? I started left, but to the right a gap like a doorway swirled open in the mist and I thought I saw something moving over that way. I changed direction, lurching badly now because each step sent splinters of pain up into my crotch. Ten feet, fifteen . . . and there he was, just out of reach of the frothy tongues of surf. Not running anymore; down on hands and knees, crawling through a scatter of flotsam and jetsam.

I plowed toward him, swiping at my eyes to keep him in focus. He heard me coming. Pulled himself around and then, when I was only half a dozen strides away, heaved staggering to his feet. He had something long and dark and bulky in one hand—

Piece of driftwood, watch out

—and I broke off to one side an instant before he sprang

at me, swinging the driftwood club at my head. I heard the rush of it going past close; heard him grunt and curse. The unchecked thrust had put him off balance. I twisted back, down to one knee, and pitched myself at his legs. My shoulder caught him a glancing blow over one knee, sent him spinning away into the surf.

I made it to my feet, saw him trying to do the same. A wave broke against the backs of his legs and toppled him again. Without hesitation I went out there after him.

It was like wading into Arctic waters. The surf boiled around my ankles; the sand shifted under my feet, so that I had to flap my arms to maintain balance. There was a treacherous undertow along here; if you got caught in it it would drag you straight out to sea. Vega fought free of its pull before I reached him, came all the way up shaking his head and blowing like a sea lion. He still had the piece of driftwood clenched in his hand. As soon as he located me he lunged, arm upraised—and another wave smacked him, a big one this time, and hurled him past me and then knocked me tumbling after him.

Salt water poured into my mouth and throat and took my breath away. The churning surf roughed me this way and that before it finally let me go. I flopped over, fighting for air, and dug my hands into the running sand to keep from being dragged backward. I couldn't get my legs under me before the next wave broke; instead I scuttled forward crablike, so that when the surf foamed around me again I was far enough up on the beach to avoid being submerged. When that wave receded I crawled another few feet, lay still in a pile of slimy seaweed, gasping and coughing water out of my lungs.

Vega, I thought then, and rolled over, tensing, ready to fend him off another time. But he wasn't anywhere near me. I didn't see him at all until another breaker finished punishing the beach; then I spotted him, all humped and bobbing like some sort of sea creature. When the surf released him he made little trembly movements but didn't try to get up. Hurt? Or faking it? No, he'd been too wrought up to think of clever games, particularly when he was being thrown around by an angry sea.

I stood—and fell right back down again; my legs felt numb and wood-block heavy. I crawled partway to where he was, held myself in place as another wave mauled him, then tried again to stand. This time I was able to keep my feet. Another wave surged and ebbed. I let the receding water pull me along, leaned down and got hold of his jacket collar and started to drag him inland. The next wave and the shifting sand threw me down but it didn't make me lose my grip on Vega's collar. I got up and kept on dragging him. Maintained my balance somehow when the next one splashed down and kept right on dragging him until my legs gave out on firmer sand.

I sat there shivering, sobbing a little from exhaustion. Thinking—when I could think clearly again—that I was lucky not to be dead. Not by Vega's hand; from a stroke or a heart attack. Fifty-eight years old . . . you can't punish your body this way at my age and expect it to keep chugging along in fine shape. The pain was still there in my chest, a tightness with a little pulsating core. Not out of the woods yet . . .

When I had enough strength I crawled over next to Vega and pushed him onto his back. He was alive but not conscious, his face twisted into a grimace of pain; I could see his chest moving, hear strangulated sounds in his throat. Swallowed water, I thought, and I turned him on his side again so he wouldn't suffocate on it. He quit making the choking sound; water dribbled out of his mouth. But his breathing stayed irregular, and when I felt his pulse it was weak. Hurt when the wave knocked him down and pummeled him . . . but in the dark I couldn't tell where or how badly. Chances were he needed medical attention, and soon, before pneumonia set in.

Let the son of a bitch die, I thought.

No, I thought, no. The rage was seeping out of me now, and along with it the scum of bloodlust. There was nothing more Vega could do to me. He wasn't my real enemy anyway;

he was just a soldier, a weapon primed and aimed by a general behind the lines. The general was my real enemy. And the general had to be Coleman Lujack. How else would Vega have known where to set up in ambush for me? Nobody other than Glickman and the Lujacks had been told about my under-cover work at the Hideaway. It *had* to be Coleman.

I was shivering badly now: move or run the risk of catch-ing pneumonia myself. I got up slow, stayed up, but my legs trembled with weakness. And even though the chest pain had finally eased, my breathing was still labored and short. There was no way I could carry Vega from here to the Great High-way. Leave him where he lay, then; no other choice. I put my back to him, smudged him out of my mind, and set off through the clinging sand.

I don't know how long it took me to find the trail and climb off the beach. I don't know how many times I fell and got up again. Fatigue and the shroud of fog robbed me of any sense of time or distance. At first, when I neared the dunes, I couldn't find the path; I slogged south along the base of them and there it was. Then I didn't have enough strength left in my legs to walk all the way up the incline, and I had to crawl the last ten yards or so to where the trail crested. I stayed there on all fours, peering over toward Taraval.

An L Taraval streetcar was sitting at the line's terminus, an oasis of light in the mist. But there were no police cars, no activity of any kind. The disarming of Vega, the foot chase, had gone unnoticed by anyone except the driver of the car that had almost hit Vega, and like most urban dwellers these days, he'd chosen to pretend it had never happened.

I waited until the streetcar moved up past the Hideaway before I stood again. I walked down to the bicycle path that flanked the Great Highway on this side, turned onto it. Nearby was one of the old beachfront convenience stations, locked at night these days because of vandals. I leaned against its wall, resting, while a car pulled up to the curb on 48th and somebody got out and went into one of the buildings. Then I crossed the highway, crossed 48th into Taraval—all in a gait as tanglefooted as a drunk's.

I had dropped my keys when I took the revolver away from Vega, but I did not have to hunt for them; they were lying right there in the street and I stepped on them when I walked up alongside the car. With the key ring in hand, I fumbled around under the car and found the gun—light-weight belly-gun, from the feel of it. I had to use the door handle to haul myself up so I could unlock the door. Then I collapsed inside.

For a couple of minutes I sat with the engine running and the heater on high, rubbing my hands and face dry with the car blanket. The gun I locked away in the dash compartment. The mobile phone then: 911, a terse message in a voice that didn't sound like mine, telling the Emergency Services operator where Vega was and that he might be badly injured, and a fast disconnect when the operator asked my name.

It would take the paramedics and the first police car not much more than five minutes to get here, which didn't leave me enough time to hunt up Vega's Buick and search it. Just as well; I was in no shape to do any more shambling around on the street, and I had already used up most of my allotment of luck. Wasn't likely there'd be anything incriminating in his car anyway.

I put mine in gear and headed home to do more battle, this time with my own private demons.

Chapter **16**

YOU THINK YOU KNOW, based on past experience, exactly
how your mind and body will react to a certain set of stimuli
—but you're not always right. The subconscious has its own
perversities. I thought that when I was alone in my flat the
episode with Vega would trigger another anxiety attack, or at
least an edgy and mostly sleepless night. I thought that Saturday, when it finally came, would be one of the now-rare bad
days—and that I would have to spend part of it wiring myself
back together again.

None of that happened. I soaked in a hot bath for an hour
with no slippage of calm, I took some aspirin and nonpre-
scription cold capsules, I went to bed and to sleep right away
—such a deep, exhausted sleep that I neither dreamed nor
woke up until an hour past dawn. And when I awoke I felt all
right: a little shaky, my limbs full of aches and sharp pains,
my chest tender and my breathing scratchy, but with my
mind clear and my nerves at ease. I didn't even have a runny
nose from the wetting in the ocean.

I put myself through my normal routine of exercises, a
half hour's worth, taking it slow at first until cramped muscles

relaxed and the stiffness and shakiness were gone. A shower and two cups of coffee used up another half hour. By eight thirty I was dressed and on my way out of there.

No more pussyfooting around, not after last night. Coleman Lujack and I were going to have it out.

FIRST STOP: Containers, Inc. Coleman's Imperial wasn't on the lot; neither was anybody else's car. The factory was shut down as usual for the weekend.

All right.

I drove back to 101 and headed south toward Burlingame.

JUST NORTH of the airport exit, the mobile phone buzzed. When I picked up, Eberhardt's voice said, "Yeah, I figured you'd be on the move already. Where are you?"

"Why?"

"I'm asking you, that's why." There was an edge to the words. "Where?"

"Down the Peninsula. On the way to see Coleman Lujack."

"What for?"

"Ask him some questions."

"About Rafael Vega, maybe?" he said.

"Among others. Why? Something about Vega?"

"You don't know, huh?"

"No. What should I know?"

"You go to the Hideaway last night?"

"Yeah, I was there."

"Anything happen? Say between ten and eleven?"

"Like what?"

"Like Vega, goddamn it. You have a run-in with him?"

"What's this all about, Eb?"

"Vega's in the hospital," he said. "Found on Ocean Beach last night, half-drowned, with a concussion and a couple of compressed vertebrae in his neck. Somebody put in an anonymous call, told Emergency Services where to find him."

"What's his condition?"

"He's alive. If he's lucky he won't be permanently para-lyzed."

"He do any talking?"

"No. Able but not willing."

"Police find his car?"

"Not far away and nothing much in it. Don't you want to know which part of the beach?"

"I can guess."

"Yeah. You didn't have anything to do with it, huh?"

"What would you do if I did?"

"Knock some sense into your head—that's what I'd like to do. What happened out there?"

"I'm not going to talk about it on the phone, Eb."

"Come over to my place, then."

"No. Not now."

"When?"

"Later. Later today."

"What're you up to? What do you want out of Coleman?"

"I told you—the answers to some questions."

"You think he sicced Vega on you, is that it?"

I didn't say anything.

"Listen, you rock-headed bastard, you do anything to him . . ."

"I'm not going to do anything to him. I'm just going to talk to him."

"Like you talked to Vega last night?"

"I didn't talk to Vega last night. I didn't hurt him either."

"But you were out there on the beach with him. You're the one made the anonymous call."

I didn't say anything.

"What's the matter with you lately?" Eberhardt said. "You used to play things by the book. Now you go around busting laws left and right. You want to lose your license again?"

I didn't say anything.

"You still there?"

"I'm still here."

"Well then talk to me, for Christ's sake. Tell me the truth for a change. Every time we talk lately, you either lie through your teeth or futz around with half-truths. I'm your partner and your friend; I'm on your side. Don't you know that?"

"I know it," I said.

"Then tell me what the hell's going on."

"Later. After I talk to Coleman."

"If it's not too late by then."

"It won't be too late."

"I'll be home all day," he said, and banged down the receiver at his end. Hard.

What's the matter with you lately?

Rhetorical question, Eb, I thought. How can I explain it to you when I don't fully understand it myself?

COLEMAN LUJACK'S HOUSE was a two-story mock Tudor just across the northwestern dividing line between Burlingame and exclusive Hillsborough. The fact that his was a Burlingame address probably saved him a couple of thousand dollars a year in property taxes, woodsy Hillsborough land being worth much more per acre than that of its neighbors.

Before I got out of the car I took Vega's gun—a Charter Arms .38 Special—from the glove compartment and flipped open the gate. All five chambers were full. I emptied out two of the cartridges, rotated the cylinder until one empty chamber was under the hammer and the other next to it in the firing line; then I slipped the piece into my jacket pocket. I might need the threat of it, but I did not want to use it except as a last resort. The empty chambers were a buffer against another onslaught of black fury and sudden impulse. A man who doesn't respect his weaknesses, new or old, is a damned fool.

I went up through a formal rock garden to the front porch. There was a burglar alarm system wired into the house; the tiny red warning light on a panel next to the door indicated it was switched on. I rang the bell anyway. Rang it two more times before I gave up and walked around to the driveway. At the garage I found a window to peer through. There was a car inside, but it wasn't Coleman's Imperial; it was a low-slung white foreign job. His wife's probably.

I quit his property and began canvassing the neighbors, telling them it was urgent that I get in touch with Coleman. The third one I tried, an athletic young woman in jogging clothes who lived across the street, told me Coleman and his wife had gone off about six o'clock last evening. As far as she knew, they hadn't returned.

"They took suitcases," she said. "I happened to notice him putting them into the trunk of his car. So I guess they went away for the weekend or longer."

"Would you have any idea where?"

"No, I'm sorry."

I spoke to three other neighbors. None of them had any idea, either.

I wondered if Eileen Lujack did.

SHE WASN'T HOME. Or at least she didn't answer the bell, even though I worked on it pretty good.

Out with one of her friends, probably, I thought. She wasn't the type who would be comfortable alone, especially at such a painful time in her life. The question was how long she'd be gone—a few minutes, an hour or two, the whole day?

Back in the car, I rolled the window down and sat there waiting. The sky was clear down here, the day warmish for January; people were out in the yards of two of the neighboring houses, normal people doing normal Saturday morning things like gardening and tossing a football around. A couple of them began to pay attention to me after half an hour or so. It doesn't take long for curiosity to turn into apprehension, and I wasn't up to any hassle on a day when I was not one of the normal people myself. I gave Eileen Lujack another five minutes. When she still didn't come, I went.

THERE WAS SOME SUN and blue sky in Daly City too, though it was fighting a losing battle with the fog. By mid-

afternoon the area would be socked in again. On Atlanta
Street, as on Sweet William Lane, people were outside taking
advantage of the good weather while it lasted. Teresa
Melendez wasn't one of them, but at least she was home. Or
her Honda Civic was anyway.

I parked across her driveway and went up and leaned on
her doorbell. No response. But when I let up on the button I
thought I heard steps inside; then the curtain in the adjacent
window flicked a little and I had a glimpse of her face as she
peered out. I pushed the bell again and said loudly, "You'd
better talk to me, Teresa. Unless you want to talk to the police
instead."

Still no response.

"Which is it going to be? Me or the cops? Make up your
mind."

I counted to six, silently, before the latch clicked and the
door popped inward a couple of inches. She was already walking away from it when I entered. Halfway across the room she
stopped and stood slump-shouldered without turning while I
shut the door behind me. It wasn't much of a room, because it
had no discernible stamp of individuality; it might have been a
living room in anybody's house anywhere, filled with nondescript furniture and nondescript trimmings and painted and
carpeted in nondescript colors. It might have been an Anglo's
living room; there was nothing Mexican or Spanish in it that I
could see. The room told me as much about Teresa Melendez
and the life she led as I needed to know.

Still without turning she said, "Rafael isn't here," in a
dull, emotionless voice.

"I know."

"He's in the hospital."

"I know that too."

She came around slowly to face me. She was wearing an
old housecoat over a slip and blouse. Her long hair had been
hastily combed; the lipstick and makeup she wore, just as
hastily applied, didn't hide the dark bags under her eyes or

the sallowness of her skin. The bored sexpot and the defiant mistress were both gone today. In their place was a shopworn, bitter woman, puffily soft and unattractive—the woman she would probably be in another ten or fifteen years.

She said, "You put him there?"

"In the hospital? No."

"You know who did?"

"Coleman Lujack," I said.

"Yeah," she said, and nodded once, and shaped her lips as if she wanted to spit. "Big Savior. Big Judas."

She moved a couple of paces, sat heavily on the arm of a shapeless couch. I stayed where I was. The room smelled of stale cigar smoke and stale liquor and fried food and something else I couldn't define. Despair, maybe.

"All night I waited for him," she said. "I knew it was bad when he didn't come. Bad for him, bad for me . . . *finito.* This morning . . . the newspaper . . . I went to the hospital but they wouldn't let me see him. They said I wasn't a relative. They wanted to know who I was and why I was there. I ran out quick and came home. Where else am I gonna go?" She looked up at me. "You think he'll die?"

"I'm not a doctor."

"I hope he does," she said.

"Why do you say that?"

"He'll go to prison if he doesn't. He's afraid of prison. He told me that once. Be better for him if he dies."

"Tell me why he'll go to prison."

"Why do you think? His work with the illegals."

"The coyotes, you mean."

"He was only helping our people," she said. "But the INS, the Anglos in their big government offices . . . they don't understand. They'd put him in prison for that."

"Not for that," I said. "For robbing your people, for feeding on their poverty."

She didn't want to hear that; she shook her head.

"That's why they're called coyotes, Teresa."

"No," she said. "He wasn't one of them."

"All right, have it your way. He's a good man, just a pawn in the Lujacks' hands. It was their idea, then. Coleman and Thomas. They financed his work with the illegals."

She made the spitting mouth again. *"El jefes,"* she said.

"Was Frank Hanauer in on it too?"

"I don't know."

"Rafael didn't say?"

Headshake.

"Why was Hanauer killed? Some kind of doublecross? Or was it because he *wasn't* involved and made a stink when he found out?"

Headshake.

"Who ran him down? Rafael?"

"No!"

"Who then?"

"I don't know."

"Did Rafael kill Thomas Lujack?"

"No! He wouldn't do nothing like that."

The hell he wouldn't, I thought. "He's been living here with you the past week, hasn't he? Since Monday."

Shrug.

"He came here late that night, after he'd been to see Coleman."

Another shrug.

"Were you expecting him?"

"No. I was sleeping. He was all shook up."

"Why?"

"Something *el jefe* wanted him to do."

"But he didn't tell you what it was."

"No."

"What did he say?"

"He said we'd go away together. He said he'd had enough of his fat cow of a wife."

"And you agreed to go along."

"I love him," she said, and shrugged again.

"Where were you going? Mexico?"

"Mexico City. He knows people there."

"Sure he does. How soon did you plan to leave?"

"When his business was finished."

"The business he was doing for Coleman."

"*El jefe* was paying him a lot of money."

"How much?"

"I don't know. Rafael, he said we would live good in Mexico City. He said I would have servants. . . ."

"Why did he want to go back to Mexico? Why couldn't the two of you just stay here?"

"They'd be after him pretty soon, he said. Here they'd find him; in Mexico, no."

"The INS?"

"Pigs," she said.

"So he was afraid of being arrested. That's the real reason he moved in with you, you know. To hide out until he was ready to leave for Mexico."

"What if it is? What does it matter?"

"Was Coleman afraid of being arrested too? Was *he* planning to leave the country?"

"He's an Anglo," Teresa said bitterly. "*El jefes* don't have to run away. They don't get punished."

"Sometimes they don't; this isn't one of them. Did Rafael talk to Coleman yesterday?"

Nod. "*El jefe* called him."

"Here? He knew Rafael was staying here with you?"

"He knew. Rafael told him."

"What time did he call?"

"Seven o'clock. Just after Rafael came back."

"Back from where?"

"Seeing people, making arrangements."

"For your trip to Mexico City?"

Nod.

"Did you tell him I'd been here?"

"I told him."

"And what I said about him and the coyotes?"

"Everything you said."

"Did it upset him? Make him angry, more afraid?"

"What you think? He called you names. *Hijo de puta. Maricon.* You know what those names mean?"

"Yeah," I said, "I know what they mean. Is that all he said?"

"You wouldn't bother us again—no Anglo would."

"Were you in the room when he talked to Coleman?"

"No. He made me go in the kitchen."

"So you don't know what they talked about."

"I didn't want to know."

"How soon afterward did Rafael leave again?"

"A few minutes." She had the hem of her housecoat bunched in one hand; she twisted it even more tightly now, so that I heard the thin tearing of threads of material. "All night I waited," she said to her lap. "No more waiting now. Just . . . *finito.* I won't see him again, never. All *finito.*"

"For him," I said, "and living good in Mexico City. But not for *you,* Teresa."

"For me," she said.

"No. You'll come out of this all right. You're not mixed up in anything illegal. The police won't hassle you, and neither will the INS as long as you've got a green card."

"You think I care? I don't have Rafael, I don't have a job pretty soon, I don't have money to go anywhere. I don't have nothing *except* a green card."

"What about this house?"

"I pay rent," she said. "Poor spick like me can't afford to buy a house in *Los Estados Unidos.*"

There was nothing more I could say to her, nothing I could do for her. I went to the door, opened it. "If Coleman tries to get in touch with you, don't talk to him. Don't tell him I was here. I don't want him to know I'm hunting him."

"What you going to do when you find him?"

"Turn him over to the authorities."

She smiled, and it was a terrible thing to see. "Then I

hope *el jefe* comes here first," she said. "If he does I'll cut his fucking heart out, feed it to the neighbor's dogs."

She meant it. Hell hath no fury like a woman left alone with the bloody remains of a dead love.

Chapter **17**

THE SERRAMONTE SHOPPING CENTER is only a couple of miles from Atlanta Street, off Highway 280 that runs down the backbone of the Peninsula. I drove over there and hunted up a coffee shop, another in an endless succession of lookalike plastic-food emporiums in which I consumed all sorts of bad grub and frittered away time. Sometimes I felt as if my whole life was an intricate series of wanderings on a giant game board, moving here and there toward some nebulous prize, and in the process perpetually finding myself on the square that said *Coffee Shop, Open 24 Hours, Families Welcome*.

I had no appetite after the session with Teresa Melendez, but the rumblings in my stomach and the dull ache behind my eyes said I had better eat something. If you don't keep putting fuel into a battered fifty-eight-year-old corpus, the thing will quit running and maybe break down for good. That was especially true after the abuse I had subjected the corpus to last night. So I ordered a bowl of beef stew and an English muffin —two items that even the worst cooks can't screw up too badly—and brooded my way through them.

I was beginning to see how things in the Lujack case fit

together, and most of what I saw I didn't like worth a damn. One element was particularly galling.

Glickman and Eberhardt and I had been as wrong as you can be about Thomas Lujack: He had in fact run down and killed Frank Hanauer.

It was the only explanation that accounted for everything that had happened since. His defense, the whole vague conspiracy theory, had been a smokescreen designed to obscure his guilt; and Eberhardt and I had not been hired to find a third witness, nor to prove him innocent, but on the thin hope that we'd come up with something in Pendarves's background that Glickman could use in court to discredit his testimony. We'd been pawns, Eb and me. Or maybe fools was a better word—a pair of fools prancing and dancing for the benefit of a desperate knave.

I figured it this way:

Five or six years ago, the Lujack brothers had conspired with Rafael Vega to finance a large-scale coyote operation in Southern California. At Vega's instigation, probably; he had the contacts on both sides of the border. For some reason, most likely plain greed, Hanauer had been left out of the deal. It had taken him five years to get a whiff of what his partners were into, and when he did, early in December, he'd taken it badly. On the evening of the fifth, after everyone else at Containers, Inc., was gone, Hanauer had confronted Thomas; maybe threatened him with exposure, maybe demanded a retroactive cut of the profits. In any case, it had been a heated exchange, and Hanauer had ended it by walking out. But Thomas had a violent temper, the kind that sometimes overwhelms reason; he'd rushed outside in Hanauer's wake and turned his car into a lethal weapon. By the time he'd come to his senses, it was too late to do anything but frantically try to cover up. He abandoned his Caddy, came back to the factory on foot through the Bayshore Yards, and arrived on the scene with his hastily improvised story. When one of the witnesses, Dinsmore, opened up the possibility of a missing third witness, Thomas seized on that and made it a major design in his fabric of lies and obfuscations.

The rest of it wasn't as clear-cut—I didn't have enough details yet—but I could see enough of it to make informed guesses about the gaps. The impulsive and very public killing of Hanauer was one major catalyst. There had to be another too, and judging from what Teresa Melendez had told me, it was that the coyote operation had recently started to break down. Any number of things could be responsible for that: greed, internal screwups, an informant, an INS or Mexican government spy. Whatever the reason, the feds were getting close to busting it wide open. And the Lujacks and Vega knew it.

Taken together, those two factors had created a pressure-cooker situation. Coleman, the nervous Nellie, would seem the most likely to break down first under the strain; in fact he was the coolest and deadliest of the lot. *El jefe.* Instead it was Thomas, a bundle of nerves under his casual facade, who had cracked first. And what cracked him was the specter of a homicide charge upgraded to first-degree when his involvement with the coyotes was made public, and a certain conviction on the basis of Pendarves's unimpeachable eyewitness testimony.

Pendarves's brush with death on Monday night, like the hit-and-run killing of Hanauer, was just what it appeared to be—a harebrained attempt by Thomas to save his own ass. Had he been stupid enough to use his wife's BMW? It wouldn't surprise me. In any case, the attempt had failed. But the dilemma Thomas faced was the same as if he'd succeeded: He needed an alibi. Same solution too: his brother. It was unlikely he'd planned it beforehand; and even if he had, he wouldn't have told Coleman, the level-headed one, because Coleman wouldn't have stood still for it. Thomas had gotten in touch with his brother immediately afterward and fessed up, and Coleman had agreed to supply the alibi.

Only he didn't do it out of brotherly love; he'd done it to buy some time. He sent Thomas home to his wife, then called

Vega and arranged for the two of them to meet that same night. It was clear to Coleman by then that Thomas was cracking, becoming a serious threat to *his* safety. So Thomas had to die—quickly, before he could do any more damage, and in such a way that no suspicion would fall on either Coleman or Vega. Coleman had convinced Vega to do the job by offering him enough money to finance his flight to Mexico City.

What kind of man plots the murder of his own brother? A cold-blooded, ruthless one, motivated by greed and self-preservation and maybe some deep-seated hatred for his weaker, handsomer sibling. A sociopath. I could see Coleman in that role with no difficulty at all.

Questions: Why had they decided to frame Pendarves? Why not just kill Thomas and make his death look like an accident or suicide? Pendarves was a threat only to Thomas . . . or was he a threat to Coleman and Vega as well? I remembered Pendarves's mention of Antonio Rivas on Monday night, and Eberhardt's guess that Rivas not only knew about the Lujacks' hiring of illegals but also about the coyote connection. Suppose Rivas had let something slip to Pendarves about the coyotes. And suppose Pendarves had gone on Tuesday to confront either Thomas or Coleman, threatened to tell the INS what he knew if Thomas ever tried to harm him again . . . maybe even attempted to blackmail one or the other of them. Pendarves wasn't all that bright; it was the sort of angry, fear-motivated thing he might do. If he had, it provided Coleman with plenty of motive for wanting to get rid of him along with Thomas.

Scenario: Coleman and Vega used some kind of ruse to lure Pendarves away from his house Tuesday night, and another ruse to lure Thomas out there. Vega then cracked Thomas on the head, drove the BMW into the empty garage, left the engine running and Thomas stretched out on the floor, and closed the garage door behind him. Exit Thomas, while Vega left the scene in his own car or via public transportation.

What was still murky was what they'd done about

Pendarves. Had they plotted to kill him too? If I was right about Pendarves's actions, then it was a good bet they had. It eliminated two threats and screwed the frame down tight.

They might have gotten away with it if I hadn't shown up at Pendarves's property that night. My investigation since had kept the pressure on; and I'd made it clear enough that I was getting close to the truth. So I had to die too. That was what the telephone conversation between Coleman and Vega last night had been about.

The big question now was where Coleman was. Had he, like Vega, decided some time ago to pack up and run? Probably, if he believed the feds were close to nailing him. It was in character for him to have salted away a large sum of cash as a safety valve; and the past week or so he could have been quietly liquidating assets. What argued against him having already fled was the fact that he'd sent Vega after me. Why bother to have me killed if he was planning to disappear as soon as last night? No, there was only one good reason he'd want me out of the way, the same reason he'd ordered the murder of his brother: to gain enough time to finish stockpiling cash and arranging to cover his tracks when he finally did run.

Then why had he gone off with his wife last night? To give himself an alibi for the time of my death, just in case something went wrong? No, that didn't add up; he could have just stayed home, surrounded himself with people. To stash his wife somewhere for a few days, so he'd be free to complete his preparations and then slip away quietly when he was ready? That made sense if he didn't intend to take her with him, if she hadn't been privy to any of his schemes, and particularly if she had money or jewelry that Coleman could appropriate. But where would he stash her? Someplace the two of them regularly frequented, maybe; some little getaway spot. . . .

A sense of urgency prodded me out of the coffee shop and into my car. I couldn't afford to just hang loose and wait for Coleman to come back home. Once he found out Rafael Vega was in the hospital and I was still alive, he'd run and run fast;

he wouldn't have much choice. I had to find him before that happened. If it hadn't already happened.

I drove over to 280 and headed south, back to San Carlos and Sweet William Lane.

THERE WAS a white Olds Cutlass parked in Eileen Lujack's driveway. But nobody came to open the door when I rang the bell. An offshoot of the front walk led around the side of the house; I followed it through a rose garden, past another of those damn gnomes peering slyly from behind a bush. On the other side of the garden, along the rear, was a stone-floored patio; a swimming pool, covered now for the winter, occupied the far end and some molded-plastic outdoor furniture was arranged on the near side. Two women sat at one of the tables, drinking out of mugs and taking in the still-warmish afternoon sun. The one facing my way was Eileen Lujack.

When she spotted me she said something to the other woman, who turned in her chair; they both watched as I crossed the patio. Mrs. Lujack said, "Oh, it's you," before I reached them. She didn't look or sound pleased to see me.

Her companion—older, dark-haired, a little on the horsey side in both dress and appearance—said to Eileen, "Who, sweetie?"

"Oh, that detective I told you about."

"Well, didn't you tell him you didn't want him bothering you anymore?"

"I told him. I left a message on his machine."

"Then why is he here?"

I don't much care for people talking about me in my presence as if I'm not really there. I said, "I want to ask you a couple more questions, Mrs. Lujack. Then I'll go away and you won't see me again. But this doesn't concern your friend, so either she can go in the house or we can. Whichever you prefer."

The horsey woman didn't like being ignored any more

than I did. She said to Eileen, "He's got a nerve. You don't have to do anything you don't want to, sweetie."

"No, it's all right, Monica. I'll talk to him."

"If you say so. But I'm staying right here while you do."

Mrs. Lujack shrugged and looked up at me. "It's all right to talk in front of Monica."

"As long as the answers to my questions come from you. Do you know where I can find your brother-in-law?"

"Well, at home, I suppose. He lives in Burlingame. . . ."

"He's not there," I said. "He and his wife went somewhere last night, with luggage. I thought you might know where."

"No, I don't."

"When did you last talk to Coleman?"

"Day before yesterday. After you were here."

"Did he say anything about taking a trip?"

"No. Nothing."

"Where does he go when he wants to get away for the weekend? Any special place?"

She thought about that, with her face scrunched up like a hound's; thinking would always be a chore for her. Pretty soon she said, "Well, he likes to go duck hunting. Carla does too."

The horsey woman said, "Ugh. I hate blood sports."

"So do I," Eileen said.

"So do I," I said. "Especially when the prey is human." I was remembering the prints on Coleman's office wall, the hand-carved decoy on his desk—things I should have remembered earlier, without help. "Where do they go to hunt ducks?"

"Up to their cabin, I guess."

"They own a hunting cabin? Where?"

"Oh . . . that marsh on the way to Sacramento, the big one."

"Suisun Marsh?"

"That's it. Tom . . . sometimes Tom went up there with them."

"Poor baby," the horsey woman said, and reached out to pat Eileen's hand. "Don't you think that's enough questions, sweetie?"

"I don't know," Eileen said. And to me, "Is that all?"

"Just one more. Do you know where their cabin is on the marsh? The address, if it has one?"

"No. I was only there once, a long time ago. . . ."

"Can you give me a general idea of the location?"

The horsey woman swiveled her head, fixed cold green-olive eyes on me, and for the first time favored me with a direct statement. "Can't you see you're upsetting her? She's just lost her husband, she's suffered a terrible personal trag-edy. . . . Don't men like you have any compassion?"

"Don't women like you ever mind your own business?"

Her mouth hinged open. "Why, you . . . you shit," she said.

I didn't respond to that. Instead I said to Eileen, "Thanks for talking to me, Mrs. Lujack. I really won't bother you again." Without looking at the mare, I left them and went back around to the front yard. Thinking sardonically of the bumper sticker you see everywhere these days, the one that says: SHIT HAPPENS.

Yeah. Pretty soon now, in one place or another, this Shit was going to happen to Coleman Lujack.

ON THE WAY BACK to the city I considered calling Eberhardt, maybe saving myself some time that way, but I didn't do it. His memory for details is poor, and I had no desire to listen to another sermon. I drove straight downtown to O'Farrell, went up to the office, and looked through the file Eb had built as part of his background check on Coleman.

And there it was on the TRW credit report, under *Property Owned:* 15678 Grizzly Island Road, Suisun City.

Chapter 18

THE SUISUN MARSH is the largest single estuarine marsh in the country—thousands of acres of tule grass, freshwater sloughs and backwaters, and unpaved roads spread out along the northeastern rim of Suisun Bay. The California Department of Fish and Game controls most of it, maintaining large sections as a wildlife refuge; those sections are off-limits to hunters and fishermen. But along the network of sloughs there are numerous privately owned parcels of land, whose owners can obtain seasonal permits to hunt certain species of ducks and birds that flock there during the winter months. For men like Coleman Lujack, to whom all life came cheap, it would be a shooter's paradise.

Grizzly Island Road is the main access into the marsh, a narrow, two-lane paved road that winds in off Highway 12. Fairfield and Suisun City, the two towns that flank the east side of the highway, used to be small, quiet places populated mainly by people connected in one way or another with Travis Air Force Base nearby. In recent years both had grown rapidly, thanks to the burgeoning cost of real estate in the Bay Area; now families had to come this far out—some forty miles east of San Francisco—to find affordable housing. Tracts and shopping centers had blossomed along Highway 12, in places butting right up against the protected marshland.

It was late afternoon when I turned onto Grizzly Island Road. At this time of year, even on a Saturday, it was mostly deserted; I saw only two other cars, both parked, as I drove through miles of low green hills and empty fields broken now and then by huddles of ranch buildings. Finally the road curved around and drew in close to the main part of the marsh—a broad, flat, lonely expanse of green and brown, of gray glistening water. The only signs of life were hundreds of birds making shifting patterns of color against a thickening overcast sky.

Montezuma Slough, the biggest of the estuaries, appeared ahead. I hadn't been out here in years and it seemed wider than I remembered, as wide as a football field where the road climbed up over a narrow humpbacked bridge. Along the far bank, scattered cabins—green and brown and gray like their surroundings—were visible among stretches of tule grass and stunted swamp growth; each had its own spindly pier and boat shed.

When I came down on that side of the bridge, the road hooked sharply left to parallel the slough. The numbers on the mailboxes along here told me I was getting close to 15678 —less than a quarter of a mile, it turned out. I couldn't see much of the Lujack cabin from the road, because of a tangle of bushes and gnarly trees. I parked just beyond the driveway, retransferred the .38 from the glove box to my jacket pocket, and then walked back and in along deep ruts.

The drive widened out in front of the cabin, where the tangle of vegetation ended. One vehicle was parked there, but it wasn't Coleman's Imperial. It was a Dodge Ram van.

The cabin was a long low affair, with brown shingled walls and a saggy green composition roof. Very rustic. Not very primitive, though: Telephone lines ran overhead and there was a satellite TV dish mounted to one side. Coleman

evidently liked his creature comforts after a hard day of killing things.

I could hear voices as I approached—at least three people
having a conversation in there. Was Coleman one of them,
even though his car wasn't here? If so, I wasn't sure how I'd
handle him with more than just his wife on the premises. Play
it by ear. I touched the revolver in my pocket. And get tough
if I had to.

When I rapped on the screen door, the conversation died
inside. I knocked again, and there was the thump of heavy
steps, and the inside door opened and I was looking through
the screen at a beefy middle-aged guy with a shock of iron-
gray hair. I had never seen him before. He had no idea who I
was either; he looked me over with a mixture of puzzlement
and mild annoyance before he said, "Yes? What can we do for
you?"

"I'm looking for Coleman Lujack."

"Oh? Mind if I ask why?"

"It's a business matter. Is he here?"

"Well, he was."

"When did he leave?"

Behind the beefy guy a woman's voice said, "Who is it,
Jay?"

"Somebody looking for Coleman."

The woman appeared at his side. Late thirties, muscular
and heavy-breasted in a man's plaid shirt; short brown hair,
plain features. "I'm Carla Lujack, Coleman's wife," she said.
She gave me a quick appraisal through the screen. "I don't
believe I know you."

"We've never met."

"Are you a friend of Coleman's?"

"Business acquaintance."

I hadn't offered a name and she didn't ask for one. There
was no wariness in her voice or manner; interest, yes, but of
the polite wifely sort. I figured it right, I thought. As with
Eileen Lujack, she'd been kept in the dark all along about the

coyotes. Nor did she figure in Coleman's future plans; he intended to do his running alone.

"When did your husband leave, Mrs. Lujack?" I asked.

"What time was it, Jay? Around eleven?"

"Closer to noon," Jay said.

"Well, between eleven and twelve, then. Earlier than he'd expected to go back to the city today."

"It wasn't you he called, was it?" Jay asked me.

"No. Why?"

"Would've been a funny coincidence if he rushed off to see you. I mean, the two of you getting your signals crossed and you coming all the way out here and him on his way to meet you."

"Very funny."

"Sure was in a hurry when he left," Jay said. "Didn't even say good-bye."

"He has a lot on his mind," Carla Lujack said.

"Don't I know it? Poor Tom." Jay shook his head. "I guess it wasn't easy for him to sell this place either. Even if it does remind him too much of Tom."

"He sold this property?" I asked. "When?"

"Just yesterday. The wife and I bought it—that's why we're all here this weekend."

"You pay cash for it, by any chance?"

"As much cash down as I could raise. How'd you know that?"

"Just a guess."

"You wouldn't be in on that stock deal with him?"

"Stock deal?"

"That's why he wanted cash. I wouldn't take a flier like that myself, but I guess Coleman knows what he's doing."

"He's always been very careful with our money," his wife said. "I'm sure he'll be careful this time too."

Yeah, I thought. "Did he say where he was going today?"

"No, he didn't."

"What time did he expect to be back?"

"Well, he probably won't be back at all. He thought he might have to work through the weekend."

"We'll take Carla home," Jay said magnanimously. "No problem."

"Is there any message I can give him when he calls?"

"No," I said, "no message. I'll get in touch with him later."

I smiled and did an abrupt about-face to avoid any more questions. I had to force myself to walk at a normal pace out to the road; there was a sharp driving urgency in me now. That call Coleman had made . . . to Teresa Melendez, no doubt, because he hadn't heard from Vega and was getting anxious. In spite of my warning, she must have told him what had happened to Vega. That was the impetus for Coleman leaving early and in such a hurry. He knew I'd be after him, and that if the authorities weren't also on his trail, they would be soon.

He was already on the run, or damned close to it.

And he had a three-hour head start.

IT TOOK ME better than two hours to get from the Suisun Marsh to Burlingame, because of moderately heavy traffic and earthquake-related detours. Night had closed down when I finally pulled up in front of Coleman's house.

It was as dark as the sky, the driveway empty.

I got out anyway, first unclipping the flashlight from under the dash, and went up through the rock garden. Alongside the front door, the burglar-alarm light burned like a bright red hole in the darkness. I walked around to the garage, put the flashlight up against the window I'd looked through earlier, and briefly flicked it on.

Still only one car parked inside, but now it was Coleman's Imperial. The sleek white foreign job was gone.

He'd been here, all right, and switched cars when he left —another effort to buy himself more time. It was as much confirmation as I needed that he was on the run.

In my car again I sat with my hands tight around the

steering wheel. I was tired from all the driving, drawn tight inside. And frustrated and worried. Maybe I should go to the police, lay everything out as I saw it, let them and the feds take up the chase. The only problem with that was, I didn't have any proof. The INS might have gathered some on the Lujacks' coyote activities, but not enough to make formal charges stick or they'd have pounced already. And until Vega could be made to talk, there was no evidence, hard or soft, to prove that Coleman had conspired to murder his brother, me, and probably Nick Pendarves. Without proof, the wheels of justice grind slow. Coleman could be in South America or the Antarctic by the time the authorities got around to putting out a dragnet for him.

All right—he was still my baby until I'd exhausted all the possibilities. There was at least one other place he might have gone before leaving the Bay Area entirely; check that first, and then start backtracking.

I drove over to 101, went north again. Heading for Containers, Inc.

HE WAS THERE.

By God, he was there.

He'd parked his wife's car at the rear of the lot, in heavy shadow beyond the last of the sodium-vapor arcs. I couldn't see it clearly from the deserted street, but it was the only car on the lot and therefore a dead giveaway. So were the lights burning in the office wing. Who else was likely to be here at this hour on a Saturday evening?

I drove on past, made a U-turn, parked alongside a weedy vacant lot that blended into the abandoned railroad yards, and fast-walked into the factory lot. There was no fog here tonight, just a high overcast, but the wind was sharp and gusty across the flatlands from the bay. It created odd, disturbed sounds—flutterings, purlings, murmurs, low moaning cries. I could have made all sorts of noise and Coleman wouldn't have heard me coming.

The car back in the shadows was the white foreign job, all

right. I got close enough to make sure, avoiding the puddles of greenish light from the arcs, then changed direction and went to the office entrance. The door was unlocked. Careless, Coleman, I thought; you're in a big hurry, huh? I took Vega's .38 out of my jacket pocket. The odd thing was, now that the hunt was almost over, the tension had gone right out of me and I was calm to the point of detachment. The hatred was still there, but it was like a core of heat inside a casing of dry ice.

I rotated the knob with my left hand, eased the door open and myself inside. The waiting area and outer office were dark. But he'd left the door that led to the private offices partially ajar, and light showed back that way. I stood still for a few seconds, listening. Silence at first; then, above the wind, I heard some sort of thunking noise. I moved again, heel and toe, through the open doorway and along the wall. Now I could hear other sounds: papers being hurriedly shifted around.

The door to his office was wide open. I stepped into the outspill of light with the .38 at arm's length, saw where he was and what he was doing, and said, "Hello, Coleman."

He nearly jumped out of his skin. He was down on one knee in front of his safe, transferring stacks of currency from there into a leather briefcase. The sound of my voice brought him up so fast, in a twisting about-face, that he cracked his elbow on the upper edge of the safe, staggered, had to brace himself against his desk to keep from falling down. As soon as he focused on me and the .38, his eyes bulged as wide and terrified as Vega's had last night. He stood clutching his elbow and shaking—literally shaking, head to foot.

"End of the line, Coleman," I said.

He said, "No," squeakily, as if trying to deny it.

"Too bad for you you decided to keep some of your run-out money here. But then, I'd have just caught up with you somewhere else."

"What . . . what are you going to do?"

"Well, let's see. I could turn you over to the cops. Or I

could do to you what you tried to have Vega do to me last night—I could blow your damn head off."

"You wouldn't . . . Jesus you wouldn't . . ."

I was tempted to keep on tormenting him, the way a cat will torment a cornered rat, but I didn't have the stomach for it. One little twist of the knife was as much cruelty as I could muster, even for a piss-poor human being like Coleman Lujack.

I said, "Finish what you were doing. Hurry it up."

Two simple commands, but I might have spoken them in Arabic; he didn't comprehend because he was thinking about dying. He stayed where he was, wagging his head, trembling as if with a fever. His face was paper-white. Sweat stained it, ran like melting parentheses around the corners of his mouth. Thief, killer, sociopath—and underneath it all, coward.

"Come on, Coleman." I waggled the gun. "Finish loading the briefcase."

"Briefcase," he said.

"Right. Put all the money into it. *Now.*"

He moved all at once, jerkily; went to one knee and clawed up handfuls of currency and shoved them haphazardly into the open case. At first his hands were so palsied he dropped or spilled as much as he stuffed inside. Then he seemed to gather himself, regain part of his control. When he finished emptying the safe and looked around at me again, I saw a small desperate cunning mixed in with his fear.

"There's more than a hundred thousand dollars here," he said. "But it's not all I have. There's another hundred thousand . . . some bearer bonds and jewelry. You can have it, all of it . . . I'll take you to it . . . just let me go."

"Still trying to buy time. You're a pistol, you are."

"No, I mean it, I swear . . ."

"I'm not selling, Coleman."

"Take what's here, then. I don't care about the money. I don't want to die, I don't want to go to prison. . . ."

"You should have thought of that before you murdered your brother."

"No! It wasn't me, it was Vega . . . all Vega's idea."

"Sure it was."

"It *was.* I swear to God—"

"Shut up, damn you." I was sick of him—of what he was, of the sight and sound of him. I wanted Coleman Lujack out of my life as fast as possible. Take him out to my car and handcuff him—I keep a pair of handcuffs in the trunk, along with other emergency equipment—and then drive him to the Hall of Justice. Even if he refused to talk, the money in his briefcase and what I had to say would be enough for the police to hold him until the INS could be brought in and Vega cracked open. "Get on your feet."

He did that, in the same jerky movements. "Now close the briefcase and pick it up."

He did that too—and then held the case out toward me as if it were a pagan offering. His half-popped eyes begged me not to sacrifice him.

"Uh-uh," I said. "You carry it."

"You . . . you won't kill me?"

"That depends on whether or not you do what I tell you."

"I'll do anything you say. Just don't kill me, please. . . ."

"Walk out of here, not too fast, not too slow. And keep your mouth shut from now on. I don't want to hear another word out of you."

I backed off to one side as I spoke. Immediately he came away from the safe and around the desk in jelly-legged strides; he was no longer looking at me. He went through the door, turned along the hall with his shoulders hunched, as if he expected a bullet in the back at any second. I followed by several paces, warily. I doubted he had the guts to try jumping me and the .38, but you never know. Even a coward will fight if he's desperate enough.

Through the darkened waiting area, outside into the cold rackety wind. Coleman kept walking; I paused to reach back and pull the door shut. Then I saw him break stride, half-turn toward the rear of the office wing. A second or two later I saw what he saw: the shadow breaking away from other shadows along the wall.

Coleman screamed, "No!"

Then the shooting started.

Chapter 19

I DON'T KNOW how many shots there were—at least three, maybe as many as five. I went down flat on the ground after the first one, in tight against the wall, whacking my chin on the asphalt. For a second or two my vision was cockeyed. When it cleared I was seeing Coleman buckled forward at the waist, falling . . . and out ahead of me, the flash of the shooter's weapon as he fired once in my direction. Instinctively I pulled my head down and in, but it was a wild shot, the bullet smacking wood somewhere high above me an instant before I heard the report.

When I looked up again the shadow was running away, back along the wall in swift pounding steps. I leaned up on my elbows and squeezed the trigger on Vega's .38—and the hammer fell on the first of the two chambers I'd emptied earlier. Cursing, I pulled on the second empty chamber, but by the time I had a cartridge in firing position it was too late. He was gone around the far corner of the office wing.

I pushed up against the wall. Ran wobbling to the corner and poked my head around it. No arc lights back there, just three widely spaced night spots in metal cages mounted on the factory wall; the reach of them wasn't far. He was already out beyond both the light-spill and the Containers, Inc., property, a moving shadow among stationary ones, heading deeper into the war-zone desolation of the old SP yards.

Let him go, you're not up to another chase. . . .

But I was on my way by then, driven by anger that wasn't as black or volatile as the rage I'd felt toward Vega, but was just as urgent. I plunged across the backstrip of asphalt, running in a low crouch, avoiding the direct glare of the night spots. I could hear myself breathing as I ran, a kind of wheezy panting that was louder in my own ears than the blustery natterings of the wind.

He was well out into the yards now, where the heavy overcast night pressed down and the shapes were inky and formless. I could barely make him out; he was just a moving blob. Beyond the asphalt, the ground was flat and overgrown with weeds and high grass; in low places, puddles left by the recent rains gleamed faintly. I blundered through the grass, sidestepped the puddles as best I could. But I couldn't generate any speed because of the uncertain footing. He had thirty or forty yards on me already, seemed to be gaining.

He knows this area, I thought, he's been out here before.

Off to the left, the burned-out, quake-damaged hulks of the old roundhouse and warehouses reared up ghostlike against the dark sky. It appeared he was heading that way . . . but then I saw him veer off in the opposite direction, around what materialized out of the gloom as a series of low, irregular mounds. I stumbled over something hidden in the grass, lurched, nearly fell; when I regained my balance I could no longer locate him. He'd vanished somewhere behind or near the largest of the masses ahead.

I slowed to a crouching walk, trying to get my breath. *Stupid bastard, drop dead of a heart attack, serve you right.* It was eerily quiet out here, except for the wind. Like wandering across an alien landscape. And yet surrounding this dead acreage there was light and movement and teeming life—cars rushing along the 101 freeway, on Bayshore Boulevard;

chains of lights in hillside houses and the buildings along Industrial and Bayshore and Sunnydale. The city and its neighboring communities all around, thousands of people . . . but this was a piece of nowhere, a corner of the twilight zone, and I was alone in it with somebody who had just committed a cold-blooded act of violence.

Nearing one of the mounds now, close enough to make out broken chunks of concrete and other rubble. I went around past it, warily; didn't see or hear him and kept on going toward the larger masses farther out. They coalesced into piles of rotting wooden ties, left here when most of the rails were taken up and removed years ago. I cut between two of the piles, looking left and right—

Something made an audible slithering through the moist grass on my left. I dropped to one knee, stiff-armed the .38 in that direction. But it wasn't the shooter. Small animal, or maybe a rat. These ruins were probably crawling with rats.

I straightened again, eased forward. In front of me now was flat barren ground, no obstructions or cover for sixty or seventy yards to where a short string of forgotten cars—flats, boxcars, oil tankers—stood on a rusty siding, faintly backlit by streaking headlights on the freeway a quarter of a mile beyond. He wasn't out that way—or if he was, I couldn't pick him out. He'd had enough time to get all the way to the cars, hide somewhere among them.

I made myself stand still, briefly, to listen for sounds of him moving. Useless; all I could hear was the wind and the stuttering beat of my heart. I went on, parallel to the string of dead cars, then out toward them. Power lines on spindly poles angled through the yards here, feeding the buildings on Industrial Way; I passed under them, still heading toward the cars.

Motion off to my right, toward the far end of the factory property: shadow gliding among shadows. I cut over that way, running now; stubbed my foot against a chunk of rock and went down on all fours, almost losing the gun. The shadows were still. I got up and bulled ahead, came off flat ground into a bumpy section clotted with grass and weeds and patches of sharp-smelling anise.

Ahead was a low cluster of trees. And beyond them was Industrial Way, the part of it where I had parked my car. I gave the trees a wide berth, plowing through tangles of vegetation, but they weren't where he was. I knew where he was as soon as I saw the shape of another car drawn up in front of mine, one that hadn't been there before.

Suckered me, led me out into the yards and then doubled back here to pick up his wheels. . . .

I yelled when his car jumped ahead—a roar of frustration that was lost in the howl of tires biting into pavement. He didn't switch his lights on until he was out of range of my vision, if he put them on even then. I hadn't been able to tell what kind of vehicle it was, just that it was shorter and more low-slung than mine. Shadow man in a shadow car.

Who?

Why had he shot Coleman?

I slogged through a puddle of water and the last of the high grass, onto the street next to my car. He was long gone by then. I had a crazy impulse to hammer on the hood with the butt of the .38. Controlled it and walked stiffly around to the driver's door, put myself inside.

For a time I sat there, fighting off delayed-reaction shakes, putting a tight wrap on my emotions. Tonight was not the first time I had been shot at, but like an earthquake, it is nothing you ever get used to. Each time is like the first; each time is bad, because once you begin thinking clearly again, you realize how close you came to dying and how fragile your life, all life, really is.

When I felt steady enough I started the car and got it under way. Drove slowly along the empty street . . . where the hell were the goddamn security patrolmen all this time? . . . and turned into the factory lot. Near the office wing, my headlights picked out the huddled motionless body on the asphalt. I stopped a few feet away with the lights bright on him.

Coleman lay where he'd fallen, ten feet or so from the entrance to the wing. I squatted, turned him a little. Shot at least twice, once in the belly and once in the middle of the chest. His eyes were open, staring glassily. I put my finger on the artery in his neck, to make sure he had no life left in him. There wasn't a pulse, hadn't been a pulse, I thought, since right after the first bullet hit him.

The briefcase was there, too, near one of his legs; I took hold of it before I straightened. The shooter may not have known what it contained, but even if he had, he might not have come back to pick it up. He'd been after Coleman, focused only on Coleman. His one shot at me had come after he was sure he'd bagged his quarry, and it had been designed to keep me down while he made his escape. If he'd cared about taking me out, he'd have fired at me again here or out in the yards. Revenge, then, or some other personal motive. I hadn't been the only one hunting Coleman Lujack today. And chance had brought the three of us together here, on a convergent path within minutes of one another.

Somebody mixed up in the coyote operation, somebody I didn't know?

Paco Vega?

Nick Pendarves . . . if Pendarves wasn't dead after all?

Teresa Melendez? Eileen Lujack? It *could* have been a woman, even though I'd kept thinking of the shooter as a man. A woman runs differently, uses a more fluid kind of stride, but it had been too dark, the period of time too confused, for me to be certain of anything about the person. . . .

You're wasting time, I told myself. Besides, it wasn't up to me to pursue the shooter's identity. I'd avoided dealing with the authorities twice this week; I couldn't do it again even if I wanted to. And I didn't want to. I was in deep enough as it was.

I took the briefcase to my car, used the mobile phone to make the call.

IT WAS almost midnight before they finally let me go home.

Long, wearying sessions at Containers, Inc., and then at the Hall of Justice. Conversations with patrolmen, inspectors, a homicide lieutenant named Cousins. (Nobody from the INS, though, despite the fact that they had a strong vested interest. On weekends, especially weekend nights, government-agency bureaucrats are as hard to find as a Democrat in the White House.) I told them everything, with one exception. I had to own up about Vega, his attempt on my life and what had happened on Ocean Beach to cause his injuries; if I'd held that back, my story would not have hung together and they might have decided to lock me up. They might also have decided to lock me up if I'd admitted to shirking my duty twice in the span of a few days, which was why I kept quiet about being the first on the scene of Thomas Lujack's murder. There was no reason they had to know about that anyway.

Early on I'd tried to call Eberhardt, get him down to the Hall to back me up, but he hadn't been home. He hadn't been at Bobbie Jean's, either. Out somewhere together, the two of them. But as it turned out, I hadn't needed his help to keep things from going badly for me. All I got from the cops was a lecture and a warning to play by the rules if I wanted to keep my license—what amounted to wrist-slapping. I'd lost my license once, a few years ago, but that had been under a different city administration and a different chief of police; the current bunch were more tolerant of private detectives. Also weighing in my favor was the currency in Coleman's brief-case, a total of one hundred sixteen thousand dollars, and what they found when they searched his wife's car: three packed suitcases, another ninety-seven thousand in cash, thirty thousand in bearer bonds, a jewelry case full of valuable pieces, and the name and address of a small flying service down near Needles—Coleman's way out of the country, evidently.

I got a beer from the refrigerator and sat with it in the

front room. I was so tired I felt numb, but I was not ready yet to ride my nightmares.

Who? I kept thinking.

Why?

I finished the beer and went in to use the toilet. When I came back through the bedroom I realized that the message light on the answering machine was lit. I ran the tape back—three messages—and pushed the PLAY button.

The first one was from Kerry. She sounded mildly frazzled but not unhappy. "It's me," she said, "and it's midmorning. I've got some news I want to share in person. Call me. I'll be home all day."

Cybil, I thought. And the news was good, judging from her tone and phrasing.

The second message was from Eberhardt. A predictably angry Eberhardt. "So why the hell didn't you show up? It's seven o'clock and I waited the whole frigging day. Sometimes you piss me off royally, you know that?"

I smiled a little. Yeah, Eb, I thought. Sometimes I piss myself off royally too.

Number three was Kerry again. "All right, who is she? I'll scratch her eyes out." Making a joke—another good sign. "Call me, okay? As soon as you can. I really need to see you. And not for the reason you think, you horny old goat."

I laughed at that. Just hearing her voice could make me feel better, a bad time easier to deal with.

I reset the machine, switched it off. Another beer? Something to eat? TV for a while, just for the noise? None of the above. A shower, I decided. Wash away the lingering smells of Coleman Lujack and Containers, Inc. and sudden death.

The shower made me feel even more tired and dull-witted. Enough so that I could sleep right away, maybe. I crawled into bed and held Kerry's image close in my mind, like a crucifix against the night's evil. And pretty soon I slept.

But not well and not for long.

. . . Running, running, shadows lurking in shadows, guns firing, things behind me with claws that scratched the ground and jaws that snapped the air, dark places, cold places, dead men lying huddled in rows, dead men rising and chasing after me in a pack, raw terror, screaming, running in sand, caught, trapped, dunes with gaping mouths and green-and-brown witches' hair, cold, cold, waves of blood lifting and crashing down, dark places, cold places, shadows lurking in shadows, and running running running . . .

I WAS AWAKE for good an hour before dawn. The bedclothes were gamy with my sweat, cold-clammy against my skin, and before long I got up and stripped the bed and lay back down on the bare mattress with just a blanket over me.

Kerry was no longer uppermost in my mind. Now it was the two questions, chasing themselves round and round.

Who?

Why?

By the time the first pale light showed at the window, I knew I wasn't finished with it yet. Wouldn't be finished with it until both those questions had answers.

Chapter **20**

I LEFT THE FLAT at seven thirty, before the media and other parties began their inevitable assault. Down on Lombard there are a number of interchangeable coffee shops . . . or maybe that's a redundancy. I picked one in Cow Hollow, bought a copy of the Sunday *Examiner-Chronicle,* and scanned through it while I waited for coffee and orange juice.

The shooting of Coleman Lujack was a featured story on the front page of the Metro section. I was mentioned as an eyewitness, but the reporter didn't dwell on my involvement —probably because the police hadn't yet released certain pieces of information, such as the Lujacks' connection with the coyotes and the particulars of Rafael Vega's injuries. A rehash of Thomas's death by carbon monoxide poisoning, and of the hit-and-run killing of Frank Hanauer, took up the last third of the article, with the correct implication being that the violent demises of the three partners were interrelated. Nick Pendarves's name was trotted out as a possible suspect in Coleman's murder. But "police sources" admitted that there was no direct evidence linking Pendarves—or anyone else—to the shooting.

It was a few minutes past eight when I finished reading that. I drained my orange juice and took my coffee back to the rest room area, where I used one of the pay phones to call Kerry. Before Cybil came to live with her, she would have been fast asleep at 8:00 A.M. on a Sunday morning; now she answered on the first ring, wide awake and a little edgy. As soon as she heard my voice she said, "Why are you calling so early? Are you all right?"

"I'm fine. I just didn't want you to think the worst."

"About what?"

"Haven't you read the paper yet?"

"No. I just woke up a little while ago. My God, don't tell me you're all over the news again. . . ."

"Not exactly. There was some trouble last night and I got caught up in it, that's all."

"That's all? If it's in the paper . . ."

"Don't read the Metro section, all right? I'll explain when I see you."

"I can be over there in an hour or so—"

"I'm not home," I said. "And I have some things to take care of this morning. Later today would be better."

"Well, I've got an appointment at one, but it shouldn't take more than a couple of hours. Three thirty at your place?"

"Good. If I get hung up for any reason, I'll call you there."

"You're sure everything's all right? I mean—"

"I know what you mean. Don't worry."

"Don't tell me not to worry. I started worrying when I didn't hear from you yesterday."

"I got home too late to call. What's your news? Something about Cybil?"

"If I have to wait to hear yours," she said, "you can wait to hear mine."

"Fair enough."

"Oh God, she's calling me. . . . I'd better go."

"Don't let her read the paper either."

"She hasn't looked at a newspaper since she's been here.

She's just not interested." I could hear Cybil's voice now, rising querulously in the background. "Three thirty," Kerry said, and rang off.

I called Eberhardt's number. Still no answer, which was just as well; I didn't really feel like talking to him yet. We'd connect later in the day. He'd see to that, if I didn't. He read every news item in every edition of the local papers, as if he were moonlighting as a researcher for a clipping service.

I DROVE OUT to Daly City first. Teresa Melendez struck me as one of the least likely possibles; might as well eliminate her first if I could.

As usual, fog crawled over its hills and flats, put a shiny wetness on the streets: giant formless gray slug and its slime trail. I had to use my windshield wipers on the way across from 280 to Atlanta Street. Teresa's Honda was under the carport, but I didn't get a response when I rang the bell. I pushed it again, listened, heard nothing, and tried the door. Unlocked. Not smart, Teresa, not these days. I opened it and went in calling her name.

Silence.

On the floor near the couch was an empty fifth of vodka, lying on its side in a wet spot where some of it had dribbled out. An empty glass and an ashtray full of cigarette butts was on an end table. The place smelled of booze—and of stale tobacco and, faintly, of sickness.

I moved into the rear of the house. She was in one of the bedrooms, lying face down across a rumpled king-size bed, the same housecoat she'd worn yesterday bunched up over her hips. Dead drunk in a dried patch of her own vomit. I called her name again from the doorway; she didn't stir. I went and leaned over the bed and shook her, hard. That got me a low mumbling groan. One of her hands came up, twitching, as if she were trying to brush away a bothersome fly, and then flopped down again. She didn't wake up. Without help she wouldn't wake up for hours yet.

Brew up some coffee, haul her into the shower? No. Instead I tugged the housecoat down over her hips and thighs, covered her with a tattered quilt that was lying at the foot of the bed. Then I set about searching the room and the rest of the house.

Coleman Lujack had been shot—and I had been shot at— with a 9mm automatic; that was what I was hunting for. I didn't find it. Nor any other type of handgun. Nor anything at all that linked Teresa Melendez to Coleman's murder.

Her car keys were on one of the kitchen counters. I took them out through the back door, over under the carport to the Honda. The driver's door was open; I leaned in and looked through the glove compartment, under the seats. No gun. I unlocked the trunk and poked around in there. No gun. She could have gotten rid of it, of course, but I didn't think so.

Back inside the house, I put the keys where I'd found them and went to look in on Teresa again. She hadn't moved. Let her be, I thought. She's not the one. If Coleman had come here, she might have tried to do what she'd said she would— cut his heart out and feed it to the neighbor's dogs. But she wasn't the kind to go stalking a man, even one she hated as much as her former boss, and then blow him away with a 9mm cannon. She was the kind to cry and wallow in self-pity and drink herself into a puking oblivion.

Not a killer, Teresa Melendez. Just another lost soul.

SOUTH to the San Carlos hills. But it was an hour's worth of wasted time and effort: Eileen Lujack was away somewhere again.

ALBERT ALLEY was a little hive of activity this Sunday morning. The sun was out here—the Mission has the best weather in San Francisco—and so were the residents: young guys working on cars, kids playing ball, kids hanging out, well-dressed families on their way to and from church. Spanish music clashed with heavy-metal rock, each issuing loudly from an unseen radio. On one of the stoops, two men sat drinking beer out of cans and watching a pro basketball game on a portable TV.

There was nobody in the little garden fronting the Victorian where the Vegas lived, nobody on the stoop. I went up and worked the bell for more than a minute before I got results. When the door finally opened, it was Mrs. Vega who peered out at me.

Like Teresa Melendez, she, too, had spent Saturday night soothing her love for Rafael in an alcohol bath. Her face was puffy, her eyes bloodshot and sick with pain both physical and emotional. The smell of sour red wine blew off her like a bad wind. What was it about that son of a bitch that made his women grieve for him so intensely? Maybe he had admirable qualities underneath; maybe he was gentle and loving and kind to animals. Or maybe it was just that his women were lousy judges of men.

At first there was no recognition in Mrs. Vega's gaze, probably because she was seeing me through the soft focus of her hangover. I watched the knowledge break in on her as I spoke.

"I'm sorry to bother you," I said, "but I need to talk to your son. Is he here?"

"No." She spat the word at me as if it were a bitter-tasting seed.

"Can you tell me where I can find him? It's important that I—"

She slammed the door in my face. And locked it. And went wherever it was she went to nurture her pain.

LA MODERNA MARKET was open for business, but the butcher shop part of it was closed; no fresh meat on Sundays. I spoke to both grocery checkers, one of whom referred me to a stockboy named Manuel. Manuel said maybe I should try the Café Guitarra on Guerrero Street. Paco hung out there sometimes, he said, because a *chiquita* he liked waited tables.

CAFÉ GUITARRA turned out to be one of the funky products of the Mission's New Bohemia status—a combination coffee house and music hall that featured folk, rock, punk, and flamenco guitar players. Paco wasn't there. Three waitresses bustled around, all of them wearing white blouses and colorful peasant skirts; the second one I talked to was evidently the *chiquita* Paco was interested in, because her eyes got bright when I mentioned his name. He hadn't been in so far today, she said. Had I tried La Raza?

I said, "La Raza? You mean the graphics center?"

"No. Centro Legal."

That surprised me. "Why would he be there?"

"He works there sometimes on weekends."

"Doing what?"

"Helping out. You know, volunteer stuff."

"How long has he been a volunteer for them?"

"A long time, I think."

As I left the café I decided that I shouldn't have been surprised. La Raza Centro Legal is a legal assistance and referral group, and is deeply committed to making sure that the IRCA amnesty program for undocumented aliens is properly administered. Rafael Vega had become a coyote who preyed on his own people; his son, who knew or suspected this, and who hated him as a result, had taken the exact opposite route and become a La Raza volunteer. No, I shouldn't have been surprised at all.

LA RAZA CENTRO LEGAL has its offices on the 2500 block of Mission Street. I spotted Paco Vega as soon as I walked in, sitting at a table with two other young Latinos; they were stuffing envelopes from stacks of some kind of document or flier. He didn't see me until I called his name. His first reaction was anger, but it lasted only a couple of seconds; what replaced it was a kind of disgusted resignation. He got up and did a slow walk to where I stood.

"Man," he said, "you're like a dose of the clap. You just don't go away."

"You get around pretty good too," I said. "I didn't know you were an activist volunteer."

"Yeah, well, there's plenty you don't know about me. What you want, pancho? You didn't come here to talk about La Raza."

"Let's go outside."

"Yeah," he said, "get it over with."

By Mission Street standards, the sidewalks were un-crowded today; so were the bus-stop and rest benches, which were usually the domain of drunks, homeless citizens, and little old ladies when they could squeeze out a seat. Paco and I found an empty bench and sat down.

I said, "How's your father?"

"He'll live, so they tell me. But he won't use his right arm again." Paco's face betrayed no emotion of any kind. "You have anything to do with putting him in the hospital?"

"Would it matter if I did?"

"Not to me."

"You don't care that he's badly hurt?"

"No."

"No feelings for him at all?"

"Not in a long time, man. My mother's hurt bad too"—Paco tapped his head—"up here. He don't care about her, why should I care about him? Be better for everybody if he'd died out on that beach."

"You feel that way about Coleman Lujack too?"

"What way?"

"Better for everybody that he's dead."

"He's a pig. I don't think about pigs."

"You help butcher them, though, don't you?"

"What's that supposed to mean?"

"Come on, Paco. *Somebody* killed him last night. Why not you?"

He looked startled; and the startlement seemed genuine. "The hell," he said. "How'd he get killed?"

"You don't know, huh? It was in this morning's paper."

"You think I read the damn paper these days?"

"If the cops haven't been around to see you yet, they will. Any time now."

"Jesus Christ, you and the cops think I did it, you all been smoking angel dust. Why would I kill that *marrano*?"

"Revenge. He's the main reason your father's in the hospital and in big trouble with the law."

"Bullshit," Paco said. "I wouldn't kill nobody for my old man. I wouldn't kill a mad dog that was biting his leg."

"No? You own a handgun?"

"Not me, man. Guns aren't my thing."

"But you'd know where to get one if you wanted it."

"Sure. Lots of guns on the streets. But I told you, I didn't kill Coleman Lujack. You want proof? What time'd he get wasted?"

"Around six thirty."

"Yeah," he said. "Six thirty last night, I was at Mission Dolores with my mother. Six o'clock Mass—she was praying for my old man's soul. Ask the padre, ask fifty other people, maybe that'll satisfy you."

"I'm already satisfied," I said. And I was. I'd started being satisfied as soon as I found out Paco worked as a volunteer for La Raza.

He wasn't the shooter either.

EBERHARDT WAS HOME when I stopped by his Noe Valley house at one thirty. In a snarly mood and none too happy to see me. He started an up-tempo harangue as soon as I walked in, and if Bobbie Jean hadn't been there, we'd have got into a hell of a row; my mood wasn't much better than his. But Bobbie Jean is the unflappable sort of Southerner and exerts a calming influence on Eb, and she got him settled to the point where he could speak to me without yelling and calling me "a stubborn goddamn wop" at the end of every third sentence. He didn't stop glaring at me though. He would probably go on glaring at me for days.

Bobbie Jean made us some coffee, and while we drank it we managed to discuss things in a more or less rational man-

ner. When I got done telling him why I had pretty much
scratched Teresa Melendez and Paco Vega off my list, he said,
"All right, smart guy. If neither of them shot Coleman, then
who did? Thomas's widow?"

"I doubt it."

"Pendarves?"

"Maybe, if he's still alive."

"And if he isn't?"

"I don't know. Somebody who's mixed up in the coyote
business, maybe some friend of Vega's."

"But you don't have any idea who it might be."

"No."

"So you're going to drop it, right? Let the police and the
feds do their jobs and haul your ass out of it, right?"

"Maybe," I said.

"Maybe? Chrissake, *maybe*?"

"I want to talk to Antonio Rivas."

"What the hell for? You think *he* shot Coleman?"

"No."

"Well? He doesn't know anything about Pendarves. I already told you that."

"I still want to have a talk with him."

"You don't trust my judgment, is that it? You stubborn
goddamn wop . . ." And he was off again.

Bobbie Jean stepped in to do another calming job, but I'd
had enough. It was about time for me to go meet Kerry anyway. I said as much, thanked Bobbie Jean, gave her a peck on
the cheek, and then asked her glowering fiancé if he minded
coming to the door with me.

"What for?"

"Humor me, all right?"

He went along, grumbling. "So?" he said when he'd finished yanking the door open.

In lowered tones I asked, "Everything okay with you?"

"Huh?"

"You know, physically."

"I'm fine. Why?"

"I worry about you, Eb. I know you spent the night with Bobbie Jean, and I know how clumsy you can be sometimes."

"What the hell're you talking about?"

"Well, I'm just wondering about your rotten disposition today," I said. "You didn't have one of those freak accidents last night, did you? Miss the target and ram your dingus into the mattress?"

For the second time that day I got a door slammed in my face. This time I didn't mind a bit.

Chapter **21**

————————

KERRY WAS WAITING when I arrived at my flat, even though it was still fifteen minutes shy of three o'clock. A different Kerry than the last few times I'd seen her—not quite her old self, but with some of the old optimism and assurance. A good part of the strain had been eased. Whatever she'd done on Friday, it had had a profound effect on her.

She said after she kissed me, "My appointment didn't take as long as I expected. I've been here half an hour." She gave me a long appraising look. "You look tired, my love."

"Not much sleep lately. I'll be okay."

"I wish I could help you sleep." Gently she rubbed my cheek with her fingertips. "I'm better than calcium lactate."

"You're telling me? Right now, though, we need to talk. And before we talk, I need a beer."

"I helped myself to the wine," she said. "You mind?"

"Nope."

"Good. I was afraid you might go all grumpy and mother-hennish on me. You do that sometimes, you know, when you're under stress or in a bad mood."

"I'm not in a bad mood today. Not anymore."

She kissed me again. "Go get your beer."

I went and got my beer. When I came back into the living room, she was sitting on the couch with her shoes off, her skirt hiked up on her thighs, and her bare feet tucked under her. She has terrific legs, long and slender, with very small and well-formed feet. Dirty old man that I am, I find her feet as erotic as the rest of her. Sometimes just thinking about them gives me urges. But not right now. Right now I was much more interested in what had brought about the change in her.

I said as I sat down, "You first. Tell me about Cybil. I can use some good news. It *is* good, isn't it?"

"Well, positive. Very positive."

"You went to see somebody?"

"Yes, and I wish I'd done it a lot sooner."

"Geriatric doctor?"

"No. A support group," she said.

"What kind of support group?"

"It's called Children of Grieving Parents. One of B. and C.'s clients told me about it. A couple of dozen people like me who have or had parents, usually elderly, that reacted to losing a spouse the way Cybil has. They've found ways to cope themselves, and ways to help the parents learn to cope."

"What do they advise? In the long run, I mean."

"Getting Cybil into a care facility."

"But how, with her fear of being put in a home—?"

"Not that kind of care facility. Not a nursing home."

"What other kind is there?"

"One that's set up as a seniors complex. There are a number in the Bay Area. They're not hospitals or places with rooms like cells and nurses and doctors in the halls; they're virtual condos—separate and private apartments, with recreational facilities and organized activities that are completely optional."

I asked, "What if the individual needs medical attention?"

"Part of the facility is a clinic staffed by medical personnel and counselors. They're there if needed, but only if needed.

The resident—not *patient,* that word is never used—makes the decision. The staff periodically looks in on the residents, of course, to see if they need anything and to make sure they're all right. But they don't interfere except in cases of medical emergency."

"Sounds fine. But will Cybil agree to an arrangement like that?"

"I think so," Kerry said. "Not immediately, but eventually. The one thing she's most afraid of, that almost all grieving parents are most afraid of, is the loss of self-sufficiency. That's the first insight the people in the group gave me. She's been in control of her own life for nearly sixty years; she can't stand the prospect of losing that control, becoming dependent, because to her it means losing her freedom, her will, and ultimately her identity."

"But she's dependent on you right now," I said.

"Yes, morbidly so, and that's a major part of why she can't cope. She hates it—I've only made things worse by pandering to it. Yet the only alternative she sees is an even more terrible form of dependency, the impersonal kind. What I have to do is help her understand that there's another alternative, the only sensible one . . . and then back off and let *her* decide to make the move. Working with the group, I can do that. They've prepared literature that I can get Cybil to read. And some have recruited their surviving parents who now live in care facilities to work as support counselors; the next big step is convincing Cybil to talk to one of them. It'll take time and patience, but underneath her grief she's the same rational and intelligent woman she's always been. She'll accept the truth sooner or later. I know she will."

She wasn't trying to talk herself into believing it; she already believed it. And because she did, I did too.

I said, "I wish there was some way I could get involved in the process. But I guess there isn't."

"Not until she realizes you're not to blame for your feelings about Ivan. Then she'll stop hating you."

"I hope so. I not only like her, I admire and respect her—you know that. I always have."

Kerry smiled and squeezed my hand. "You couldn't like me if you didn't like Cybil," she said. "I'm my mother's daughter."

"I wouldn't want you to be anything else."

We sat for a while without saying anything. It was good companionable silence, the kind we used to share all the time. The awkwardness, the tension between us was finally gone.

At length she stirred and I looked over at her, and her eyes were moist. I asked, "What's the matter? Are you crying?"

"A little."

"Why?"

"Women cry sometimes," she said, as if that explained it. "It doesn't have to mean anything bad, you know."

". . . If you say so."

"God, you sound so dubious." Now she was laughing as well as crying. "You really don't understand women, do you?"

"Not a lick," I said.

She got up, still laughing and crying at the same time, and said, "I love you, you big goof." Then she said, "I'll be right back," and went off to the bathroom.

I sat there wondering why I was such an ignoramus when it came to women. Sex shouldn't make that much difference; people were people, right? All of us *Homo sapiens* under the skin. I understood men, sometimes too well, so why didn't I understand women? The fact that I didn't and never had made me feel inadequate and somehow ridiculous, as if I were the butt of some secret cosmic joke.

Kerry came back pretty soon. She was no longer either crying or laughing; she'd fixed her face and the expression on it now was serious and businesslike. She sat down, drank some of her wine. "All right," she said, "now it's your turn. What happened to get you written up in today's paper? The Lujack case?"

"The Lujack case."

"Talk," she said.

I talked. She already knew some of the facts; I generally confided in her about what I was working on, to keep things open between us and because now and then she came up with an insight or a piece of information that proved useful. I filled in the details, then went through the events of the past few days. I did not want to tell her about the incident with Rafael Vega, but it was bound to come out in the media eventually; so I settled for whitewashing it a little, making it seem less deadly than it had been. I didn't say anything at all about being shot at last night. She didn't need to know how deadly that had been either.

She sat through the whole recital without interrupting. Her face was grave when I finished, but whatever she was feeling was hidden away inside. And when she spoke she had nothing to say about Vega or the shooting of Coleman Lujack. Experience had taught her just how dangerous my profession could be sometimes, and that there was no point in carrying on about it. I was still around, still in one piece; that was what mattered.

Quietly she said, "It's not over for you yet, is it?" She knew me so well—so much better than I could ever know her.

"It won't be over until whoever killed Coleman is identified and locked up. It has to come full circle; there has to be a closing."

"But why do *you* have to close it? Why not the police?"

"It's not that I have to be the one," I said. "It's that I have to keep trying until *somebody* does it. You understand the distinction?"

"I think so."

"I thought you would. Eberhardt doesn't."

"That's because he's uncomplicated."

"I wish I were too, sometimes."

"But you're not." She smiled—a little wistfully, I thought. Then she asked, "Who shot Coleman, if it wasn't Paco Vega or Teresa Melendez? Thomas's widow?"

"Probably not. She just isn't the type."

"Any woman is the type, if she wants revenge badly enough."

"I suppose so. More likely it's somebody mixed up in the smuggling racket. Pendarves would be a good candidate too . . . *if* he's alive."

"But you don't think he is?"

"Everything I know about Coleman and Vega says they plotted Pendarves's murder along with Thomas's."

"Maybe they did, and something happened to prevent it."

"You mean there was an attempt on Pendarves's life and he got away? Sure, it's possible. It would give him another reason for hiding out, and an even stronger motive for shooting Coleman. But if that's it, where has he been holed up since Tuesday night? He has few friends, none close enough to risk prison on an accessory charge."

"No woman in his life?"

I shook my head. "I thought for a while he might've been having an affair with one of the women regulars at the Hide-away, but that idea didn't pan out."

"Why not?"

"According to Lyda Isherwood, who claims to have once been a madam in Nevada, he's been paying for his sex ever since his divorce five years ago. Plus there's the fact that he's a hard-core sexist and a psychological abuser. Women don't seem to want to have much to do with him."

"Then why did you think he was having an affair?"

"The shape his house was in. I had a glimpse of the kitchen; it was spotless. Pendarves is or was a slob, and much too cheap to hire a housekeeper. Somebody had to do the cleaning up for him."

"Why does it have to be a woman?" Kerry said.

"What?"

"The person who cleaned his house for him. Why does it have to be a woman? Why couldn't it be a man?"

". . . I don't know, I just assumed . . ."

"Men clean houses too. And cook and wash clothes and change diapers . . . all sorts of things like that."

"Okay, okay. But in this situation . . . hell, Pendarves isn't gay, I'm positive of that. . . ."

"Who said anything about gay? It doesn't have to be a sexual relationship. You said he's a psychological abuser. Why couldn't he have a male friend, somebody weak and easily manipulated, that he could have bullied into doing his housecleaning for him? *And* bullied into hiding him from the police?"

I stared at her without speaking. Then I got off the couch and took a couple of turns around the room, working on what she'd said. Somebody weak and easily manipulated. Well, why not? Another Hideaway regular; the tavern was the most likely place for Pendarves to have formed such a relationship. But why hadn't anybody there mentioned it?

They don't know, I thought. Pendarves is close-mouthed, keeps to himself. The friend could be that way too. Either that, or . . .

Weak and easily manipulated—and withdrawn, uncommunicative. A man who had expressed a deeper concern for Pendarves's well-being than any of the other regulars the night of the abortive hit-and-run . . . a man fastidious in dress and habits, who would undoubtedly keep a fastidious house and could be talked into keeping his friend's house the same way . . . a man who, now that I thought about it, hadn't been present at the Hideaway during my last few visits, even though he usually came in every night to play chess.

Douglas Mikan.

The sad-eyed, painfully shy mama's boy—Douglas Mikan.

Chapter **22**

I TOLD KERRY she was wonderful, briefly explained about Douglas Mikan, and went after the telephone directory. He was listed. Or at least there was a D. Mikan at 2316 Great Highway, which would be just a few blocks from the tavern.

There was an edge in me now, but not the bad kind; a controlled excitement, a sense that thanks to Kerry I might be nearing that final closing off. "I'd better go out there and check on this right away," I said.

"You won't take any chances?"

"No."

"I mean, if Pendarves is at Mikan's and he's the one who shot Coleman Lujack, he'll probably be armed."

"I know. I'll go slow and easy."

On my way Out There at the Beach, I did some more thinking about Nick Pendarves and Douglas Mikan. At first consideration, they seemed like strange bedfellows. Pendarves —blue-collar, minimally educated and unsophisticated, no interests beyond his work, his bar time, maybe some TV, and a hooker now and then to satisfy his biological needs. Mikan— white-collar, younger by more than fifteen years, sensitive, intelligent, probably asexual, interested in chess and history and world travel and any number of other things. When you looked a little more closely, though, there were similarities between the two, and strong character traits in each that made it natural they would gravitate to each other. Both were loners, yet both craved the company of others; their "regulars" status at the Hideaway proved that. One was an abuser who didn't care if he was liked or respected, just so long as he got what he wanted. The other was withdrawn, malleable, a man-child who had been cast adrift by his mother's death and who would typically yearn to be needed as she had needed him. . . . All in all, a perfect foil for an abusive personality.

Pendarves and Mikan—why hadn't I seen it before? Too busy trying to make things fit into convenient patterns; and too willing to accept a sexual stereotype, as Kerry had pointed out. A product of my generation, that was me. Even though I did not believe in any form of sexism, fought against it in others, there were times when I was as unintentionally piggy as Eberhardt. . . .

Between Taraval and Sloat Boulevard, before the Great Highway enters its newly landscaped stretch, its east side is just another strip of mismatched private residences. Number 2316 was one of them—a weathered, green-shingled cottage squeezed so tightly between a two-unit apartment building and a two-story house that it looked as though it was trapped there. A concrete walk bordered by two neat, slender rows of artichoke plants led in to it. Across its narrow front porch was a wrought-iron security gate. And in one of the facing windows, a light showed palely behind drawn monk's cloth drapes.

I felt a momentary longing for Vega's .38. But it was just as well that I had turned it over to the police last night. I wouldn't need a weapon if I handled things right. There was no reason I had to bring Pendarves in myself; all I had to do was determine his presence, get away clean, and notify the authorities. I ought to be able to tell if he was there by trying to talk my way inside—Art Canino come from the Hideaway to find out if Douglas was feeling all right, since he hadn't been in the past few evenings—and then gauging Mikan's reaction. It would work if I was careful and did or said nothing to arouse suspicion.

A stiff sea wind beat at me as I got out of the car. No fog out here today, and none lying in wait offshore; the sky was coldly clear to the horizon, turning a dusky indigo now as the last of the sunset colors bled out of it. I let the wind push me along the walk to where the gate barred my way. It wasn't quite latched, I saw then. But I didn't touch it. I stopped and laid my finger on a round white button set into the frame.

No one buzzed me in. Or opened the front door. Or showed himself behind either of the curtained windows.

Empty house? Or somebody in there, hiding?

I rang the bell continuously for part of a minute. Then I pushed on the gate, and it swung inward, and I climbed three steps onto the narrow little porch. Carefully I tried the door, using two fingers on the knob; it was locked. I banged on the panel, loudly, and called Mikan's name, identifying myself as Art Canino. Still no answer.

If I break in, I thought, and they're in there, Pendarves is liable to start shooting. But it's just as likely there's nobody home. Otherwise, why wasn't the security gate locked tight? And why wouldn't Mikan just answer the door, find out what I wanted, and then get rid of me? Keep me from coming back again, that way. And ease their minds about why I'd come.

Just as likely, too, that Pendarves is dead and this is a wild-goose chase. Don't forget that.

I bent for a close look at the door latch, and that made up my mind. People nowadays think a security gate and window bars are all the protection they need, so they don't bother to put dead-bolt locks on the doors. Then they leave the house and go away and forget to make sure the gate is secure. No wonder the burglary rate in this city was so damned high.

With one of the blades in my pocket knife, I tripped the spring lock. Took me less than thirty seconds. I went in slow and wary, but not being furtive about it.

Nothing happened.

Nobody home.

I let out a long breath, shut the door, stood looking around. I was in a tiny foyer that opened on my left into a living room lit by a ginger-jar table lamp. And what a living room it was. The furnishings were few and functional, of the forties Sears, Roebuck type but well preserved and gleaming with polish; the carpet was rose-patterned, threadbare in places, very clean. That much was ordinary. The rest of the room was extraordinary: It assailed the eye in a riot of color and imagery.

Postcards. Picture postcards.

There must have been thousands of them covering every inch of wall space, fanned out on top of the furniture, hanging from the ceiling on lengths of white ribbon like bright flypaper strips or homemade mobiles. Most looked to be of recent vintage and the photographic, wish-you-were-here sort, depicting scenes from foreign lands and the more interesting parts of the U.S. There were also hand-painted cards, some evidently quite old; poster and advertising cards; cards featuring boats, trains, other forms of transportation; cards showing people, animals, birds, monuments, buildings. Holiday cards, religious cards, patriotic cards, novelty cards . . . just about every conceivable type of picture postcard ever manufactured except the erotic and the pornographic. Nearly all of the hanging ones had been written on and sent through the mail; one of the old cards, of the Steel Globe Tower at Coney Island, bore a 1907 postmark. I glanced at the names of the senders and addressees on a few of the others. None had been written by or sent to Douglas Mikan, nor by or to anyone bearing his family name. Only one had been mailed to someone in San Francisco; the others bore such far-flung addresses as Baltimore, London, and Fiji.

He buys them through dealers, I thought, or picks them up in junk shops and secondhand stores. And they're more than just a hobby; they're his secret fantasy life. All the places he's never been and probably will never go. Other peoples' dreams fulfilled, shared vicariously and long after the fact by a sad, shy, lonely little man named Douglas Mikan.

I turned out of there, made my way down a central hallway. But there was no getting away from the postcards; they were everywhere, on every wall including those in the hallway, bathroom, and kitchen. The place was alive with them . . . and yet there was no life *in* them, only the static memory of life. It was like wandering through a mausoleum filled with bright, shiny, two-dimensional corpses.

Two doors off the hall were shut. The first one opened into what must be Douglas's bedroom: as neat and clean as the rest of the place, the bed made up with military precision, the concentration of postcards the heaviest. He'd affixed some directly to the ceiling—his favorites, I thought, so he could lie in bed at night and look up at them and dream his impossible dreams. On the dresser was a big silver-framed photograph of a pinch-faced, unsmiling woman with gray hair and hard little eyes. His mother. If the photo was an accurate reflection of the woman herself, it was little wonder he'd turned out the way he had.

Behind the other door was a guest bedroom, furnished with a single bed, a dresser, a couple of nightstands. The bed was made, though not quite as carefully as Douglas's own. Postcards coated two of the walls; the other two had cards only just below ceiling level, out of reach of a normal-sized man—yet the bare parts bore discolored squares and rectangles and clinging bits of adhesive where cards had been mounted. They bore something else too: gouge marks, deep in places, as of fingernails dug hard into the plasterboard and dragged downward.

I peered closely at some of the gouges. Then I got down on one knee and looked under the bed. Something was caught under one of its rollers; I slid it loose. A piece of jaggedly torn postcard of the old hand-painted type, the stiff paper yellowed and the inked words on the back faded. Douglas wouldn't have torn one of his prized possessions that way; and it didn't look as though it had been done accidentally. . . .

I left the room, went through the kitchen and then out a rear door into a tiny backyard. Near a narrow walkway alongside the cottage were a brace of garbage cans, each lined with a black disposal bag. Inside the first I opened were hundreds of torn-up postcards—the ones that had formerly decorated the spare-bedroom walls.

Pendarves, I thought. Who else but Pendarves, in a fit of pique or sudden anger. And afterward, Douglas the tidy, Douglas the timid and abused, had swept up the mutilated remains and put them in with the garbage.

Two minutes later, I had proof that Pendarves was alive and had been living here recently. And that he was the one who had shot down Coleman Lujack last night.

In a nightstand drawer in the guest bedroom I found a nearly empty pack of Pall Malls—Pendarves's brand. Mikan was a nonsmoker. In the scuffed dresser was a gray work shirt and a pair of gray work pants, both laundered and neatly folded. Pendarves's customary outfit. His size too. I had never seen Douglas except in a suit and tie, and these clothes wouldn't fit him anyway.

Another drawer in the dresser yielded a large cigar box, inside of which I found some gun oil, a couple of chamois cloths stained with the oil, several cleaning brushes, and a spare clip for a 9mm automatic pistol. I rummaged through the rest of the drawers, the closet, but there was no sign of the gun itself, or of any other type of weapon.

Before I left the room again I paused to stare at the stripped and gouged walls. What had thrown Pendarves into such a destructive fit? Being cooped up here for so long, probably. He was the same type as Thomas Lujack, a man who bottled things up until he reached an explosion point of sudden violent rage. Five days ago he'd become the object of a police manhunt, with no way to prove his innocence and no place to run. Trapped here all that time, in the home of a weak man he no doubt despised, the pressure building, building . . . and finally, early yesterday or maybe Friday night, he'd erupted. First, he had destroyed the postcards. Then, when that wasn't enough of a release, he'd got his hands on a 9mm automatic, taken Douglas's car, and gone hunting the man who may have tried to kill *him,* who'd turned his life upside down and put him in this intolerable position.

But where was he now? Had he come back here after the shooting, spent the night here? And where was Mikan?

I went back through the cottage, poking into closets and drawers and cupboards. There was no gun anywhere on the premises; either Pendarves had gotten rid of the automatic, or more likely, he was still armed with it. Nor was there anything in any of the rooms to give me an idea of where he might be.

As for Douglas . . .

The Hideaway? I thought.

If the two of them were no longer together, if Pendarves had taken off again in Mikan's car, alone, the tavern was the natural place for Douglas to go—his home away from home, the one other spot he could find a measure of solace. And if anyone knew Pendarves's whereabouts, it was Douglas. It wouldn't take long to check out.

The gaudy, mock-cheerful corpse faces of the postcards had become oppressive; I avoided looking at them as I moved to the front door. I could understand the impulse that had led Pendarves to attack the ones in the guest room. After five days of being surrounded by all these cards, I might have done the same thing.

I cracked the door to make sure nobody was on the walk or on the street in front. Then, hurrying, I left the house to the static vistas and trite messages and never-to-be-realized yearnings that made it—for me, anyway—a museum of sadness.

THE BLOCK of Taraval on which the Hideaway stood was Sunday-evening deserted. There were vacant parking spaces directly in front of the tavern; I fitted my car into one of them. It was dark now but the blue-neon cocktail glass above the entrance wasn't lighted. Burned-out tubing, maybe,

I thought as I locked the car. The place was open for business, because the familiar shine of lights was visible through the upper third of the window.

I was wrong on both counts.

When I opened the door and walked in, I didn't do it warily because I expected to see a tableau as familiar as the lights. The Sunday night relief man, Sam Cotter, behind the bar mixing drinks, polishing glasses; some of the regulars in their customary places and little groupings, not too many of them yet since it was still early—talking and laughing, reading and knitting, bending elbows in their illusory safe place. I expected the ordinary; I had no reason to expect otherwise.

What I walked into was a hostage situation.

Chapter **23**

I STOPPED just inside the door, the hair pulling all along my scalp. There were an even dozen people in the place, ten of them in a tautly seated bunch at the side tables and wall. Nine of the ten were regulars, among them Frank Parigli, Harry Briggs, Ed McBee, old man Vandermeer, Lyda Isherwood; the tenth was a thin bald man—Sam Cotter, the bartender. Numbers eleven and twelve were on the bar facing the others, like a pair of poorly matched lecturers about to address a small but intent audience. *On* the bar, not at it—haunches planted on the polished mahogany, legs dangling over the edge.

Douglas Mikan, pale, sick-looking in a dark-blue suit and tie, rocking a little with both hands pressed tight against his wishbone.

And nearest me and the door, Nick Pendarves in his usual gray work clothes, three or four days of beard stubble flecking his cheeks, the backbar lights glinting off the barrel of the 9mm automatic in his hand.

It was dead quiet in there. And dead still. All of them were frozen in position, looking at me. You could smell the fear; it came off all but Pendarves in a thick shimmer that was almost palpable. You could feel the tension too, as brittle as a layer of frost on grass.

Pendarves broke both the stillness and the silence. He waved the pistol in my direction—a sudden, convulsive movement of his arm. It seemed to set off a spasmodic reaction in the right side of his face; nerves and muscles twitched riotously from temple to jaw, like a nest of worms stirred up under a thin covering. The effect was chilling.

He said, "Canino, right? Art the fart," in a thick, slurred voice. But he wasn't drunk. The thickness was the product of emotions writhing as chaotically as the nerves and muscles in his face. "Come on in, Art the fart. Join the party, the water's fine."

He'd cracked completely under the strain—the last breakdown in a catalytic string that so far had demolished the Lujacks and Frank Hanauer. But Pendarves's was the worst of all, the kind that creates monsters out of men and situations like this one. It happens so often nowadays that it has lost its once-stunning edge of horror, become almost a cliché: Just another crazy with a loaded gun and a mad-on against the world.

Unless the crazy happens to be sitting ten feet away, and the loaded gun is pointed at *you.*

My body seemed to constrict, draw in on itself—so sharply that I could feel the pressure in my head like a sudden migraine. I took half a dozen slow stiff paces, angling away from him toward the tables. I could see the rest of the room then: empty booths, empty floor. It didn't look as though he'd shot anybody yet.

Before I got to where the others were clustered I stopped; I wanted a little distance between me and anybody else. "Hey, Nick," I said, and licked my lips, and put on a bewildered little smile. "What's the idea of the gun?"

"We're having a party," he said. He wasn't smiling; he didn't sound happy about it. He sounded mad as hell.

"Sure, Nick. A party. What you need a gun at a party for?"

"Stupid question. What's a gun good for, huh?"

"You tell me."

"Shoot somebody with," he said. His eyes, underslung by sacs of loose gray flesh, were bright and hot. "That's what a gun's good for. Shoot people with, right?"

Douglas Mikan made low moaning sounds. He was still cradling himself, eyes squeezed tightly shut.

"Shut up, Doug," Pendarves said.

The moaning stopped.

I said, "How long's the party been going on?"

The question seemed to interest him. His gaze flicked past me to the others, settled on Ed McBee. "Hey, Ed. How long's the party been going on?"

"Hour and a half," McBee said in a dull, bruised voice. His face, and the faces of the others, showed the terror and strain of those ninety minutes. But there was something else reflected in each face, too—betrayal and utter despair. They had trusted Pendarves, believed in him, and he had turned on them in the most terrible of ways. No matter what else happened here tonight, an integral part of their lives—their sanctuary and their carefully nurtured illusions—lay in ruins around them.

"What's it going to be, Nick?" I said. "An all-night party? That what you have in mind?"

"All night? Uh-uh. Not that long."

"How long, then?"

"Until I get tired of it."

"Then what?"

"You'll find out. Everybody will."

"Sure. But while it lasts, what do you say we keep it small, just those of us here now? What do you say we lock the door, don't let anybody else in?"

"No," he said.

"Too many people spoil a party—"

"No, goddamn it, I said no!" The right side of his face

went through another series of spasms. His arm jerked a little too, and I was afraid he might fire the gun involuntarily; he had it aimed in my direction. Rusty Tin Man of Oz gone haywire: unpredictable, deadly. "Sit down, Art the fart. What the hell you standing up for? Sit down like everybody else."

I didn't argue with him. I pulled a chair away from one of the tables, positioned it so that nothing separated us but a dozen feet of empty floor. When I sat down I put both feet flat on the linoleum and both hands on my knees, bowed my back forward, and held that position.

Pendarves watched me with his hot eyes. Then he said to Mikan, "Doug, I need a smoke. Get me a smoke."

Douglas just sat there rocking.

Pendarves elbowed him, hard enough to make him grunt and pop his eyes open. "Oh, God," he said.

"Shut up. Get me a smoke. You know where they are."

"Nick, please, I'm sick—"

"You fat slob, do what I told you!"

Whimpering a little, Mikan fumbled a package of Pall Malls out of Pendarves's shirt pocket, shook a cigarette loose, and managed to insert it into a corner of Pendarves's mouth.

"You want me to smoke it dry, fatso?"

Douglas fished a Bic from the pocket, lit the cigarette. It took him half a minute; he dropped the lighter twice, flicked the wheel half a dozen times before he was able to spark the flint. Then he had to hold the Bic in both hands to keep the flame steady.

"Stupid bastard, you almost singed my eyebrow. What's the matter with you, Doug? Huh?"

"I'm sick, I'm sick—"

"And I'm sick of *you,* whining all the time. Be a man, for Christ's sake. Art the fart's a man, aren't you, Art the fart?"

I didn't say anything.

"I asked you a question. You a man or what?"

"Yeah," I said, "I'm a man."

"Hear that, chubby? He's a man. You be one too."

Mikan mumbled something that I couldn't hear.

"Right," Pendarves said. "Now go get me a beer. I'm thirsty. Make it a Bud . . . no, what the hell, something imported. A Beck's. Make it a Beck's."

Douglas pushed himself off the bar. One of his feet struck a stool and nearly upset it; he fell heavily to one knee, moaning again. Pendarves said, "Clumsy bugger. Get up, get my beer," and Mikan got up and stumbled away to the far end of the bar where the hatch was.

Pendarves quit looking at him; his eyes were on me again. "Hey, Art the fart. You want a beer too?"

"Sure," I said. "I could use one."

"Beck's or Bud?"

"Beck's."

"Anybody else want a snort? On me?"

Silence. Then old man Vandermeer said, "Let us go, Nick. We've never done anything to you, we're your friends. Please let us go—"

"Shut up, old man. You and your fucking history. Shut up, you hear me?"

Vandermeer shut up. He seemed to shrink and shrivel where he sat, like a slug doused with salt.

Douglas was behind the bar now. Sweat shone on his round face, stained the front of his shirt. The beer cooler was almost directly behind where Pendarves was sitting; Mikan got it open, bent out of sight, came up again with two bottles. Pendarves still wasn't looking at him. He could have leaned forward with no effort at all and cracked Pendarves over the head with one of the bottles. But even if the idea occurred to him, he didn't do it. Poor sad broken Douglas Mikan did not have enough courage to act to save his own life.

There was an acrid taste in my mouth—the taste of hate. I made myself sit poker-faced, so what I was feeling wouldn't show; Pendarves's gaze remained fixed on me, left eye half-closed in a squint. The cigarette was still pasted wetly in that corner of his mouth, the smoke from it curling upward into a kind of obscene halo.

Mikan had the two bottles of beer open. He took a clean

pilsner glass off the backbar, poured beer into it, set glass and bottle down carefully to Pendarves's left. Then he picked up a second glass, started away toward the hatch.

Pendarves was still staring at me. Abruptly his expression changed and he sat up straight; jerked the weed out of his mouth with his free hand and threw it on the floor. The blaze in his eyes was hotter now.

"Doug," he said. "Doug!"

Mikan was at the open hatch. He stopped, turned.

"Put that other beer down. Don't bring it out here."

I said, "Come on, Nick, I'm thirsty too—"

"Shut up! Doug, you hear what I said?"

Douglas mumbled something. Then, louder, "I heard." He rid himself of bottle and glass, came through and back around to where Pendarves was sitting.

"Get up here. Move that fat ass of yours."

Mikan had difficulty getting his bulk onto the bar; he had to use one of the stools as a stepladder. His chubby hips quivered, jostled the bottle there. Pendarves snatched it out of the way without removing his flat stare from me.

"What's the idea, Nick?" I said. "How come I don't get my beer?"

"You know what I ought to give you? Huh? A bullet, that's what. How'd you like a bullet in the head, you dirty bastard?"

The sweat on me turned cold, clammy. I sat forward a little more, watching his finger on the automatic's trigger. It hadn't whitened yet; if it started to whiten I would have to try jumping him . . . *if* he didn't just jerk off a shot . . . *if* he gave me enough time. . . .

"Why would you want to shoot me, Nick?"

"Art Canino my ass. You're that damn detective."

"What detective?"

"The one I read about, the one at the factory last night. Chrissake, I should have known. Fucking Lujacks hired a private eye to come around spying on me. Should of blown *you* away last night too."

Little rustlings and throat noises from the others. They were figuring it out too, now, just as Pendarves had.

His face was twitching again. The gun remained steady, his finger still not quite tight on the trigger. I came close to launching myself out of the chair anyway. The only thing that stopped me was the fear that if I rattled him into firing once, he might keep right on firing before I could get to him, spray bullets all over the room. The automatic looked to be a military model, the kind with a double-action trigger.

"Nick," I said, "I'm not your enemy. I hated Coleman Lujack as much as you did. I'm glad he's dead. He deserved to die."

"Bullshit. You were working for him."

"No. Not for him, for his brother's lawyer."

"Bullshit."

"Nick, listen. I know he killed his brother, him and Vega, and framed you for it. I know all about that. You had a right to shoot him. He had it coming."

"Dirty bastard," Pendarves said, and I thought that now he was talking about Coleman Lujack. "Dirty lying bastard."

"How did he lie to you?"

It was ten seconds before he said, "I shouldn't of done it. But I was pissed. I'd had enough. Damn brother of his tried to run me down like he run down Hanauer, run me down like a dog. You can only take so much, by God. Then you got to start pushing back."

The facial spasming had stopped again. And the muzzle of the automatic had dipped a little. I'd gotten through to him, all right, deflected some of his anger away from me and back to Coleman Lujack. Keep him talking, I thought. Get him off his guard.

"Sure you do," I said. "How'd you push Coleman?"

"Leave me alone, that's all I asked. His brother leaves me alone, I keep quiet about the wetbacks. I never asked for no money. That was *his* idea. Five thousand bucks. I didn't even have to say I'd been wrong about who was driving the car.

backs."

"You take the money, Nick?"

"What kind of man you think I am? Huh? I told him shove his money up his ass."

"So instead he made up his mind to get rid of you and his brother both."

"Killed his own brother, what kind of son of a bitch kills his own brother? Him and that spick Vega. Then the dirty bastards tried to kill *me*."

"How'd he get you away from your house that night?"

"Called me up, said we had to talk. Real urgent. Didn't want to come to my place, didn't want me to come to his, wouldn't be good for either of us if we was seen together. Why didn't we meet up at Stow Lake. I said what the hell you trying to pull. Nothing, he said, just want to save you some grief. Dirty lying bastard. I didn't think he'd try and kill me. His brother, but not him. Place like Stow Lake, ten o'clock at night . . . ah, Christ, I should of known."

"Who showed up there? Vega?"

"Knew something was wrong when I seen that spick. Car full of kids hadn't of gone by, I hadn't of seen he had a gun and run like hell, I'd be dead too." Pendarves's cheek started to tic again; he reached up and scratched it with his free hand, digging his nails hard enough into the skin to draw blood. "Couldn't find me in the fog. But I didn't know where he was neither. Might of still been hanging around, waiting for me to go back for my car. Only one thing I could think to do."

"Find a phone and call Douglas and have him come pick you up," I said.

"Good old Doug." He prodded Mikan with his elbow. "You're my buddy, hey, fatso?"

Mikan kept his eyes shut; he was rocking again.

"I told him drive us by my house," Pendarves said. "Cops all over the place . . . Christ! Right there in my garage they killed him. Knew I couldn't go to the cops. My word against Coleman's, they'd never believe me. Nothing I could do but hide out at Doug's. Wait until they quit looking for me and then take off, get out of the state. Doug scraped some cash together for me, didn't you, chubby? Good old Doug. Good old Doug and his lousy goddamn postcards."

"But then you got to thinking," I said. "Why let Coleman and Vega get away with what they'd done to you. Why not fix them like they tried to fix you."

"Yeah. Fix 'em good."

"Doug buy the gun for you?"

"This baby? Had it since I was in Korea, locked up in a box in my basement. Sent fatso over to see if the cops found it but they didn't. He didn't want to bring it, did you, Doug? But I convinced him. He does what I tell him. Fetch, Doug, and he fetches like a fat old dog."

"You fixed Coleman, Nick," I said. "And the cops have Vega so he's fixed too. It's finished now. Why come in here with that gun, why hurt your friends?"

"Friends? Like you, huh?"

"Not me. All these other people—"

"I got no friends, I don't need no friends."

"What about Doug? You needed him, didn't you?"

"Not no more. Look at him. He's just a fat old dog. They're all old dogs, no good to nobody. Best thing with mangy old dogs is put 'em out of their misery." Bitter anger thickened his voice again. He shifted his gaze to the far wall. "How about it, huh? Put you old dogs out of your misery."

Lyda Isherwood made a thin keening noise. A look of desperation crossed Ed McBee's seamed face; he put both hands on the table in front of him, getting ready to rise. Pendarves swung the automatic his way, his finger pad just starting to flatten on the trigger. I lifted my heels off the floor, tensing.

And the front door opened and Kate and Bob Johnson walked in.

They came in jauntily, loud as always, laughing about something. Pendarves rotated his hips on the bar top, brought the gun arcing back past me to them. Kate Johnson saw it first and her laughter broke into an astonished gurgling cry. Her husband yelled, "Hey!" and Douglas shrieked, "No, Nick, no!" I came up out of the chair, fast and low—a couple of seconds too late.

Pendarves fired twice at the Johnsons.

Panic, chaos: screams, shouts overriding the echoes of the shots; people tumbling out of chairs and off the wall bench, scrambling for cover. Pendarves saw me coming, swung the automatic again, fired wildly . . . and I was on him, left hand coming up under the gun, driving it ceilingward as he squeezed off a fourth shot, right hand clawing a hold on his shirtfront and dragging him forward, down off the bar. He slammed into one of the stools; it collapsed under him and we both went to the floor.

I let go of his shirt, used both hands to go after the gun. I couldn't get hold of it at first because his arm was pinned under him and he kept squirming and kicking to free it, hurling words and spittle into my face. Finally I managed to close my left hand around the barrel and trigger guard, twisted it against his hip so he wouldn't squeeze off again. With my other hand I found a grip on his wrist, bent and wrung it hard enough to crack the bone. He yelled, his fingers relaxed, and I had the piece.

I slammed the butt of it against his jaw. That made him quit squirming. I hit him twice more in the face, both times with my right fist. Caught a handful of his hair and slammed his head against the floor once, twice, three times, hard enough to crack the bastard's skull—

No! That's enough, he's out, he's out!

—and let go of him abruptly and shoved back off his body and knelt there panting, clutching the automatic against my chest.

My mind cleared, like a dark haze lifting, and I was aware again of what was going on around me. No more screams but voices babbling, weeping, moaning; shifting movement, people milling about; somebody leaning over me, then backing off quickly when I tilted my head to look up that way. Sweat stung my eyes. The stink of burned gunpowder fouled the air, led me to breathe through my mouth.

Over by the door Bob Johnson's voice rose shrill and frightened, saying, "Kate, oh God, Kate!" as I got unsteadily to my feet. Most of the others were over there, too, or moving that way, and when I joined them I saw Kate Johnson down on the floor, blood staining her coat and dress. One of the bullets had struck her high on the chest, under the collarbone —too high to be fatal, I thought. She was conscious and in shock, making liquid sounds that had no meaning.

"Somebody call an ambulance!" her husband pleaded. He was on his knees beside her; he hadn't been hurt. "Hurry, please, somebody get help!"

I turned back to the bar, but Sam Cotter was already behind it with the telephone receiver in his hand.

Pendarves lay where I'd left him, crumpled, unmoving. Alongside him on the floor, Douglas Mikan sat crying into his hands. I looked around to be sure nobody else had been hurt; then I made certain Pendarves was going to be out for a while; and then I pushed my way through the crowd near the door. All of the regulars shied away from me, and I realized I still held the automatic in my hand. But that wasn't the only reason.

I put the gun into my coat pocket, went outside and opened the trunk of my car and got the set of handcuffs. Back inside, I shackled Pendarves's wrists behind his back. Some of the regulars watched me do that, but when I was done they turned away. None of them said anything to me—not a word.

Reaction was setting in: shaking, sweating, shortness of breath, faint nausea. I made my way to one of the back-wall booths, sank down there to wait alone.

Now it's over, I thought. Now the circle's closed.

They were the last thoughts I permitted myself until the police and the ambulance arrived.

Chapter **24**

THE OLDER I GET, the more it seems I've lived my life not in a linear fashion—day to day, year to year—but in blocks and scraps of time. These exist in my memory like an archipelago, some large islands, some small, each made up of a momentous event, a deep impression, a profound insight, a living nightmare. With each passing year, a few of the tinier islands sink and never resurface, and a few others become distorted as if by mist. The larger ones will be there to the end, waiting for me to inhabit them again, even if I never do.

The aftermath of the Lujack case was a series of little reefs and atolls, adjuncts to the one big island. All of them, unlike the island itself, would eventually sink or be shrouded in obscurity. But not for a while. Not for a long while, some of them.

DOUGLAS MIKAN was arrested along with Pendarves and charged with harboring a fugitive and being an accessory in the slaying of Coleman Lujack. He collapsed while in custody and had to be hospitalized. Acute neurasthenia, the doctors said, compounded by fear-psychosis and guilt. Add another breakdown to the list.

I spoke to Paul Glickman about the charges against Douglas. Glickman said that given the extenuating circumstances, and the fragile state of Mikan's mental health, it was doubtful that the DA's office would move to bring him to trial. And even if they did prosecute, no jury would convict. Douglas Mikan, he said, would never see the inside of a prison.

But he was wrong. Douglas Mikan was already in prison, and he would stay there for the rest of his natural life. Solitary confinement, with no possibility of parole.

PENDARVES and Rafael Vega, fittingly enough, were held under guard in adjoining rooms in the prison wing at S.F. General. Made calm and rational by an antipsychotic drug, Pendarves signed a full confession. So did Vega, on the advice of his public defender, so he could cop to a second-degree murder charge.

I was privy to both confessions, thanks to Eberhardt's influence at the Hall of Justice. It had all gone down pretty much as I'd surmised and as Pendarves had indicated at the Hideaway. Vega confirmed that part of Coleman Lujack's plan had been to murder Pendarves that night at Stow Lake and then dispose of his body. Pendarves's escape had prodded them into hurrying up their run-out preparations, with Coleman's final destination being South America. They were afraid that if Pendarves were caught, and he spilled what he knew about the coyote connection, they would be detained pending a full investigation.

They had argued long and hard, Vega said, over the necessity of killing both Thomas and Pendarves; Vega hadn't wanted any part of it at first. But the decision to kill me had evidently been made with little or no argument. One more murder didn't matter much to either of them by then.

There are all kinds of crazies with guns.

THOUGHTS WHILE LYING in bed waiting for sleep:

Was *I* a potential crazy with a gun? Something of a loner, tendency to brood, given now to sudden black rages and monomaniacal pursuits and the breaking of laws I had once obeyed to the letter . . . I wasn't all that different from Nick Pendarves and others like him. Did I have the capacity for the same terrible type of breakdown, like a poisonous seed growing in the new, dark side of me?

No. No. There is a line between change and collapse, self-awareness and self-delusion, monomania and psychosis, and it's not such a fine or easy one to cross. Not for a man like me. I would never willfully harm an innocent person, under any circumstances. I have too much respect for life, too much empathy for the victims of wanton violence, too much love of justice and order. These are the things that make me who and what I am; they are too deeply rooted to ever be blighted, to ever allow the nurturing of an evil seed.

I had changed, no question of that. But no matter how profound the changes were, I would never break down.

KATE JOHNSON survived her gunshot wound. I couldn't bring myself to visit her in the hospital, but I did send flowers. They were not acknowledged.

TEN DAYS after Vega's confession, INS field agents and members of the Border Patrol's elite antismuggling unit, working in cooperation with the Mexican government, made a sweeping series of arrests that broke the back of the coyote operation financed by the Lujacks. Fifty-seven people on both sides of the border were taken into custody.

The ironic thing was, the INS had had only sketchy information on the ring until I came along and until Vega supplied the details. Their investigation, which had only just begun, would have taken months; and even then they might not have come up with enough hard evidence to convict the Lujacks. Coleman and Thomas had panicked prematurely. Done all that they'd done without any real justification.

The INS hadn't broken them down, nor had anybody else including me. They had simply self-destructed.

I DID NOT GO BACK to the Hideaway. I would no longer have been welcome. In my own way I had betrayed and deceived the regulars too, and such sins could never be forgiven. But the main reason was that I didn't want to see it or its denizens again—the same reason a man might not want to walk through the rubble of a quake-collapsed building he had once frequented. Some places, some states of mind, can't be reconstructed once they've been battered down. The Hideaway would never be the same for the regulars, so how could it be anything at all for me?

But I kept thinking about the ones who had been there that Sunday evening, Kate and Bob Johnson and Douglas Mikan in particular. I kept wondering if they would ever feel safe again.

THE NIGHT BEFORE Kerry's birthday in early February, she and I had dinner together at my flat—our own private celebration. Her birthday, like Christmas, would be spent with her mother.

While we were eating Kerry said, "Cybil finally read the literature from Children of Grieving Parents. I talked her into it last night."

"Well," I said, pleased. "How did she react to it?"

"Skeptically. She's still afraid. But she'll think about it, if I know Cybil, and then she'll want to talk about it some more. If I can just get her to see one of the volunteer parents . . ." Kerry sighed. "Nothing's going to change before late spring at the earliest, I'm afraid."

"But it *will* change. That's the important thing."

"Everything changes," she said. "Including my building."

"Your building?"

"It's going condo."

". . . Are you sure?"

"Yep. On June first, unless I decide to make the other

tenants hate me by trying to block it. They think it's a great idea. I love my apartment but I don't know if I love it enough to buy it, or even if I can afford the probable asking price. What if I can't, and Cybil won't go to a care facility after all? I'd have to find a new place and then move her and me both—"

"Hey," I said, "don't start fretting prematurely. It'll all work out. Even if there are problems, we'll get through them."

"We?"

"You and me together. Look at what we've been through in the past. One crisis after another, and we've weathered them all. Care facilities and condos are a piece of cake."

"Since when did you become such an optimist?"

"I've been an optimist," I said, "ever since I fell in love with you."

She fixed me with a long silent look. Then her face scrunched up and she burst into tears. Then, bawling and snuffling, she hurried off to the bathroom.

I'm damned if I know what I said to upset her.

M   (EXT)

Pronzini
    Breakdown